CW01500827

Lexie Winston has been an astronaut, rock star, princess and time traveller. In her dreams. But none of the dreams have lived up to what becoming an author has been like. She gets to live in a world of pure imagination, and her heroines get to do the things she's always wished she could.

When not writing books, Lexie is a mother of two gorgeous teenagers and the wife to a patient and understanding man. They live in Western Australia and are lorded over by a black toy poodle. She loves camping, reading and if her iPad was stolen, her world would explode. (It has the kindle app on.)

And check out my website at lexiewinston.com

Also by Lexie Winston

The Collectors Division

(Reverse Harem Series)

Guardian

Guardian's Blood

Guardian Ascending

Collectors Division Omnibus

Neighpalm Industries Collective

(Contemporary Enemies to Lovers Reverse Harem)

Abandoned Girl

Broken Girl

Tormented Girl

Wanted Girl

Cherished Girl

Loved Girl

Superficial Girl - Jacinta's Story

Seductive Sins Collection

(Paranormal Reverse Harem Series)

Glorious Gluttony

Gangs, Guns, and Glory

Galaxy Circus

(Sci-Fi Reverse Harem Series)

Apprentice

Stagehand

Broken Promises

(Dark Poly Romance Series)

Secrets Kept

Lies Untold

Standalone Reverse Harem Romance

Spies Like Me

CHERISHED GIRL

LEXIE WINSTON

NEIGHPALM
PUBLISHING

First published by Neighpalm Publishing in 2022

Copyright © Neighpalm Publishing 2022
The moral right of the author has been asserted.
All rights reserved. This publication (or any part of it) may not
be reproduced or transmitted, copied, stored, distributed or
otherwise made available by any person or entity, in any form
(electronic, digital, optical, mechanical) or by any means
(photocopying, recording, scanning or otherwise) without prior
written permission from the publisher.
This is a work of fiction. Names, characters, businesses, places,
events and incidents are either the products of the author's
imagination or used in a fictitious manner. Any resemblance to
actual persons, living or dead, or actual events is purely
coincidental.

Cherished Girl: Neighpalm Industries Collective

Mobi : 978-0-6489412-0-0
Print: 978-0-6489412-3-1

Cover design by Breakout Designs
Edited by Inked Imagination

For Jillian and Kerry the best alphas an author could ever want.
(Happy now, Kerry?)

Chapter One

Harlow

I follow Thomas to the master bedroom, hoping that I might be able to convince him to have a nap with me, maybe make out a little bit, as we wing our way toward Connecticut. But there's no way in hell that's happening right now.

My mouth drops open at the words I just heard coming out of that annoying woman's mouth. Nothing kills the mood like hearing that your boyfriend might have fathered someone else's child.

"But we used condoms," Thomas argues, "and I checked it out before I threw it in the trash. I know it didn't split or tear." His distress is already changing his words, letting that accent of his peek through, so I push the door open a little more to see what's going on. Not to mention leaving enough space to angle my phone's camera to record their conversation. Veronica is sitting on the bed, a smirk on her face. A smirk that makes me seethe as I imagine punching it off of her face.

"Yes, but you both passed out as soon as you disposed of them, so you have no idea what happened after that. It was all too easy to grab the condoms out of the trash, cut the knots off, suck everything out with a turkey baster, and inject it into myself. Who knew watching all of those daytime soap operas would come in handy?" *Holy fuck! Is everyone around these guys unhinged?* "I don't know for sure who the father is, but it's most definitely one of you. Feel free to challenge me on it, give me any test you want. All that will do is give me the concrete proof I need to milk your asses dry. If you play your cards right, at least we can have a good relationship and raise this baby together."

"Did you just admit to stealing their sperm!?" I can't keep quiet any longer, nor can I stop myself from pushing the door open and stepping in. From the look on Thomas' face, he's about to have a meltdown. I press stop on the recording and tap out a quick SOS message to Declan, hoping he still has his phone in his hand like he did when I left them.

She shrugs, not looking one bit concerned, and I'm more than willing to take advantage of her overconfidence. It's easy enough to turn the camera back on and hit that little red button, especially since she's staring Thomas down, an expectant eyebrow raised. Well, this bitch is about to get a lot more than she bargained for.

"I sure did, and no court in the country is going to rule against me when I give them a sob story about being harassed at work and coerced into sex to keep my job. You've even done half my work for me, thanks for that! Your relationship with them is the cherry on top of the situation. No one will believe them when they try to claim they're not the deviants I say they are. Neighpalm Airlines is going to be fifty percent mine before you know it."

I stare her down in the ensuing silence, only looking away to end the recording and make sure the video is stored in the cloud, nice and safe.

"Thanks for that confession. I'm sure our lawyers will be absolutely *thrilled* to see it." I wave my phone at her, and her face falls right before she leaps up. Thankfully, despite his shock, Thomas is quick to react, and he restrains her before she can tackle me. The pounding of feet running down the corridor tells me the cavalry is on its way, and the entire contingent of Summers brothers bursts into the room.

"Oh my god, the baby!" Veronica screams, and Thomas instantly lets go of her, holding his hands up to show that he's no longer touching her. Making a severely ill-advised play for sympathy, she claps a hand over her stomach and looks at the other five. I'm not sure if she's going for fear or sadness, but honestly, the woman looks constipated.

"What the fuck is going on in here?" Declan asks, pulling me out of the way and shifting us so that his body is shielding mine. And hey, I am a firm advocate that women can fight their own battles, and I am 100% willing to smack a bitch down, but there's something a little swoonworthy about the way he's trying to protect me. I'm not a damsel in distress, but I'll still ogle the fuck out of a white knight if he tries to fight the dragon for me.

"Turns out that Veronica here isn't opposed to a little garbage diving and sperm stealing in her spare time, and I caught her admission on my phone." Leaning around Declan, I wave the thing in the air, and she lunges for it again, which is a little ridiculous considering there's now a wall of Summers men between her and me.

"Whose sperm and what baby?" Jaxon sounds bewildered, and I don't blame him at all. This is the kind of shit that only happens on tv. I'm just waiting for someone's look-a-like to show up, complete with a sketchy beard, claiming to be a long-lost evil twin.

"Mine and Kai's." There's nothing but defeat in Thomas' voice, so I edge around the musclebound wall in front of me and find him tugging at his red hair, doing nothing to hide his agitation.

"Fucking what?!" Kai bellows, sounding more disturbed than I've ever heard him.

"That time a couple of months ago when we were drunk... After we fell asleep, she dug the condoms out of the garbage, sucked out the sperm with a turkey baster, and fucking inseminated herself!" The room explodes into noises of disbelief, giving me the full surround-sound effect. It's impressive how many different ways the word *fuck* can be exclaimed.

Thomas, I can tell, has started to retreat into himself, damn it. Just when he's starting to trust me, she reinforces his fear that all women can be sly as fuck. I push through Declan and go over to Thomas, grabbing his hand and tugging it into mine. I'm not going to let him lump me in with her; she's obviously off her fucking rocker.

Declan finally gets his shit together, which really doesn't surprise me. His ability to pivot has been quite clear since I've known him. He's Mr. Cool Under Pressure, but I guess he has to be given he's the CEO of a multi-million dollar business. One doesn't make it in an industry as capricious as movie production unless they can steel their spine and stand their ground when it comes to stressful situations. "I think it would be best if you returned to the staff quarters and stayed there for the remainder of the flight, Veronica. You may want to look at getting yourself a lawyer because you're going to need one."

Her smug smirk turns confused. "Why would I need a lawyer?"

Oliver scoffs, that haughty curl to his lip telegraphing just how far below them she really is. "You can't possibly think we're just going to believe you. No, bitch, there will most definitely be a paternity test before anything goes any further."

"Yeah, you think nobody has ever accused us of being the baby daddy before? Please, I think every one of us has been there. And each time, it's been proven not to be ours because we always wrap it before we tap it." Holden looks at her with disgust. "Though no one has been low enough to do what you did. Fuck I didn't even know it was possible for sperm to be viable after that period of time."

She bites her lip in concern but quickly shakes it off, which doesn't exactly bode well for us. Even if it's not theirs, we need to be careful with how we handle her. God knows we don't want any stories out there about the guys mistreating a pregnant woman. My eyes zero in on her torso, trying to determine if there's anything to see. If what she says is true, she's three to four months along, so she should be showing something by now, but her fitted skirt is tight across her flat stomach. Maybe there's a slight bump there, but I very much doubt she's as pregnant as she says she is.

"Hey, what's going on in here?" A few of us turn to the door where Jilly's waiting, a concerned frown on her face. I'm sure she can feel the tension in the room. Fuck, I have no idea how Jacinta's not in here yet, ready to claw Veronica's eyes out with her bare hands.

"Veronica isn't feeling very well. She's going to spend the rest of the flight resting in the staff quarters," Declan tells Jilly, and some of the stiffness leaves her body with that simple answer.

"Oh, okay. It's not like you guys are hard work," she says with a smile. "Come on then, Veronica. Let's leave them alone in case what you've got is contagious. We don't want you giving it to the bosses."

Oliver snorts as Jilly hustles Veronica out of the room.

Kai shakes his head. "What a crazy bitch."

"Fuck, how is it that we always end up with the crazy ones?" Declan moans, pulling me away from Thomas and into his side before kissing the top of my head. "You are the best decision we ever fucking made. Please don't turn out to be crazy. Princess and I wouldn't be able to stand the loss."

The room fills with chuckles as I look up into his green eyes, detecting genuine warmth despite the teasing tone. "Oh, and here I was about to ask you to tattoo my name above hers on your chest." I flutter my eyelashes at him, and he growls at me and snaps his teeth.

"Keep that up, and you'll be over my knee getting a spanking." The men in the room all throw out encouragement at Declan's words as I push him away and hurry back down to the lounge area, a smile on my face. Is this the most dramatic thing we've experienced together? Unfortunately not. Is it still possibly a big fucking deal? Yes, of course, but if I can get them to smile a bit in the midst of this impending bullshit, I've earned a smile of my own. See? I can totally do this relationship thing.

The rest of the flight is drama-free, apart from one almighty meltdown from Jacinta when she hears what Veronica has done. Jax had to physically restrain her from storming off to confront her. Declan and Thomas disappeared into one of the offices to call their lawyer and advise him of what had occurred, and when they returned, the two of them looked like children in a candy store, mile-wide grins on both of their faces. They refused to give anyone details, no matter what we promised in return. All we got were assurances that we'd find out as soon as we landed in Connecticut, which can't come soon enough—for many reasons.

The plan is to visit Chuck and Melinda for a few days so that Thomas can poke around and ask some questions about my mother. There have also been some not-so-subtle reminders from Oli that he wants to be introduced to my tattoo artist before we move on to New York with the intention of checking how the build for his new location is going. His friend Jonah, who will be running the place, moved there a week or so ago, and Oli wants to catch up and make sure he's settling in okay.

Technically, we're gaining time as we fly home, but it's about one in the morning when we arrive in Hartford. We had planned to stay on board and sleep until a more reasonable time then make our way to Chuck and Melinda's, but not long after I feel the plane land, there's a knock on my bedroom door. Kai had snagged the other side of my bed, and it's him that gets up, pulling on sweats and opening it up.

Holding up my hand, I shade my eyes against the glare of the lights in the corridor, but I can still make out Declan standing there, grinning maniacally. "Hurry, or you're going to miss it."

Confused, I get up and pull on my own sweats and zip-up my hoody, then Kai and I follow him to the plane's open door, eyeing the stairs that have been pushed up to meet the doorway. The entrance foyer thingy is filled with everyone but Jilly and Veronica. It's a tight squeeze, but I sidle up to Oliver.

"What's going on?" I ask him, and he shrugs. Neither he nor Holden have bothered with a shirt, which would usually be pretty damn distracting. But the flashing red and blue lights, accompanied by a pealing siren of the police cars tearing across the tarmac, quickly steal my attention away from the boys' naked chests.

What the fuck? The low rumble of voices tells me everyone is thinking similarly to me, but all we can do is watch Declan make his way down the stairs, gesturing for us to follow. So, like obedient children, we gather around the bottom, not far from the stairs. I wrap my arms around me to protect myself from the chilly night air and shuffle closer to the guys, eager to steal the comfort and protection their bigger bodies give from the elements.

Two plainclothes police officers get out of an unmarked vehicle and head toward Declan, where they have a few words before making their way up the plane steps.

"Jilly!" Chris cries, but James shakes his head and holds him back, stopping him from following the officers.

"It's ok; she knows what's happening. She just had to stall her for a moment or two."

Sure enough, a couple of minutes after the two detectives disappear, Jilly appears at the top of the steps and hurries down to join us.

"What's going on?" Oliver hisses, but before she can respond, there's a commotion at the plane's entrance. The detectives exit with a struggling Veronica between them, the woman handcuffed and screaming profanities. They transfer her to the uniformed police officers who help her into the back of one of the marked vehicles.

We watch on in amazement as they depart, leaving the detectives to shake hands with Declan, then Thomas, before they take their leave.

"Will someone please explain what the fuck just happened?" Jacinta demands, hugging herself against the cold Connecticut nighttime air.

"Come on, let's go back into the plane where it's warmer, and I'll explain." Declan climbs the stairs, expecting us to follow, and, well, it's butt monkey freezing outside and I forgot to put on shoes, so he doesn't have to tell me twice.

When we all get comfortable in the lounge, he tells the story. "When Veronica announced she was pregnant and the circumstances surrounding it, I, of course, got on the phone to Forrest immediately. He's already filed some injunctions against her—something along the lines of stealing your sperm, entrapment, and one for paternity. Forrest says he doesn't think they will stand up in court because there doesn't seem to be a precedent, but he's sure he can have at least the paternity test enforced. While he was doing that, he discovered there was a warrant out for her arrest. It turns out her roommate had to go to the hospital, where they discovered she had strychnine poisoning, and the only person she had been in contact with for the twelve hours before falling sick was Veronica. When they searched the house, they found a bottle of rat poison in Veronica's room with her fingerprints all over it. She'll be going to jail for a long time, so even if the baby turns out to be either of yours, she won't be able to have any contact with it. Forrest is making sure of it."

The room explodes. I hear Jilly ask Holden about the baby and his mumbled reply in return. Jilly looks decidedly ill by the time he finishes, and Chris and James wear twin appalled expressions.

"Holy fuck." Jace just looks stunned, his expression almost comical. Poor guy is getting a trial by fire. At least he'll have an idea of what it means to be close to a Summers; Jacinta deserves to have a guy chase after her despite the attached baggage, and this family comes with an entire warehouse of suitcases.

"Yup, this is what all of us have been through our whole lives," Jaxon explains sadly. "It's why we don't trust easily and have a very, *very* small circle of friends. We prefer the company of each other more than anything. The only people who've managed to break it are Hope and these guys." He points to the two pilots and Jilly.

"Yeah, if your friendship with Harlow, and by extension of that, all of us, is going to last, you need to prepare yourself to weather the storm." It's probably the nicest way he could tell the guy that he'd better find his balls if he's going to start something with Jacinta. They do one of those man nod things, ya know, where there's some kind of unspoken understanding, so at least Jace seems like he's getting the picture. I think? Fuck, for all I know, it could mean 'dude, I need to piss,' though I'm betting on the whole brother and possible suitor approval thing as the winner.

"How long until we can get that paternity test?" Thomas asks Declan.

"It depends on how long it takes to process her and if she lawyers up. It could be a couple of weeks, or it could be a couple of days, especially if they imply that by cooperating, they might go easier on her. Forrest has organized an OB to be available as soon as she consents."

"Will they really go easier on her?" I ask, hoping that's not the case. The idea of her doing what she did is despicable, and I'm feeling a little protective and possessive of my men. The idea of them being so violated in this way is making something murderous peek out of me.

"Nope, but she doesn't need to know that. She's looking at attempted murder for what she did to her roommate. There's not a lot that's going to make them more lenient."

"Well, now that that's done with, how about we all head back to bed so we can get started early in the morning? I've arranged for you guys to stay at the Neighpalm Hotel here," he tells James, Chris, and Jilly. "Take a couple of days off. I advised Dad of the situation, and he let me know that Chuck and Melinda are thrilled we're coming and have rooms waiting for us all. I've arranged for a security company to check over a couple of rental cars for us and deliver them in the morning."

Despite the late hour and everything that just occurred, a wave of excitement thrums through my body. I've been so busy I haven't had time to dwell on it, but god, I've missed my family. My brief visit with Max just wasn't enough. I have no idea how I'll cope with living on the opposite side of the country if I decide to stay in California, and that's something I need to seriously start considering if I'm committing to this seven-way relationship.

I wish everyone good night and head back to my bed, followed by Kai. When we climb under the covers, I let him spoon me, but both of us are quiet. I'm sure he's thinking about the possibility of being a father despite what I believe are slim odds. And, well, I can't wait to sleep in my own bed tomorrow night. Will there be a fight about who gets to sleep in my little apartment with me? Because goodness knows there's not enough room for all six men. Kai's breathing evens out, his arm growing heavy as he falls asleep, but my mind is restless.

It's playing over the last few days—my date with Thomas, the dinner with the Dobrov's, Veronica's dropped bomb, and then the utter satisfaction I felt at seeing her taken away by the police. Poor Thomas and Kai, what a horrible thing to be happening to them. And a selfish little part of me also whispers, *But what does that mean for me*?

I know if it turns out that the baby is one of theirs, they will embrace that challenge and love that baby like no one has been loved before. A funny feeling sits in the bottom of my stomach as I think about a baby in our lives. One that's not mine. Although I hadn't considered children at this moment in my life, there's a small part of me that's sick with jealousy. *Is that a deal breaker?* Almost as soon as that thought enters my mind, I mentally kick myself. I can't let that jealousy eat away at me and make me bitter, or I'm no better than the woman who gave birth to me. No, I promise to myself that the baby, if it *is* Kai or Thomas', will never experience anything but love and kindness at my hands.

I smile as I think about the Summers family with a baby in their lives. Holy crap, maybe I'll have to be the hardass mom because every one of them will be squishy marshmallows. That baby will have everyone wrapped around its finger the minute it's born. Someone's going to have to keep it grounded, and I have just the thing for that. Cleaning animal cages is a great way to instill some humility *and* keep a kid out of trouble. I know first hand. I was an expert at cleaning stables by the time I was ten. Chuck and Melinda were amazing role models and loving parents, and I only hope I can do as good a job as them if it's needed.

My eyes grow heavier, and I snuggle back into the warm body behind me, sleep coming far more easily now that my head is filled with warm thoughts of a drama-free future where we get to focus on simply being a family.

Chapter Two

Harlow

I don't even have a chance to step away from the car before Melinda throws herself at me, her body practically shaking when she envelops me in her arms and hugs me tight. Now, I'm pressed between the vehicle and her body, holding on for dear life as she half reams me out for not calling enough and half sobs with joy. Honestly, it's a wonderful feeling. How can I leave behind these people who have been more of a family to me than my biological one? Well, my mother anyway. Dad is well and truly stepping up to the plate.

When she pulls back, her eyes are red, and she's busily wiping tears from her cheeks before smacking me on the arm. "Damn you, Harlow. You've always tried to do everything for yourself! Why won't you lean on us and let us help you?"

I know she's referring to the stalker issue, but Jacinta is pushing her way in to run interference before I can answer. "Hello, Melly, it's so good to see you!" She pulls her into a hug. "Don't worry, Dad and the boys have got it all under control. Harlow isn't allowed anywhere unless *that* big lug escorts her." She points to Thomas, who sends her a smile and a wave.

Melinda runs her eyes up and down his length before turning to me and wiggling her eyebrows. "Damn, it's been a couple of years since I've seen the boys; they sure did grow up nicely. And look at you, pretty girl. All woman now, aren't you?" She holds Jacinta at arm's length and sighs. "Goodness, where has the time gone? We don't see you all nearly as much as we would like."

A hand on my arm has me spinning to find my foster dad glaring down at me. "Harlow, I swear you've managed to turn my hair gray over the last few weeks. Look at it," he demands, pointing at his head. "Melinda and I have both developed a drinking problem. You are the last person I would expect to cause me to worry. Always with your head down studying, never any trouble. God, there were days I would say to Melinda, 'is something wrong with Harlow? She's so good.'" He's full-on scolding me now, but I know it's coming from a place of affection, so I wrap my arms around him and squeeze. That familiar scent of horses and Chuck makes a tear well in my eye, but I wipe my face on his shirt and pull away.

"Just luck, I guess?"

He snorts. "Well, come on then. Bring your gear, and Melinda will show you to your rooms."

I let everyone go ahead of me, and as Thomas passes, I grab hold of his arm, stopping him. He looks down at me questioningly. "I want to go to my apartment, but I know I shouldn't go on my own. Will you come with me?"

"Sure. Should I leave my bags here?" he asks, and I glance down at his case before looking back up at him. "There's enough room in my bed for another person, and of course it would be responsible for me to share it so that Chuck and Melinda aren't *so* overrun inside." Thomas snorts as his gaze goes toward the large mansion. Yeah, it's not quite as big as the Summers', but it definitely has enough space for everyone.

"Are you suggesting that I should be the one to share your bed? By all means, we should be responsible." He grabs his bag and follows me around the back of the house and over to my stables.

Before we can get too far, Chuck shouts after us. Stopping, I turn, grumbling at being caught. As he approaches, though, the look on his face sends chills down my spine.

"Harlow honey, I'm afraid we have some not-so-nice news. I wanted to wait until you got here before I told you." It's all I can do to stop myself from racing for the barn to check on DS and Jenny. I know Chuck and Melinda are okay. Shit, what about Max? She wasn't in the picture the stalker sent me, though.

Chuck grabs hold of my hand, squeezing it to reclaim my attention. "It's about Luke."

Luke? My heartbeat returns to normal, and I can feel my body relax again. "What about him?"

"I had to identify his body for the police. He washed up along the river a couple of days ago."

A gasp leaves my mouth. "Oh no. Suicide?"

"No, the police suspect foul play." He looks at Thomas, his eyes saying much more than his mouth is. "Harlow, Detective Brown found something else, and I asked him to let me tell you. When they added Luke's prints to the system, they got a hit."

A grunt escapes Thomas' mouth like something just occurred to him. "Luke was her stalker, wasn't he?"

Chuck nods his head, and even though his eyes are flashing with anger, he sounds sad. "Yes, it looks like it. His prints match the partial they got off the last package that you received, and his DNA is a match to the *samples* left behind when your room was trashed." I screw my nose up at the thought. Gross on so many levels.

"The police came here and searched his room; they found a diary where he kept track of the things he did. Since everything was found on the property and out of respect for our connection with you, he clarified a few things for me."

Chuck pulls out his phone and swipes his fingers across the screen before reading from a text message. "According to Detective Brown, Luke was responsible for the cut in the saddle, pushing you into the pool, the threatening photos of DS, the destruction of Oliver's car, the attack on Holden, the note at the hospital, and the destruction of your room. He was also watching you and Declan in the stables after the shooting incident. It seems that he was *not* responsible for the dummy of Jacinta with the bullet hole and covering DS and Jenny in whatever it was, nor the death of Declan's PI. We also know he wasn't responsible for Hawaii because he was here, so, like they initially suspected, there are definitely two people responsible for all the incidents." Chuck's more somber than I've ever seen him. Melinda was always the disciplinarian in our family, and Chuck was the softy who let us get away with everything. Seeing him like this is a shock to my system.

A kind of numb sensation creeps over my body. I don't know whether to be relieved that part of the mystery has been solved or terrified that there's still someone else out there. Someone else has a problem with me, and this one seems even more determined to see me out of the way. There had been talk about the possibility of there being two people responsible, but to have it confirmed and to realize that this still isn't over is a smack in the face.

"Did his diary say why? Anything as to why he was doing this to me?"

I can see it in his eyes before he even opens his mouth. "No, honey, there was nothing." He hugs me and leaves me to digest the news, promising he'll let everyone else know and will keep them away for a little while.

"Come on." Thomas picks up both our bags. "Let's go lie down for a while. I find news like this is best dealt with when I'm not so fatigued and emotionally unbalanced."

I decide that his idea has merit, so I lead him to my barn. Today, we've both been hit with crappy news, and I know my mind will run wild with what-ifs or whys. Snuggling with Thomas will be an excellent way to calm myself. I also want to take a moment to check in on him, find out how he's dealing with Veronica's announcement. I'm thrilled that this hasn't caused him to pull away, and I'm hoping that if I check in with him without an audience, I might be able to make another crack in that wall of his.

The barn doors are closed, and the aviary alongside it is decidedly empty. I pull open the heavy doors, and when the familiar smells of hay, dust, and horse poop meet me, I smile. God, I've missed this. I should have spent more time with

Prada and Coco in the stables, but I hadn't wanted to bug Thomas.

A shrill whinny and an incessant braying tell me my entrance has not gone unnoticed. Dropping my bag on the ground, I hurry over to the stable and fling open the door. I'm being charged before I can even step into it. With a shout of joy, I hold my hands up, and the two rascals come to a stop just in front of them. Even Devil Spawn is happy to see me, nuzzling against my stomach as I rub Jenny's velvety ears. A gentle nip to my stomach tells me DS isn't pleased with the amount of attention, so I move one of my hands to her ears.

"I've missed you guys too," I coo as I feel tears prickle my eyes. I need to do something about my lack of animal interaction. Sure, Princess and the kittens are nice, but they're still a little small to be fun yet, and Coco and Prada are great, but they're Jacinta's, and she's on top of their care. Can I volunteer somewhere? *If anywhere will take me on now that the media is slamming us...* Thankfully, word that we're here hasn't gotten out yet, so the airport was media-free this morning. I doubt it will stay that way though.

Heat at my back tells me Thomas has joined me, and DS's ears and head prick up at the possibility of a new target. His hand reaches over, and I'm just about to warn him, but then she does the strangest thing. There are no threatening teeth or aggressive flat ears; she nudges me out of the way and starts to rub her face against him, a quiet nickering sound leaving her mouth. "Who are you, and what have you done with my demon?" I chuckle at her affection, which Thomas is easily returning, scruffing at her mane and whispering pretty words to her.

"DS and I became good friends when she came to visit; she's quite the affectionate little thing. I can't understand where she got her name from."

I raise an eyebrow and try to insert myself between the two of them. Her ears flatten back, and she bares her teeth as she lunges for me.

"Holy shit!" He snatches me out of the way, and as soon as I'm no longer competition, she turns on the charm again.

Shaking my head at her, I give Jenny one last hug before grabbing her and DS's halters and leads. I hand him the demon's and put Jenny's on before leading her out to her day paddock, with Thomas and Devil Spawn in tow. We let the two go, and they canter off into the middle of the paddock, stop abruptly, and start to eat.

"Come on. I'll show you my place." We head back into the stables, but he stops as we pass the clinic room. Beyond it is the horse crush and the two stable boxes I had converted to a cage.

"What's this?" he asks.

"Oh, Melinda and Chuck had it built for me so I could treat their injured horses. I've taken care of some of the neighboring farm animals too. We don't have a vet super close, so it was easier for people to bring them here once they all found out I was getting my veterinary degree. The stable boxes were converted into a cage because we have a few wild cats in the area. If they're injured, we can't return them to the wild, so I treat them before releasing them. I had a bobcat last year that had been shot in the shoulder by a hunter. I dug out the bullet and stitched him up, and he spent a couple of weeks recuperating here until we released him." I chuckle when I think back. "I had to keep Jenny and DS in the newer stables with the rest of the horses because they were freaked out by the smell of the cat."

"You know, you really light up when talking about animals," Thomas murmurs, pushing a lock of my hair back from my face. My cheek warms where his fingers brush across it, and I revel in that soft touch. Knowing he's choosing to touch me, seeking out opportunities to have contact between us, is a heady feeling.

"I think Chuck was kind of hoping that I would start my own practice here once I'd done my internship. I hadn't told either of them about my desire to work with exotic animals. Really, I kind of never told anyone that until just recently. I mean, don't get me wrong, a lot of horse farms surround us, and equine breeding fascinates me, so I would be perfectly happy doing that." My heart sinks as I think about the media. "Well, I guess that might not even be an option now either."

I trudge my way up my stairs as I think about the possibility, but Thomas stops me with a hand on my arm. I spin to face him and discover we're now eye to eye due to the stairs. Wow, he has a smattering of freckles across his nose that I hadn't noticed before. It's cute.

"Harlow, I know you're worried about everything that the media is saying, but I promise you it will die down and go away. Ninja Starfish's media conference on Friday will be enough to drag the attention away from all of us. You *will* get an internship, I guarantee it, even if Dad has to throw money at someone. No, don't roll your eyes; we know how you feel about it, but that's what family does. They help one another. It just so happens that your dad has more money than most. Let him help; you will make him the happiest man ever. Heck, find a zoo about to go bust or one that's abandoned, and he'll buy it for you. You're lucky he hasn't done so already."

His words make me think about the one practically on their doorstep. I really want to find out more about what their eccentric neighbor kept there.

"As for the remaining stalker, he'll slip up. We know about Luke now, which means we know so much more than before. I'll give Jake a call and get him to trace Luke's whereabouts while he was in

LA. It will lead to something, and Cecelia must know something too. She can't hide forever. This whole clusterfuck is starting to unravel. Whoever is responsible will get careless, and they will panic. We will get through this." He leans his forehead against mine. "Have faith in the system and us. Please tell me you're not going to run away. Dad would be so sad; we all would be. I'm going to be selfish and beg you not to do that to us. Please. Not with what we've started here. I'm pretty sure you'd destroy us all if you decided to run away and leave us all behind."

My heart aches from the pain in his voice. Thomas, after being so hesitant to start, is actually putting his emotions on the line. He's probably the last Summers I would have predicted making an emotional declaration, but I'm going to savor whatever he's willing to reveal of himself, his thoughts about us, to me. For Thomas, if I understand anything his brothers or he has told me, this is huge. How could I do anything but cave to his wishes? I already knew I was going to stay, but I guess until I pack up everything here and move it there, they're not going to see the truth in it. I'll just have to prove it to them.

But first, now that I'm here, at least I can have a much-needed conversation with Chuck and Melinda. I need to tell them face to face. I owe them that, at least.

I have no words to offer him at the moment, so

I lean in and place what's meant to be a small reassuring kiss to his lips, but his big hands circle my waist, and he deepens it. My body melts against him like putty in a hot hand. Holy hell, the man can kiss. It's like he's trying to imprint himself on my soul to ensure that I won't be able to leave. I'm breathless and lightheaded when he finally pulls away. Blinking a couple of times to clear my mind, I turn and head up my stairs.

"Come on, let's dump our stuff. If I know your family, once they hear about Luke, Chuck won't be able to hold them off for long." I reach the landing of my apartment, and a funky smell hits my nose.

"Gross, what is that?" I look around, trying to ascertain what it is. After I left, Melinda would have sent one of the cleaners up to clean out the fridge and tidy up, so where is it coming from?

By the time my eyes complete a circuit of the small space, I notice a vase of dead flowers sitting on the little dining table I have. The water is mostly gone, with sludge sitting in the bottom, and the petals are all withered and dry, most of them scattered across the table.

"Huh, where did they come from? You would have thought the cleaning service would have gotten rid of them." Thomas moves me out the way, plucking the card out of the dead stems and pulling it open.

"I'm sorry about your mother, Harlow. I wish she could have been a better one." He flips the card back and

27

forth. "There's no name signed to it. It seems innocent enough, but it's strange that Melinda or one of the staff would put them up here knowing you weren't returning any time soon. I'll just hang on to the card; who knows if we can have the handwriting analyzed." He plucks the dead stems out of the vase and carries them over to the garbage, opening it and tossing them before pulling out the bag and knotting it. "We'll take them out when we leave, but I think you'll find it's the water that smells." He places it on the landing near the stairs, so we remember to take it.

"Maybe they were from Luke?" I suggest, and he nods.

"Could have been."

I grab the vase and empty the remaining water into my sink before grabbing some detergent and using it quite liberally before filling it with water again. Leaving it to soak, I crack open one of the windows in the apartment. Once the fresh breeze takes care of some of the smell, I grab my bag and take it into my bedroom. But before I can unpack, Thomas leans against the door way with a serious look on his face.

"Come on, then. Might as well be comfortable if we're going to have a serious conversation." I pat the bed next to me and try to keep my voice light, but I have a feeling I know what's about to come. He comes over and takes a seat, grabbing my hand.

"Harlow, your other stalker has proven to be

more elusive than we had thought. They're smart, whoever they are. We still have no clue what this is about or why or anything really. Luke's death answers one of the whos but not the whys, and right now, that could be an important part to figuring out who this second person is. If we figure out Luke's motive, we can determine who else might have shared in that and helped him. There was a business card found in the dead PI's office and it's for a biker bar not far from the trailer park your mom lived in. I'm going to head over there a little later today and poke around, see what I can dig up. I'm almost a hundred percent sure it starts here and has something to do with your mother."

I'm sure he prepared for the worst, figuring this might be something that I'd freak out about, but I'm honestly not sure if I could be surprised by anything connected to my mother. I squeeze his hand, trying to reassure him as best I can that I'm here and I'm safe. "What I don't understand is how he got the card. Why did he have it? And why was his file all hard copies? Was there no computer or electronic evidence stored anywhere?" Okay, maybe I'm not as cool as I thought; by the time I voice the last question, there's a small hint of hysteria in my voice. But it's not my mother's involvement that's the upsetting part. It's just kind of hitting me again that we just know so little about this, and one of the people who was *supposed* to have some answers is dead, leaving behind no solid trail as to what he discovered, or how, or from whom.

Thomas sighs again. "According to Jake, the PI had taken a trip out here not long before he was found dead. And there *was* a computer, but it looked like someone had tried to destroy the hard drive. He's having Forensics see if they can get it working again. Until that happens, we won't be able to check for back-up copies."

"Can I come with you? It might help to have an extra pair of eyes." He adamantly shakes his head, his hand already clenching mine more tightly.

"No, I'll take my brothers, and I would really like it if you stayed here, inside, where it's safe, for now. This could be the epicenter of it all, and I don't want to make it easy to get at you. Plus, there's no way that Jacinta would let us leave her behind if you came too."

A small sigh of disappointment escapes me even though I know he's right. "Okay, but I want to know everything when you get back."

He smiles, looking a little relieved that I didn't argue. But I'm not that stupid girl in a horror movie who doesn't listen and gets themselves killed. I like my life even more now with my new family. I won't risk that, and I certainly won't risk Jacinta. He's one hundred percent correct that she'd never let the family go on some kind of sleuthing adventure while leaving her behind.

"Thank you." He leans in and kisses me, and

without a second thought, I wind my arms around his neck and try to encourage him to lie back on the bed with me. I never did get my make-out session on the plane.

But a bang down below has him jumping up, pulling a gun out of the back of his pants, and moving to check the noise out. Shit, I hadn't even noticed it tucked under his shirt in the back of his jeans.

I stay put until he calls me, but I can hear more than one voice. "It's okay; it's just Holden and Oliver," he shouts.

When I get down the stairs, I find them poking around in my clinic.

"Hey, babe, are you okay?" Holden looks up as we enter, concern clouding his eyes, his jaw taut with tension. "It must be a bit of a shock to realize Luke was behind so much of what happened." He comes over and pulls me in his arms, and I relax into his hold.

"I'm okay, I promise," I mutter into his chest, and I feel him reassuringly run his hands up and down my back. Oliver is still poking around, peeking in drawers and opening cupboards.

"What's that?" Oliver asks, pointing to a locked and barred cabinet.

"That's the drug cabinet. Mostly tranquilizers and sedatives for the horses, but there are also antibiotics, vaccines, and things for smaller animals too." His eyes widen in surprise, and I chuckle.

"Did you think it was all pretend? I *am* licensed here, and I'm sure Chuck will have me checking over everyone as soon as possible. Not to mention how busy I'll be if the neighbors hear that I'm home."

"Well, as long as you can do all that with me around, that's fine," Thomas warns, and I roll my eyes.

"Yes, General Hardass." I salute him, and the sound of Holden and Oliver's laughter follows me out of the stables as they hurry behind me.

Chapter Three

Thomas

Leaving Harlow behind at the Bostons' house was harder than I had imagined. Lunch was a fun and rowdy affair until Chuck's parents arrived. They were cold and rude to Harlow even as they kissed my and my siblings' asses. Maybe it's a bit of the pot calling the kettle black, considering our initial reception of Harlow, but it grated on me to see people treating her that way.

"Fucking hell, how are Nana and Poppy friends with those two?" Jaxon grumbles, his nose wrinkled in disgust. I only partially listen to him, having no real answer to give and needing my attention focused on the directions the navigation system is giving me.

"To be honest, I think it had nothing to do with

them and everything to do with Chuck and Melinda being friends with Dad. And on some not-so-small level, Harlow herself. Poppy once told me that when she moved in with them, Chuck's parents were awful to her, so they took it upon themselves to treat her very differently. I think that's the reason they kept going back. Nana and Poppy spent more time with her than they ever did those old stuck-up assholes," Declan says. He's sitting next to me in the passenger seat, his body turned to look at the others in the back.

"Well, surely that's a tick on the plus side of her coming to live with us." Kai sounds happy about that, but Jaxon clears his throat.

"About that… How serious are you all about her? I mean, we haven't had a conversation since we started to 'woo' her."

"Fucking Jacinta," Oliver cuts in, but we just ignore him.

"How are we all feeling about this harem thing we've got going on? Especially now that it's in the media?" At Jaxon's words, the car erupts into chaos. Everyone's talking over one another, their shouts loud enough that I can't hear myself think.

"Hey. Hey!" I shout before pulling into a vacant parking spot on the side of the road. His timing is terrible, but Jaxon has a point; it's something we need to talk about, and I have a feeling it's going to be a short conversation. Turning so I can see every-one, I take charge. "One at a time, alright? Are we all in with Harlow?" The loud yes echoes in the car despite my one-at-a-time instruction, and smiles simultaneously appear on my brothers' faces. "Well, I guess that says it all."

"I have a proposal then." Jaxon squirms, looking a little nervous. I'd tease him if that weren't so significant. I'm not sure I've ever seen him *nervous* about a woman before. In lust? Definitely. Smarmy and totally self-satisfied after a hookup? Fuck yeah. But nervous… That's a new one. I kind of like seeing him that way because it says to me that my brother is being sincere, not that I really needed confirmation of that.

"She was so devastated when she got those rejection letters, and my heart almost broke for her. We're all doing what we love, and the thought that she can't is unacceptable." There are murmurs of agreement from the rest of my brothers, the sound quiet enough that none of us really interrupt Jaxon. "Jacinta wants nothing to do with the count's house across the road. I'm not entirely sure why. It's not like it's a connection to our mother or anything, but anyway, she's more interested in the overseas properties. Plus, you know she loves our place. Dad isn't ever going to be able to budge her, and whoever manages to keep up with our sister is going to have to accept the fact that they're going to have to live there. Being that there is a potential relationship on the horizon if Harlow's matchmaking works, that puts us in an awkward position. I don't want to hear my sister having sex. Oh, fuck, now I'm *thinking* about my sister having sex!"

"For god's sake, Jaxon, get to the point," Oliver growls between gritted teeth. He's never been able to handle suspense, and with the way this conversation is going, we're all going to need brain bleach if he doesn't refocus.

"Right. The point. Okay, so I'm suggesting that we move into the count's property, or I guess it's mine now... with Harlow, renovate the zoo part of it, and let her start her own animal sanctuary or something. She got so upset at that idiot on the tv last week, the guy with all those tigers, and maybe we could help stop that kind of shit from happening. She could rescue them, start a proper conservation program, and we could do school tours and everything." He breaks off and raises an eyebrow when everyone gapes at him. "What?"

"Holy fuck, dude! It's perfect." Kai claps him on the shoulder while Holden and Oliver continue to stare at him in shock. Declan has a slight smile on his lips, and I can see his brain working on it already. I'm glad he's not feeling a little salty. Our youngest brother just came up with the perfect scenario, but it's usually Declan who comes up with all the plans.

"We'll have to hire someone to train her through her internship and find staff to run the day-to-day things." Declan pulls out his phone and starts making notes, an excited gleam in his eye.

Really, he's got the best mindset for this stuff, so now that we have an idea, we can hit the ground running.

"None of us know anything about zoos or sanctuaries or anything, so let's find a consultant to help with design or whatever else we need." Holden points a finger at Declan, who writes it down.

I chuckle before I can stop it, and they all turn to look at me.

"What is it, General Hardass?" Oliver asks sarcastically. "What are you going to say to rain on our parade now?"

"Well, don't you think asking Harlow first might be a good idea? Not to mention we should have a tour through the house and see if it's livable after all these years." Declan is so practical it's a little scary, but I don't think he means it negatively. He's just cautious and would hate to see them disappointed if Harlow didn't like the plan or the place was deemed unlivable.

Looking a little sheepish now, Declan tucks his phone away, though I do see him save the notes, and the others kind of just squirm under my gaze.

"Yeah, you've probably got a point. But at least we've got some kind of a plan, right?" Jaxon points out, and yes, he is right. We have a consensus that we all want to stay in this relationship, and now we've got a plan to make Harlow as happy as we are. That's pretty damn good for a bunch of guys with terrible relationship experience and intimacy issues, if I do say so myself.

"Okay, but before we can get a happily ever after, we have to deal with this stalker crap, so how about we check out this bar? I'll ask the questions, so you're just there for backup. Have a drink or play a game of pool, but don't start anything," I warn them, and thankfully, they're all intelligent enough to let me lead.

The bar is smoky, the smell of stale beer is prevalent, and the fact that it's a biker hangout is glaringly evident thanks to all the bikes parked out front and the patched leathers inside the bar. But it's a quiet, relaxed atmosphere that we walk into. No one but the bartender pays particular attention when I take a seat at the bar and order beers for the six of us. When they arrive, the others take theirs to a booth near an empty pool table, where Declan puts some coins in and racks up the balls.

"Visiting?" the barman asks conversationally after he goes back to polishing glasses. He's wearing a leather vest and has tattoos all over his arms, with a long red beard and matching hair on his head. He looks like he's tough, but he's certainly not putting out any fuck-off vibes.

I take a slow sip of my cold beverage before

answering. "Kind of. I also might be looking for some information if you're willing to help."

"Well, I guess that all depends on the information you might be looking for," the bartender says, putting down the glass and cloth, his eyes narrowing and his vibe becoming a little less casual.

"This was found on the body of a dead PI back in California." I pull out the business card and flick it onto the bar. The man raises an eyebrow, but I've got to give him credit; he doesn't even flinch.

"So what? Do you know how many people come in and out of this bar every day? That doesn't mean shit."

I take another long pull of my beer. "Nope, you're right, but I'm hoping when I say who the PI was investigating, you might give me a little more to go on."

He scoffs, not so friendly now. He leans against the bar, trying to intimidate me, but I don't scare so easily. "I doubt it, but sure, let's give it a whirl." The sarcasm is thick, but I rush on, ignoring it.

"Does the name Diane Stubbs mean anything to you?" I watch the man over the top of my bottle very carefully. He's obviously had practice, but the tic in the corner of his eye tells me everything I need to know. "Look, I'm going to be straight with you. She's dead, but her daughter is being stalked, and this bar is one of the better leads we've had. Now, I could have given it to the police, and they'd be busting in here and messing shit up, but I haven't, so how about we cut the crap, and you share with me what you know."

I can see him contemplating whether he's going to pull a gun on me or cooperate with me. When his hands shift, I tense, ready to grab the weapon I've got tucked into the back of my jeans, but he just turns, moves out the bar, and disappears down a corridor.

Now, either he's about to ambush me with more men, or I might be getting some answers to my questions. Either way, I wait and drink my beer. I'm alert and ready for anything, but I'm really hoping it's the latter, not the former.

Five minutes go past, and when he returns, a large man follows him. He's probably my dad's age, maybe a little older, and this guy has some fuck-off vibes radiating off of him. His jeans are ripped at the knees, and he's got shit-kicking motorcycle boots on his feet. He's wearing a shirt with the bar's name on it, so there's no saying who this man is, but if I had to guess, this is the President of the MC.

He looks me up and down before nodding in the direction of a booth. "Come on, let's talk over there." He grabs the two new beers the barman has just slammed down, and I follow him to the secluded corner. He slides in, and I take the opposite side as he passes one of the new pints over.

"I saw you on the news. Some gossipy piece of shit that said you and those other pretty boys are in a relationship with Harlow. Is this true?" The voice is gravelly, but there's no aggression, just curiosity.

"Yes, it's true, but it's nothing as evil as the media is claiming. We all know about each other. She's not cheating on us, and she is most definitely *not* related to us."

The man nods. "Yes, I know that she's not even remotely related. Polyamory is cool, man." My eyebrows jump. Well, that wasn't what I was expecting. "I have two wives and a husband."

Fuck me, I think my eyes just about pop out of my head at his admission. He chuckles at my reaction and takes a sip of his beer. "You said she has a stalker. Is she okay?" He kind of looks over at my brothers, almost like he was expecting her to be here.

"Yes, she's fine. We left her at her home," I tell him cautiously. "Mind sharing how you know Harlow?"

He sighs and runs a hand through his hair. "When I knew Diane, I had just become President of this club after my old man had had a freak car accident. Diane was a regular in the clubhouse, one of the club whores, I guess, but she was also turning tricks on the side to make money. For me, she was safe because she was usually too coked out of her mind for sex. I was hiding the fact that I was bi, and she was an easy cover, but that ended as soon as I realized how she treated her kid. Harlow was a good girl, but at fourteen, she was starting to develop into a woman, and I saw how her mom's clients looked at her. I bought her a gun and taught her how to use it. I wish I could have done more, but like I said, I had just taken over and was trying to muddle my way through running an MC that was old school. It's different now, but it was hard for a couple of years. Most of the time, Harlow was safely out of the way, staying with her foster parents. I must admit I did try to stoke the flames of Diane's jealousy, telling her how pretty her daughter was, and last I heard, it worked. She had stopped having Harlow visit."

Ahh, this is the guy Harlow told the family about back when she first arrived. "Do you have any idea who might have killed Diane?" He blinks kind of owlishly a couple of times, something like surprise showing on his face.

"Someone killed her? I thought she had over-dosed. I mean, it was only a matter of time." Another big sigh leaves his mouth. "Diane would often rant about Harlow's father and how he had just dumped her out of nowhere. I think she really loved the guy, and she had worked at staying sober while they were together, but she never could understand that her partying ways weren't for everyone. Then she just got mean, nasty, and spite-ful. I think she had a little bird whispering in her ear, and with the drugs, well, there was no coming back from that."

"Bird?" I jump on that. "What bird? We haven't

been able to find any definitive information about friends, and there was no family."

"Ah yeah, there was. Diane had a sister. They were super close before Diane got pregnant with Harlow, but then something happened. She wouldn't say, but I think it had something to do with Brad. When she was high as a kite, she would ramble about her sister being to blame for Brad and everything that had gone wrong, but then she would usually pass out, and, to be honest, listening to her wasn't high on my to-do list."

Holy shit, a clue. How is it Harlow doesn't know she has or maybe had an aunt? "Does she live in the area? Did either of them know who my dad was? I don't see Diane being the type to let sleeping dogs lie if she could get an easy paycheck. Harlow said as much. Her mom used to come and beg her for money."

He shrugs. "No, she never put two and two together. The drugs really did fuck with her mind. I can't say how surprised I was when there was that scandal with the billboard a month or so ago, and her relationship with your family came out. You're right, though. Had Diane known, she would have milked it for all it was worth. As for the sister, I don't know. I never met her, and I banned Diane from the clubhouse after I saw her hit Harlow one afternoon when I was there. I had no clue she was physically abusive, and I won't stand for child abuse of any kind."

"Is there anyone here at the club who continued to see Diane once you kicked her out? Anyone who may know more about her sister?" I can see him thinking about it before he slowly nods.

"Yeah, there's this one guy. He was a new pledge at the time, maybe just turned eighteen, and he was obsessed with her. Even once I made it known she wasn't welcome, he blew most of his weekly paycheck on her. He never ended up patching in because he was more about partying and drugs, and I was moving the direction of the MC away from that. I mean, we're far from squeaky clean, but I stopped running girls. Last I heard, he got in with a drug cartel, Russian maybe? He was their go-to man on the East Coast. Not sure whatever happened to him. He had a weird Russian name—Pierre, or Pietro, or something. I can probably find out for you."

"That would be great, thanks." He gets up and heads back down the way he came while I finish off my beer and check on my brothers. Declan raises an eyebrow, looking for a nod that I'm okay. Once they're reassured, they go back to playing pool.

When he returns, he hands me a piece of paper. "His name was Peitre Baciu; here's his last known address."

"Thanks, man, I appreciate it."

"How is Harlow? I hope you guys are being good to her. She was always such a good girl. She had such a fascination with animals. She found a kitten under one of the trailers once. Diane wouldn't let her keep it; crazy bitch even tried to drown it. Harlow was beside herself, so I took it home. Monster lived to the ripe age of fourteen and was one of my stepson's shadows when he arrived with his mother." He smiles at the memory, and there's a genuine affection there, which makes me happy.

"Well, Harlow became a vet and desperately wants to work with exotic animals. We're going to make it happen for her."

He looks at me like he's trying to stare into my soul, then he smiles. "Good. Can you tell her that Bear says hello? And hey, if you ever need advice on living a polyamorous life, hit me up." He's chuckling as he walks away, which is totally not what I was expecting when we came here, but I'm happy. I've got new information, we're making it out of the biker bar unscathed, and this could actually help Harlow for real. But then I think of something that dims a tiny bit of the light that started to fill me.

"Hey, man." He stops and looks back. "Did you ever send Harlow flowers when her mom died?" His brow creases in a frown, and he shakes his head. "Okay, thanks," I tell him again, and he continues on his way, stopping to talk to the bartender before disappearing out the back.

Standing up, I signal to my brothers. Instantly, they abandon their game, and we head out the door once I try to settle up the tab. Bear has already taken care of it, though, so we leave quietly.

A thrill of excitement runs through me as we step out into the cool afternoon breeze. Maybe, just maybe, we might get somewhere now. I'll give Jake a call and get him to run this name through the system, see if he can come up with any information for me.

Chapter Four

Harlow

Lunch was fine until Mr. and Mrs. Boston showed up, proceeding to throw passive-aggressive comments in my direction while simultaneously fawning over the Summers like they were the latest reincarnation of Christ. Chuck's cheeks were growing pink in embarrassment, and I could practically hear Melinda's teeth grinding together every time Mrs. Boston opened her mouth. Eventually, I asked to be excused. I hid outside on the patio, still in sight of Thomas but away from that awful couple. I do *not* know how Chuck turned out to be so lovely, but apparently, his granny had quite a bit to do with raising him, so maybe she's the reason why. It's something Chuck, Melinda, and I have talked about many times over the years.

Unfortunately, the elder Bostons never grew to like me much.

"Honey, we're so sorry about them." I look up from my phone to Melinda and Chuck's apologetic faces, but all I can give them is a shrug.

"Nothing I'm not used to."

Melinda grimaces. "No matter how many times we both tell them that you're family, they just don't listen. They're such assholes and always have been." She passes me one of the mugs she's carrying, and the smell of coffee hits my nose.

They both take a seat, and Chuck leans forward to pat me on the knee. "You're a better person than most, and I'm thankful to see that there are at least some others who understand how special you are. Why, I thought Jacinta was going to implode. You could practically see the steam coming out of her ears!" He chuckles, bringing his mug up to his mouth.

"But Brad raised them better, so they kept their mouths shut." Melinda growls, "I would have paid to see Jacinta put them in their place. God knows they think they're better than they truly are. Ungrateful parasites." I don't think I've ever heard her speak this way about them before. Sure, she's always made it clear that she hates their attitude toward me, but it's like something in her has finally snapped just enough for some big cracks to be showing through.

"Look, we've never told you this, but when

Chuck's granny passed, she left everything to him. David had already received his trust fund from his father, and you cannot imagine their shock and Margaret's absolute horror when they discovered she had left them nothing. They had blown through most of his fund already and were counting on the top off from Granny," Melinda explains before Chuck takes over.

"That's why they live with us. They have enough money to keep up appearances for their friends but not to own the things that they want, and I didn't want to be responsible for my parents being homeless."

Melinda scoffs, "They wouldn't be homeless. They would just have to adjust to a considerably less extravagant lifestyle." Although her point is completely true, Chuck is already squirming in his seat at just the thought. He's always been too generous for his own good, completely undeserving of the kind of parents he's stuck with.

"Chuck, you shouldn't have to apologize for their behavior. Neither of you should. I know an asshole when I see one. It's nothing I haven't experienced before, and the world is certainly not short of them."

"Listen, that's not why we came out here. We wanted to talk to you about something." She exchanges a glance with Chuck, and I feel myself starting to tense up. Is this where they give me the third degree about my relationship? Was everything they said about being okay with it a lie? Now that I'm here, they're going to try to talk me out of it.

"We're thinking about selling up and moving out to California." I feel my mouth drop open, and the nerves I was feeling are taken over by shock. That was *not* what I thought they were going to say.

"Look, it's not definite yet, but it makes sense for us to be on the West Coast. We have to send horses out there so often for filming, making Max more in demand there, and, well, of course there's you, Harlow." Her eyes are all misty, so I grab her free hand with mine. "You're finding your own feet, and I know it hasn't been long, but I can tell you feel something for these boys. Long-distance relationships aren't fun, and we can tell you love Brad as much as we do. We don't want to miss out on everything, and nothing is keeping us here with both of our daughters gone more often than not. Family is what's important to us."

"But what about Mr. and Mrs. Boston?" I argue, earning a snort from Melinda and a heavy sigh from Chuck.

"Although it's probably going to cause some huge drama, I wasn't planning on inviting them to live with us. I don't think they would be happy in California, so I planned to buy them a small place here—hire them a housekeeper, which hopefully they won't run off within days, and wish them the best. I know it may seem like it, but I'm not blind to who my parents are, and as much as I wish things were different, I know that they'll care more about their 'severance package' than my absence in their lives."

"Not that they will be happy with anything we buy for them or any housekeeper we choose, but they're fucking adults, and I'm sick and tired of paying for them to live above their means. It's going to be such a culture shock, but I think we all need a fresh start with less toxicity in our lives." Melinda almost sounds gleeful at the idea of cutting out her toxicity, namely, her in-laws, and Chuck scolds her with a single look.

"Mel is right, no matter how inappropriate her joy is. The way they've treated her and you over the years has gone on far too long, and no matter how many times I say something to them, they don't listen. This is going to be a rude wake-up call." He looks resigned, but I know they've worn away at his good nature. They deserve to reap everything they've sown.

"Well, I have to say I am so happy to hear your news. I was just thinking about how hard it would be, moving out to California and not seeing you, but you just solved my problem. Does Max know yet? Does Dad? Dad is going to be so excited when you tell him."

They both shake their heads. "No, we kind of only came to a decision last night. Melinda will call Max and let her know, and I'm going to call Brad and see if he knows of any places around them that have spaces for horses. Once that's figured out, I guess we'll get the ball rolling. We'll need to put this place on the market and find somewhere for Mom and Dad, and…" Chuck trails off, looking a little lost, and Melinda giggles.

"You worry about finding us somewhere to live on the West Coast, and I'll worry about getting everything here ready to move."

"Ah, just one thing." They both look at me as I interrupt their plans. "Can we wait until I'm gone to tell Mr. and Mrs. Boston? I do *not* want to be here when that happens."

Melinda's face screws up in a pout. "Coward."

"Yup, and I won't deny it."

Jacinta pokes her head out the glass door as the three of us chuckle to ourselves. "Is it safe to come out yet?"

"Get out here. I still haven't had a chance to tell you off for what you did to my girl when she first arrived," Melinda growls, and Chuck hides his smile behind his coffee cup as Jacinta's eyes widen. I see her take a step back inside, but Jace gives her a shove from behind, forcing her to stumble out the door. She throws him a look that could kill, but he doesn't act like it bothers him.

"Jacinta, actions have consequences, and this is one of them," he says calmly, then he wanders back inside, allowing her to be spanked in private.

Jacinta slowly takes a seat next to mine, her eyes not leaving Melinda. "What were you thinking? I cannot believe that, knowing we raised Harlow, you would still assume she was some gold-digging harlot. I am so disappointed that you allowed your distrust of everyone else to play with your mind and convince you to treat our daughter with such loathing." She reaches out and grabs Jacinta's hand, but despite the firmness of her words, the grip is gentle. "We never would have sent someone like that to be a part of your family. We know what all of you have been through, and your lack of trust in us was hurtful. What you did to Harlow hurt us too."

Damn, Melinda is not pulling her punches, and tears are already streaming down Jacinta's face. Melinda's not yelling or being hateful, but I think that's worse than the alternative. She's always been so calm when upset, and that makes it all the more difficult. I've been on the receiving end of this sort of Melinda talk once or twice, and it's not something you forget.

"I know that you and Harlow are becoming firm friends now, and she has nothing but nice things to say about you, but I hope this experience also helps you learn not to judge people so quickly in the future. I know it's hard, honey." She slides forward and pulls Jacinta into a hug. "Your mother did a real number on you, but you need to know that not everyone is out to get you or use you. Some people will accept you for who you are despite all the money and fame, and they are the ones you need to trust and stay close to. They're the ones that matter." She pulls back and wipes the tears from her cheeks. "Now, tell me all about this young man you brought with you. That Southern accent is certainly music to the ears."

"And that's my cue to leave. I'm going to call Brad. Mel, make sure you don't forget to call our daughter and let her know the news as well." Chuck hurries away before any more talk about boys can continue, all three of us laughing at his retreating back.

"What news?" It totally does not go unnoticed that she's latching on to anything that takes the spotlight away from Jace. Subtle, Jacinta is not.

"Oh no, tit for tat." Melinda shakes her head. "You tell me yours, and I'll tell you mine."

Jacinta's emotions are entirely scattered across her face, and it's just painful watching her work through them. There's panic, worry, and just plain confusion. It looks like she hasn't had a chance to process everything that has been piled on her in the last couple of days. I grab her hand. "Would you like to tell her your other news for now? I can get it started if you're not ready to talk yet," I offer, and she knows I'm not referring to Jace. She nods quickly, no sign of the confident, effervescent woman I have come to know. She's regressed into a scared, insecure teenager I'm sure she once was.

"Do you know the story of the abandoned

property across the road from Brad's place in California?"

"Yeah, of course, the owner's son Dragos was best friends with Brad and Chuck. He was a really nice guy. We were devastated when he disappeared. That happened at the same time that Brad was out here with your mom, Harlow. It's the other reason he rushed home after the two of them split up."

"Yes, well, it turns out that Dragos was the twins' biological father. Their mother sold them to Brad when they were younger." From the guilty look on Melinda's face, I can tell this isn't all news to her. I guess it's not far-fetched to assume she knew the latter. "And they're now heirs to Count Bucătaru's fortune." I go on to explain the Cecelia blackmail situation and how it finally came out, probably getting Melinda's brain closer to overload with each new detail. But now that I'm in front of her, it all just kind of spills out.

Melinda grabs Jacinta's hand again at the end of the story. "Let me tell you, even though your mother was a raving fucking lunatic, your dad would have wanted you and would have loved you. He would have moved heaven and earth to make sure you were protected from his father and his illegal business practices, and if he couldn't be there for you, then Brad would have been his first choice."

"So the twins are dealing with the fallout of everything, and I think they're handling it amazingly." Then something occurs to me. "Huh, I just realized we've both been hit with the 'who's your secret daddy' conversation in the last couple of months. We could be a whole episode of Jerry Springer."

My joke lightens the atmosphere a little, and Jacinta takes over. "On an easier topic, Jace and I are just friends, for now at least. I told him that I didn't think starting anything more serious or complicated would be fair while I was dealing with all of this. Pretty sure we all saw how well I deal with change, considering the billboard fiasco. My attention would be split and unfocused, and I'd worry about them being neglected."

"Them?" Melinda is almost giddy as she asks.

"Ah, yeah… Jace's roommates and, I guess, lovers. The three of them have expressed an interest in getting to know me better, maybe take me on some dates and see where things might go. It's not something that I ever really thought I'd have for myself, but if Harlow and my brothers can take a chance on a relationship that's twice as complicated, I think I deserve to let myself see where it all goes when I'm ready."

Melinda claps her hands and bounces up and down on her chair like the cheerleader she used to be in high school. "You're getting a harem too! Now we need to find one for my Max, and then all of my girls will be taken care of, and I won't have to worry about them."

Completely pink-cheeked at this point, Jacinta

waves Melinda's enthusiasm away. "Anyway, that's my news, so come on, share."

"Oh, nothing much… just the fact that we're going to sell here and move to the West Coast." Jacinta is silent for a moment before she starts to squeal with excitement, and then there's two of them looking like high school cheerleaders. I roll my eyes but can't help smiling, too. I mean, it *is* exciting.

"Oh my god, that is awesome! Dad is going to be so happy. Oh, and just wait until you meet his girlfriends."

Melinda stops suddenly. "Did you say girl-friends… plural?" She gives me a look that could fry me. "Why am I only just hearing about this now?"

"Because there's just been so much going on. Does it really surprise you that I forgot something? Emma, Dad's first girlfriend, rescued me when I fell." Jacinta coughs, and I correct myself. "Was pushed into the empty pool on the count's property. Anyway, there must be something in the water over there because everybody's getting lots of love. Molly is Emma's partner, and Dad's apparently a silver fox. It turns out they aren't opposed to sharing either."

She grumbles, "Damn it. I wish Chuck was interested in sharing." Jacinta and I burst into laughter, and I stand up, stretching my arms over my head. "I don't know about you guys, but I could do with a little nap. I'm going to head back to my apartment until the guys get home."

"Ahh, no, you're not." Melinda stands to block me from leaving. "Before they left, I promised Thomas that we wouldn't let you go anywhere on your own, so if you want to nap, you can use Max's room. Let's not be that silly girl in a horror movie that doesn't listen to anyone and gets herself killed."

Sighing, I agree. She has a point. As I give them both a kiss on the cheek, I hear Melinda ask Jacinta if she'd like a glass of wine, and while I contemplate turning around, the need for a nap is stronger, so I keep going. Climbing into Max's bed, the smell of her room brings me comfort, but I find that I've gotten used to sleeping next to someone now, so the bed feels awfully empty. I close my eyes, hoping the guys don't take too long with their investigations.

Chapter Five

Harlow

The next few days are a flurry of activity for basically everyone but me. Oliver and Holden take a trip to New York to check out the new Neighpalm Ink setup and touch base with Jonah. Declan has been holed up with Chuck in his office, making video calls to Dad so they can do virtual walkthroughs of properties close to the Summers' estate. Jacinta and Jace have been helping Melinda pack things to prepare for the move, and Thomas and Kai have been trying to find out more about my mother's sister.

You could have knocked me over with a feather when Thomas told me all about meeting Bear and the information he gave him. I had no clue about having an aunt, but when I sat down and really thought about it, some of her drunken, high rants actually started to make sense. She would ramble and scream about a traitorous bitch, and I always thought it was one of the whores she used to compete with for clients, but now I'm not so sure. I never did understand what a "coworker" could have done to make her that angry, but it makes a lot more sense if this was about her sister. Nothing can bring you as high or low as family can—that I know with firsthand experience.

Now I'm just left to wonder about what the hell my aunt did to piss my mom off that badly, but I guess we'll never know unless we find the damn woman. Honestly, I'm not that optimistic. Somehow, tracking her down is proving more difficult than we had thought, even with the Summers' and the Bostons' combined resources and wallets. No birth certificate can be found for a Diane Stubbs, born anywhere in the U.S. the year my mother was supposedly born, so Thomas' current theory is that wasn't my mom's real name. Unfortunately, that leaves us at a dead end because without at least a name, tracking her becomes a little tricky. But he and Kai still head out every day to ask questions in local bars, homeless shelters, and drug dens. I don't know if I admire or am worried about their dedication to figuring this out. I really don't know whether this is a dead end, and I just don't know what it might do to them if they don't find her.

Jaxon and I have spent the time packing up my apartment and helping Josh organize the stables for the cross-country trip. All of Dad's horses will need to be moved, plus the remainder of Chuck's, as well as Jenny and DS. Peter never turned back up, and Chuck has decided not to bother with hiring anyone new until they're in California.

Seriously lost in our little safe space at home, I can act like everything is normal, focusing on how excited I am to have Chuck and Melinda close by once more. I'd love to stay in that giddy place, pretending that I get to be the girl with her family, her boyfriends, and her animals all in one safe and happy bubble, but I know it will burst very soon when reality rears its ugly head.

"Who is this?" Jaxon asks, waving a photo at me. He's reached the bottom of one of my drawers, and when my eyes meet the photo, sadness overcomes me.

It's a picture of my mom, carefree and vibrant. I think it's from the same summer that I was conceived. Melinda had always told me that Mom never had a visible drug problem up until then. Sure, she was tight-lipped about her past, so Melinda didn't know much, but my mom was always health-conscious, drinking very seldomly and exercising daily. That was why Melinda was so stunned when everything changed.

"That's my mom," I tell him, taking the photo

from his hand and running my finger across the seam in the paper. I couldn't tell him how many times I unfolded that picture and stared at it, wishing with everything in me that I'd someday get that version of my mom back. I wanted so badly to have that person who would smile and laugh with me, make sure I ate healthy meals, and would maybe just sit next to me, quietly enjoying our time together.

Jaxon frowns, looking a little confused. "Wow, that's really weird. I could swear she looks like one of my mom's old friends, but I guess I was only four or five when she dumped us with Brad, so I must be remembering wrong." Shrugging, I toss the photo into the open box at his feet.

"I guess if your mom was as much of a junkie as mine, she probably had junkie friends, too. They all seem to get the same sort of washed-up, rode-hard, and hung-up-wet kind of look, or that's what my experience has been. What she would have been doing on the West Coast, I have no idea, so it's probably just some weird coincidence. I'm sure she just looks like another strung-out person your mom knew."

Despite his agreement, he's still frowning, so I distract him with a promise to let him bend me over the exam table downstairs if we finish up soon. Suffice it to say the packing is done in a whirlwind, and I'm glad that I haven't been asked to examine any local animals while I've been home because I'm never going to be able to look at my little clinic the same.

Chuck and Melinda did not, in fact, wait until we had left to tell Mr. and Mrs. Boston they were selling and moving. Let me tell you that the sight of nine fully grown adults running for my apartment was enough to have us all giggling by the time we all made it into hiding. We deserted Chuck and Melinda like the house was on fire and only returned once the coast was clear. Chuck and Melinda were drinking heavily, and there was no sign of Mr. and Mrs. Boston in sight. None of us were brave enough to ask how it went because it was obvious it had not gone well. I simply gave them both a big hug and ordered pizzas for dinner.

Yesterday, the news about Ninja Starfish broke, and our relationship seems to have become old gossip, thankfully, so we're heading home. Today the for-sale sign goes up on the property, and I promised Oliver I would take him into town to visit my tattoo artist before we fly back to California tomorrow. So, this morning, we use one of the hired cars to head into Hartford to see Tasha at Saint Ink. I'm pretty sure that Oliver wants to invite her to work for him in New York, but Tasha's boyfriend is the owner of the place, so the likelihood that she will want to leave is slim.

Thomas insists on driving us, so I'm sitting in the back when the phone rings.

"Hey, neighbor!" Max sounds more upbeat for

the first time in a while, and her contagious joy makes me smile. "I can't believe Mom and Dad decided to leave Connecticut. I'm pretty sure you're the reason why, but I'm not complaining."

"Hey, yourself. I believe being neighbors is what your dad and my dad have planned. I think they've finally settled on a place about ten minutes from Dad's. I'm pretty sure the property actually backs onto Dad's, so they may have thrown a little incentive at the neighbor to encourage him to sell to Chuck, or that's how Declan made it sound."

We chat the rest of the drive into town, catching up on everything, including Luke being responsible for most of the stalking.

"That doesn't really surprise me. He always watched with creepy eyes. Remember, I used to tell you that." Yep, can't say I'm surprised by her reaction either. Like any other sibling, Max never could resist the chance to throw something in my face, especially when it means she was right.

"Yes, but I thought that was just you being an elitist snob," I fire back, and she grunts her reluctant agreement.

We move away from the topic when she asks about the press, and I'm happy to inform her that the press have lost interest in us—for now. Luckily, she's got some exciting news that takes some of the focus off of us; she has a speaking role in the latest film she's working on. She plays a tavern wench who gets ravished by one of the male leads, which of course leaves me with a million questions, but when I try to dig a bit more, she clams up, citing her NDA as the reason, and I can't very well argue with that even though I'm a bit tired of the secrecy. We've always told each other everything in the past, and I've never judged her, not once, even when she did things that were totally opposed to what she really wanted to do. Could she be jealous of the Summers being in my life? Being the biggest recent life change, that should be the likeliest culprit, but it didn't seem that way when we dropped off the horses. In fact, the distant crap didn't really start until *after* that night. I wonder if it has anything to do with whoever was in her room.

We hang up with a promise to speak again soon, and Thomas finds us a parking spot near the shop. The bell jangles as Oliver holds the door open, allowing me to enter before him, both following close behind. The wall is decked out in art of all styles, showing off the range of what the artists can do, and the air is filled with the familiar scent of antiseptic.

There's no receptionist, with Tasha being expected to do that as part of her job, but I can hear guns buzzing, so I patiently wait for her. Thomas takes a seat in the waiting area as I look over the range of piercing jewelry and merchandise. There's a wall that separates the reception area from the front and the back, with a glass window in it so that Tasha can look out for potential clients while those same clients check out what's going on in the rest of the studio. I can see Tasha working on a client while her boyfriend drawing at a lighted table, completely ignoring us despite Tasha saying something to him. Whatever he says, she rolls her eyes, turns off her gun, and speaks to her client before taking off her gloves and coming out to the front.

"Hi, sorry to keep you waiting," she says before she realizes it's me. "Harlow! Hey, girl, shit! Haven't you been keeping busy." She comes around the display counter and gives me a hug, but her body stiffens once she takes a peek at my bodyguards—I mean, adoring and just *slightly* protective boyfriends.

"Holy shit!" Yep, I missed Tasha.

"Hey, Tasha, this is my boyfriend Oliver."

"Summers. Yeah, I know. It's a pleasure to meet you; I love your work," she all but gushes as they shake hands. Oliver is smiling genuinely, not the bland professional one he had in place when he interviewed that woman at his shop.

"Hey, Tasha, the pleasure is all mine. Your work is the reason I begged Harlow to bring me here. Her tats are incredible, and she says you did them all. Listen, I wanted to offer you a job in my new place that's opening in New York. We would help with the cost of relocation, and we've converted the aboveground levels of the warehouse into accommodation for the staff, so they don't have to find any."

Tasha's eyes widen in surprise, then she bites her lip and looks back through the glass into the back. Her boyfriend's watching, and when he stands up, she whirls back around to face us.

"Shit, please don't say anything when he comes out here," she quietly begs as the guy comes out the front, frowning.

"Tasha, your client is waiting," he all but growls, reminding me of how I feel about him. I don't like this man; he's never got anything nice to say, is super critical of everything Tasha does, and he puts off this aura of intimidation like everyone around him should bend to his will and get out of his space. I always make sure my appointments are scheduled when he's having a day off. Last time I was in, Tasha had told me that her client list was growing, making her responsible for sixty percent of the shop's clientele, while the other three artists brought in the remaining forty. Instead of being proud of her good work, her asshole boyfriend raised her seat price to compensate for his loss of revenue. So, basically, she's paying more than anyone else simply because she's a better artist and a nicer human being. Not sure why she stays with the ass, to be honest.

Oliver holds up his hands and plasters his professional smile on his face. "Hey, sorry, man, I just wanted to drop in and give Tasha my card."

"What the fuck for?" the asshole grunts back. I

can tell he recognizes Oliver, but the look he gives Tasha is positively frightening.

"Oh, she's done all my girlfriend's work, and Harlow's keen to have some more stuff done, but she's relocating to California to be with me. I was giving Tasha my card to give me a call if she ever comes out there. She can use my shop to do Harlow's work."

Oliver easily pulls the bullshit excuse out of thin air. The guy looks suspicious because of course, why wouldn't I get my boyfriend to do the work, but he doesn't say anything as she takes the card and tucks it into a pocket of her denim shorts. I know for a fact that it's Jonah's card, not his, but the asshole doesn't need to know that.

"I don't think I'll be coming out there any time soon, but I'll be sure to let you know if I do," Tasha says to the both of us, her eyes practically pleading for us not to make a big deal of the situation.

"Okay, well, like Oli said, I'm moving, so I just came to say goodbye and tell you you're welcome to visit whenever." I pull her into a hug. "Call me if you need help. Any time," I whisper to her before pulling away, and she gives me a small, nearly imperceptible nod. We say our goodbyes and leave, but before the door can close, I catch him grabbing her by the arm and squeezing. Instead of the big personality I usually see, Tasha is practically cowering before him. I start to turn around, ready to storm back in there, but Thomas puts his hand on the door to stop me.

"Don't, you'll probably only make it worse. Call her later and check on her, but let it go for now." I grit my teeth in anger but allow them to pull me back to the car.

I'm silently stewing in my rage on the ride home when my phone rings. The name on the screen brings a smile to my face, though, so I accept the call. "Doc Davies, what a lovely surprise! How are you?"

"Harlow, my girl, I saw that you were home. I have a situation, but I can't get there right now. Are you at your place?" The usually jovial man sounds stressed, which has me sitting up straighter, ready to pay attention.

"We're about ten minutes out. What can I do to help?"

"I'm not entirely sure. I got a phone call from a woman, quite distressed, saying a wild cat had attacked her. She was locked inside her car, and the cat was still there. Have you got a tranq gun? I thought you might keep one on hand in case the bobcats get too close to the horses." He sounds upset, and I know it's because he has an obligation to report it to Animal Control. Unlike our tranqs, they'll be coming with real guns because a bobcat attack during the day raises rabies suspicions. He's such a softy and doesn't like any animal to get hurt, let alone killed for something out of their control.

"Yeah, I do," I tell him, thinking about which box it's packed in.

"Can you take care of it for me? I'll be there as soon as I can, with a cage to transport it in."

"Absolutely," I reply, feeling pretty confident until he gives me the address.

"Isn't this that really weird place about ten minutes or so from the Bostons'? It has all the barbed wire surrounding it and those keep out signs?"

"Yeah, it is. Harlow, be careful, okay? I've heard conflicting things about the people who live there, and I've never actually been called out there before."

I assure him I will before I hang up and fill the guys in.

"I'm coming, too," Thomas says before I've even finished, and I roll my eyes.

"I wasn't going to exclude you. I've actually got two tranq guns, so I was figuring you could be back-up in case I miss. Also, not knowing what we're walking into makes me more cautious than if this was a bobcat bothering the horses."

"Yeah, and I might bring Declan along to protect our backs from the human element in case there's more than just the woman trapped in her car. He shoots almost as well as I do."

When we get to the Bostons', Thomas drives straight to my clinic. Oliver hops out and runs inside to get Declan while I change out my sandals for a pair of boots and grab the supplies we need. Not entirely sure what the tranq dosage should be, I go higher than normal and pack the antidotes just in case. I'd like to put down a charging bobcat fast, rather than wait twenty minutes for a slow-acting sedative to work.

Within ten minutes of stopping, we're back in the car and driving for the house, filling in Declan on the way.

"Alright, you two stay behind me and cover my back. If I miss the target, Thomas, it will take me a moment to reload, so if it starts coming for us, I want you to take a shot. Declan, if he misses and we're in danger, you are to put the animal down as a last resort. You're more for the people element. Keep an eye on our surroundings and the person trapped in the car, as well as keep an eye out for Animal Control."

My heart is racing as we pull up to the huge gate blocking the entry. It's over twelve feet high, with razor wire at the top. Behind it is a driveway that's overgrown and unkempt, and there's no visual of a house. Declan climbs out and opens the gate while Thomas drives through, then he closes it behind us and gets back in.

The tension in the car is high as we slowly creep down the driveway. The foliage opens up, and my mouth drops open as we pull up to a set of build-ings that have not been well looked after. There's an old station wagon, and standing on its roof is one *very* surprising animal.

"Fuck!!" I exclaim, rubbing a hand across my face to check if what I'm seeing is real. Sure enough, beyond all reason, when I look again, it hasn't changed.

"That's not a bobcat," Declan says, turning to look at me in horror. "That's a fucking tiger!"

Chapter Six

Harlow

"Yup, and a white one at that." I check out the surrounding buildings and shudder. God, I hope that's the only one around. The last thing we need is to have a whole heap of them loose. That would be a disaster, not to mention freaking dangerous if they're all as aggressive as this one is. The tiger jumps off the roof and paces around the car, and right now I can't do anything but watch.

"What are you going to do?" Thomas asks as I dial Doc Davies back on my cell.

"Are you there?" he asks without any pleasantries, and I can't help the sigh that escapes my mouth.

"Yeah, but we're not dealing with a bobcat."

"Well, what is it? A cougar?" he asks, sounding surprised as cougars aren't native to the area.

"It's a white tiger."

There's a moment of silence before I hear tires squealing. "Fucking hell." Now I know he's upset because Doc Davies is an old-school gentleman who *never* curses. I've seen a cow with exploding diarrhea fart when he stepped behind it and he never muttered more than a disappointed 'damn it'. "I'll call the police and ACO to update them. They should be able to call in additional support as well. I'm going to need a bigger cage, and I'm going to have to call around to some zoos, see if they've lost a tiger or can temporarily take one."

"I've got that cage I kept the injured cougar in last year. It was large enough for a few more cats, so it should be big enough for the tiger if you can't figure out an immediate solution. It might not be happy, but it'll be able to move around a little until we can make better arrangements."

"That's a great idea, Harlow. We may just have to do that." He sounds a little relieved at that suggestion, which doesn't bode well for our other options to get this taken care of quickly.

"Alright. Do you want me to wait for you, or do you want me to tranq it and see if they have some-where for it here? I mean, surely they've got to have some sort of enclosure."

"Use your judgment. I trust you," he orders, then hangs up without another word.

"What did he mean about calling the police?" Declan asks, not taking his eyes off the big cat in front of us, who is still pacing the car. My attention, on the other hand, is now on the woman trapped in it. Rightfully, she looks pretty damn terrified.

"Hmm? Oh, owning exotic animals is illegal in Connecticut. When we thought it was a bobcat, it would have been easy enough for us to tranq it, cage it, and release it. Now, that's not possible. Zoos have to be *very* careful what they take in, so a quarantine period would be needed. Otherwise, they run the risk of their permanent residents getting sick. The police need to be called in because whoever owns this place is going to go to jail, and Animal Control will search the property to see if there are any other animals here that will need to be confiscated. They'll also want to see my exotic animal license, which I have thanks to Doc Davies, before they'll let me take custody of any animals."

The whole time I've been talking to the guys I've been watching the tiger, taking in the state of its coat, which is dull and lifeless, and the gauntness of its frame. There's no way the poor thing has been getting enough meals. I'm worried that if I hit it with a fast-acting sedative, it's not going to be able to handle it, and we'll lose it. Whenever possible, I try to choose the course of action that gives the animal a chance at life, especially when it's clear it hasn't been living its best.

Making my decision, I grab my tranq gun, eject

the dart that was in it, and load in a lower dose that will act slower but will be kinder on the big cat's nervous system. I do the same to Thomas' gun then pass it to him. There's a chance that the cat could calm down if we leave it alone, but that's not really a waiting game you want to play with a tiger. The chance that it'll just become more agitated with time is too big of a risk for us to wait for ACO.

"Okay, here's what's going to happen. This sedative will act a lot slower. The cat will probably turn and charge our car when he realizes we're a threat, and we'll be trapped until it works. I'd rather that, which should only take ten minutes tops, than risk killing it because its body wasn't able to handle the most extreme dosage of the drug. Same plan as before, but I'm pretty sure I won't miss at this distance. I'm going to get out on this side and use the door as cover."

I grab the handle of the door furthest away from the enraged animal, but before I can open it, Declan grabs me, hauls me forward, and plants a kiss on my mouth.

"Good luck," he says as he pulls away, leaving me a little dazed.

"Well shit, I shouldn't miss now," I tell him with a grin and quietly open the door. Thomas copies me on the opposite side, using his door for cover as well. The tiger hasn't stopped to look at us, its focus completely on the woman inside the car.

Cocking the gun, I take aim at his haunches,

hoping to hit the meaty muscle on the back leg. I track its movement, take a deep breath, and pull the trigger. The dart flies across the clearing and hits the tiger where I wanted it to. The tranq gun isn't as loud as a normal gun, but we've definitely drawn the tiger's attention now.

"Back in the car!" I tell Thomas, but he's already climbing back in and pulling his door closed. The tiger whirls on our car and stalks toward it, but already, I can see the tranq starting to take effect. It really isn't in good condition if the drugs are working so damn quickly. Fuck, I hope I haven't just signed its death certificate. It circles our car, and I can hear it chuffing its annoyance, but it loses interest and goes back to the other car. There's no way this woman is just a bystander. She had to have played some role in the tiger's captivity for it to be so focused on her, which means we probably got here in the nick of time to save her life—whether she deserves it or not.

"Whatever that woman has done to it, it badly wants payback," Declan mutters, eyes locked on the cat's movements. Step by step, it continues to circle the car, though its movements become less coordinated until it staggers, collapsing to the ground.

"Wait a little longer," I murmur as the big cat struggles to get back to its feet. Eventually, it gives up and lays its head down.

"Okay, let's go." I leave my empty tranq gun on the back seat and take the one from Thomas. "Just keep your weapon on you. I want us to have at least one ready to go if needed." Declan hands it back to him, and we slowly get out of the car. I've got my stethoscope wrapped around my neck and the tranq reversal in the bag I'm carrying. I grabbed a couple of blankets when we left, which come out with us too. I'm going to lay them over the tiger to block out any stimulation that might force it out of sedation too soon. We've only taken a few steps away from our car when the woman in the car opens the door and climbs out.

"Did you kill it? Is it dead?" she screeches, and we get a good look at her for the first time. She's holding her arm, which looks to be bleeding, so I pull my cell out of my pocket and hand it to Declan. "Can you call an ambulance, please?" I ask him, not taking my eyes off the cat. As I get to it, I slowly crouch down, and it's definitely out.

"Not dead, sedated," I answer as I put my stethoscope to my ears so I can listen to its heart rate. Its pulse is a little slower than I'd like, and its lungs don't sound great, but I think it's going to be okay for now. Now that I'm closer, I can see that its fur is matted, and there's a distinct smell that tells me the cat hasn't had proper hygiene habits for a while. Not letting myself get caught up in those details, I scan its whole body and realize it's very obviously female. Not to mention another urgent problem. Crap!

As I pull the things out of my ears, I hear a

commotion, and when I look up, Thomas is restraining the woman. The insane bitch has her foot pulled back like she's actually under the misguided idea that kicking a motherfucking tiger is a good plan.

"You should have put a bullet between its eyes! It attacked Jim and was coming after me. I ran, but it wouldn't let me leave." Her shrill, upset voice is like nails on a chalkboard, exactly what I *don't* want filling the silence while we have a sleeping tiger in front of us.

"Sit your ass down," I order the woman, pointing to the nearby dilapidated porch. "I need to have a look at your arm. Did the tiger get you?" Now that I know it's going to be okay, I need to ask some more questions because I'm almost one hundred percent sure that the tiger has a litter of cubs somewhere, from the look of its teats.

She shakes her head but does as I said. "No. I scraped it on one of the enclosures as I was running away." She has a bit of cloth wrapped around it, and after pulling on some gloves, I unwrap it, hoping the authorities get here soon. A syringe of saline helps wash away some of the blood, giving me a better look at her. The woman has a deep slice down her forearm that's going to need stitches. She hisses in pain, but I'm not feeling a lot of sympathy at the moment.

"The ambulance will be here soon, and you're definitely going to need stitches," I say just as the sound of sirens hits my ears. "Now, are there any more animals or people on the property that we need to be worried about? Anything else that might have escaped?"

She closes her mouth and clams up as soon as the question leaves my mouth, so I press into the wound until she grimaces. It's all fun and games, owning an exotic pet, until someone gets hurt. The police will search the property anyway, but I'd rather hear it straight from the idiot's mouth first. Plus, it's a matter of safety. "Come on now, you don't want to be held responsible for anyone else getting hurt."

She snarls at me much like the cat had been doing before shaking her head. "No, it's just me and Jimmy here, and I don't think any of the other animals got out."

"Is there anything that's as dangerous as that?" I ask her. Once I see the stubborn set to her jaw, I pull the reversal syringe out of the bag. It's definitely a big needle, and it's not my fault if she assumes it's going into *her* arm if she doesn't answer me. Besides, I'm pretty sure I've got a bigger threat than sticking her with this.

"Well, okay. I guess we can just get back into our car and leave. After I've reversed the sedative, anyway."

"NO! No, please don't. Yes, there are some big snakes, a jaguar, and a male tiger."

Fuck. "Are they all locked in safely?" She nods, and I breathe a sigh of relief.

"What happened here?" I point to the escaped cat, and she groans, probably with the realization that she's not getting away with this.

"Shinto was our family pet. She used to live indoors with us, and she was lovely. But then Jim got the idea that we should breed her for profit. He got his hands on another tiger, they hit it off, and she did have a litter. Jim wanted to get them out so he could hand raise them, but she attacked him when he tried to take them away."

I just stare at her in disbelief. "You're both idiots." I stand up and walk away before I can say anything else. It's only then that I notice the police and everyone else have arrived. Doc Davies and an animal control officer are examining Shinto, and police officers are talking to Declan and Thomas. A paramedic approaches me, so I point the woman out. "If you could *forget* to give her a pain blocker; none of us would say anything." All I get is a raised eyebrow in return, but I refuse to feel bad about saying it. That woman deserves every bit of discomfort coming her way.

I crouch down with the two around the cat. "She seems fairly stable, but she was agitated and aggressive when we got here." They both groan when I explain the rest. "The male is here some-where, but I haven't searched yet. I wanted to make sure nothing else was going to surprise us."

"And is there?" the AC officer asks, and I grimace.

"They're all locked up, but aside from the male tiger, there's a jaguar and some large snakes."

Then it's their turn to grimace. "Harlow, this is Jay. How about the two of you go have a look, and I'll stay to monitor the cat. It might be best to leave the others where they are while we take her back to your clinic. She needs fluids and these mats in her coat cut out. I can see she has fleas, and she probably has worms too. Thankfully, we can treat all of that. She may have been their pet, but I'm pretty sure she wasn't loved. The other animals probably have problems too, but we can't take them all to your place. We may have to leave them here with a guard overnight while we work out what to do with them." Doc sounds upset but resigned, and it's sad to say the feeling is mutual. "Who would have guessed this was practically on our doorstep?"

With nothing else to do, I reload my gun with a rapid-acting tranq and wave Thomas and Declan off so they know I'm heading out to explore with Jay. I can see Declan on the phone, so I'm assuming he's either updating the rest of the siblings or maybe he's tattling to Dad, but Thomas hurries over and puts his hand on my back as we move away from the ramshackle house and toward the outer buildings. There's a convenient trail of blood to follow—likely the woman's.

We push through the doors of the barn-like

structure, and Jay sucks in a deep breath at the sight. Very much like a stables, it has a walkway through the middle and enclosures on either side. The roof has windows to let the light in, and one of them is broken, the sunlight just so happening to shine a beam of light down on a body. A body which has been *eviscerated*. Intestines hang out from what was once his stomach, and his left arm looks to be quite badly mauled. The smell should have given it away, but the sightless eyes confirm that Jim most definitely isn't living to see another day. My heart sinks; even though it clearly wasn't the tiger's fault, the state authorities will likely argue to put her down. Generally, any exotic pets are placed somewhere safe, but it becomes a whole issue if the animal has harmed a human. Too many people argue that the animal will be more likely to harm more people now that it's happened once.

"Fuck, I guess Jim didn't make it." The words slip out before I can stop them, accompanied by a nervous giggle, and Jay and Thomas both give me a weird look. "Sorry, I think the stress is getting to me."

On the right side of Jim, running the length of the building, are cages. I can see another white tiger pacing up and down in one that's not really big enough for him to get four paces before he has to turn around.

I step around Jim and walk past the tiger, the poor animal paying no attention to me since his eyes are locked on the corpse. What's in the next enclosure has me shuddering and stepping back. Thankfully, it's all glass; otherwise, I would be running for the hills. Not realizing the others had followed, I shriek when I touch something, whirling around and aiming my gun.

Both Thomas and Jay hold their hands up in defense. "Harlow, hey, it's just us," Thomas cajoles, and I shake my head and lower my gun, sighing.

"God, I'm sorry. This is all so upsetting, and… well… out of all the animals, I really, *really* dislike snakes. Which I know might be weird for a vet, but… ugh." I can't control the shudder as I point back to where there are three humongous pythons. I don't really want to get any closer, but Jay's face lights up as he decides to get a closer look.

"Oh, wow. I think that's a green boa constrictor, and the other two are albino burmese pythons." He sounds excited, so I'll leave him to it. I will happily take care of the big cats instead.

A sound on the other side of the shed has me spinning around and stepping forward. This cage isn't as well lit as the others, so I need to close to the bars to see into the depths. On the floor is a black form; the only reason I can see it is because Thomas takes out his cell and shines the flashlight into the back corner until its eyes light up.

"How the hell did these two get their hands on two white tigers and a black jaguar?" I'm astonished at them having not one but two rare species of big cats. Well, actually, I'm stunned they have big cats in the first place, but these are just amazing. I was expecting the normal spotted jag, not this gorgeous creature. The pitch black animal is watching us with curiosity. It stands up, stretches, and pads its way over to the bars of the fence where it proceeds to rub against the bars, purring. It doesn't look like it's quite fully grown yet, so I decide I need to get all the information I can from that stupid woman before they drag her away.

"Well, this one seems a lot friendlier than the tiger was," Thomas quietly says from behind me, not wanting to startle the animal.

"The tiger was protecting her babies, and Jim was an idiot. But yes, this one seems like it's an over-grown house cat." Then I notice something horrifying. I bend down and hold out my hand in the hope that maybe it's had some training, and the animal pushes its big paw through the bars, placing it in my hand.

"Harlow, what are you doing?" Thomas asks in a low, urgent tone.

I ignore him for a moment, and as I run my thumb along it, I confirm that the poor baby has been declawed. I try to get a look into his mouth, but he doesn't open it for me, so I can't see if they defanged him too. God, I hope not because it might be kinder to euthanize this one if they have. Declawed and defanged cats almost never have easy lives.

Another sound carries through the shed, and I give the cat back its paw and stand up. It's like a high-pitched screeching roar, and I'm pretty sure I know what it is.

I hurry over to the open cage door, gagging at the smell of Jim, even while avoiding looking at his body.

Pushing the door open, a huge smile takes over my lips when I find the cause of the sound. "Holy shit, there are five of them!"

Chapter Seven

Jaxon

Oliver had torn into the house, yelling for Declan, and we all listened breathlessly as he told us about Harlow being called out to take care of a bobcat that had trapped a lady in a car. Our older brother had hurried out to assist her and Thomas, leaving us behind.

In the meantime, I've done nothing but pace back and forth across the living room while we wait to hear how everything went.

"Jaxon, relax," Chuck says, smiling. I have no idea what the fuck life is like in Connecticut, but I have a strong feeling that he should not be nearly as calm as he is right now. "Trust me, Harlow lives for this kind of thing. Last year, she brought home a cougar to rehabilitate. It had escaped a wildlife refuge, and someone had taken a shot at it with a bow and arrow, but the arrow had hit its shoulder and snapped off. Because it was injured, it started to look for easy prey and was tearing up the neighborhood chickens. Animal Control caught it and Dr Davis had them bring it here so they could fix it, and then when it was healed, they returned it to the wildlife refuge it had escaped from. That girl loves a challenge, always has. Didn't think twice about taking in a wild cat."

"Yeah, it was all snarly and grumpy, but she was never scared. You could see the thrill in her eyes when she was feeding it. Should have known horses and domestic animals weren't going to be her thing." Melinda smiles fondly at the memory, but I'm already shaking my head by the time she's halfway through the sentence.

"It's easy to say that, and I know she's capable, but..." I don't really want to tell them all that I love her before I've even had a chance to say it to her. "It's easy to say don't worry, but we don't know what they're actually walking into."

The two of them exchange a glance, with one of those expressions that says, "Oh, isn't he cute?" Then Chuck goes over to the sideboard and pulls out a pack of cards. "Let's play a hand of poker while we wait, shall we?"

Melinda doesn't join us, but Holden, Oli, Kai, Jacinta, and Jace all take a seat at the table while Chuck deals out the first hand. I'd say he must be a brave man, but he knows all about the competitive nature of the Summers, and his own competitive streak is almost as fierce.

We play a few rounds, but my mind just isn't on the game, so I fold and take a seat on the sofa with Melinda, who's curled up with a book. At least I can be productive while I'm sitting here. With a few taps on my phone, the notes app is open, and I'm working on the notes for our wildlife rescue surprise.

There are rules and regulations and licenses that need to be applied for, feeding logistics to work out, as well as disposal of waste. So many things to consider that I bet Count Bucătaru didn't have to worry about twenty-five years ago. I'm so deep into my research that I jump when my cell starts ringing.

"Hey, Declan, how's it going?" I answer, and despite their assurances not to worry, I notice Chuck and Melinda are paying just as much attention as my siblings.

"Dude, you are *not* going to believe this. It wasn't a bobcat like Doc thought! It's a fucking tiger."

"Did you say tiger?" I ask, not sure if I heard him right. Melinda gasps and tosses the book she was reading on the coffee table in front of us.

"Yeah, it's a mess here. She tranq'd it, but it's in rough condition. I think she said she'll bring it back there while they figure out what to do with it. There may be some more animals, but she and Thomas have gone to check out the rest of the buildings with an Animal Control officer while Doc Davies monitors the tiger until they can get a transport crate here. Listen, when we get back, I think you need to tell her about your idea. This could be the start of it all. Let's do this for our girl, make her dream come true. If she hates the house, we'll gut it, and she, Jacinta, and Nana can have fun decorating. Call Dad and get the ball rolling."

Sometimes it drives me nuts when my big brother gives the orders, but this is one I can jump on board with no questions asked, mainly because it was my idea in the first place.

"Ok, I'll call Dad now, but I want to make sure the DNA results come back before I say anything to Harlow. It would be devastating if we told her, only to have the trust come back and say we weren't the count's grandkids."

"Pfft, then we'd just buy her something else or build her something else. Call Dad." He hangs up, not giving me a chance to respond.

To no one's surprise, Jacinta is the first to break the silence. "Did you say tiger?"

A loud sigh comes out before I can stop it. "Yeah, apparently. Listen, are you sure you're okay with me giving Harlow the property? I'm going to call Dad to ask about the results and get the ball rolling. I think Declan wants Harlow to be able to keep this tiger as the start to her sanctuary."

"Yes, absolutely yes! She saved the one thing that means the world to me, and I have some serious groveling to do to make up for how I treated her. I know she says she's already forgiven me, but I feel like I need to do more. I would totally make you guys do more if you messed up as badly as I did. Yes, let's do this." She claps her hands together. "It's exciting. I'm going to call Hope, so she can get the marketing department to work on a logo for her."

I look to my brothers, wanting to double check even though I know what their responses are going to be. "You all in?"

"Absolutely."

"Let's do this."

"What can we do?"

Before I can respond, Melinda throws herself at me and hugs me tight. "You are amazing. This is perfect, absolutely perfect." When she pulls away, there are tears in her eyes. "Did you hear that, Chuck? Our girl is going to get her dream. The boys are going to help her with it."

"I sure did, babe." Chuck sounds choked up, and when he looks at me, I can see the pride in his eyes. "Jaxon Summers, you sure did grow up right. I can't tell you how proud I am of you." He looks to the other guys, adding, "All of you."

"Okay, I'm going to call Dad about a few things. It sounds like they're bringing the tiger back here to the cage Harlow has, but there are other animals that need rehoming too. I need to get someone out to the property to start running an assessment on the enclosures. I know we donate to a zoo somewhere, so I'm sure we can get someone out there quickly. If not, Nana can scare up some connections pretty easily."

I make my call, and the phone barely rings before Dad picks up. "Jaxon, I was just about to call you. We got the results, and it's official. You and Jacinta are Count Bucātaru's only living heirs. Congratulations, my boy, you just inherited a fortune."

"Dad, you know that means nothing to either of us, right?" He should already know we don't care about any of it. More importantly than that, I want to reassure the man who raised us that he's the best father a man could want.

"Oh, I know," he chuckles. "I just know where I can get a loan if I find myself a little short." I roll my eyes and join in with the laughter because Neighpalm is worth about three times what we inherited. My eyes flick to my sister, and she can see by the look in mine that the DNA results were confirmed. There are a whole heap more issues we'll have to unpack, but for now, I'm going to put those on the back burner. Harlow comes first.

"Dad, I wanted to talk to you about giving Harlow the property across the road. I want to renovate it into a sanctuary for her and hire someone to help with her internship. We all want to open up a new branch to the Neighpalm Inc. family by using some of the donations from this year's fundraiser to start up the Neighpalm

Wildlife Sanctuary, or whatever Harlow wants to call it."

There's a pause, and I panic, thinking maybe I've overstepped the line. Are we allowed to donate to a company we own, even if it's not for profit? Shit, I've never paid too much attention to the yearly ball in the past. I've just shown up, shaken hands, and flirted with pretty girls and older women in the hope their daddies and husbands would open their wallets and donate to all the amazing causes we support.

"Jaxon, that sounds like an amazing idea, but let's leave the funds raised for charities who really need it. I'm going to finance the zoo's startup. It's the least I can do after missing out on her life up until now. Not to mention I funded Neighpalm Ink too. But we'll still have it registered as a charity so that other organizations can donate to it in future. We also need to get her some staff. I'll get Nana and Poppy on it. We've supported the MacGinty Sanctuary in the past, so I'm sure I can find out who their head of Veterinary Services is, possibly their head of Zoology too, and convince them to consult with us. I mean, it's the least they can do considering their board flat-out rejected our girl."

"We're going to poach their staff?" I ask, a little shocked at Dad's ruthlessness. He doesn't show that side very often, though I guess if anything is going to poke Papa Bear, it's someone mistreating one of his kids.

"Now, Jaxon, I wouldn't call it poaching. I would call it making them an offer they can't refuse." With that final smug line, we hang up so he can start working his billionaire magic.

"Okay, Dad's getting things moving on his end. I just need to talk to Harlow and convince her this is the best thing for her."

Melinda snickers next to me. "Pretty sure that's not going to take much effort at all." Her smile drops when she looks at me, and I can practically see her thoughts running through her head. "Does this place come with no strings attached, or are there strings?"

"You bet your ass there are strings," Oliver says before I can answer, and I wouldn't need to be his brother to see the irritation in his eyes. I know Melinda is just looking out for Harlow, but she could have worded it a better way. "Six strings, to be exact. Six strings that would do anything for her because most of us are halfway, if not all the way, in love with her. Six strings that will support her in anything she wishes to do, and if she doesn't want this, then those six strings will keep trying until they find the perfect fit for her."

"No offense, Melinda, but it's really none of your business. I can see your side of it, especially considering our relationship is unconventional, but it's between Harlow and the six of us. I can assure you there will be absolutely no coercion or influence from any of us. Yes, we want her to take the house and property, and yes, we would like to be invited to live with her, but that's all on her. We will abide by anything she says, and we will fight for this relationship and against anything that tries to get between the seven of us." By the time Kai finishes his spiel, Melinda looks properly chastised, if not a little surprised that two of my brothers jumped in so passionately, but Chuck's got a smile on his face.

"Good for you, boys. Melinda, leave them be. They have to make their own paths in life just like you and I did. Remember what you did when *my* parents tried to interfere."

She blushes and looks down at her hands. "Yeah, you're right, and I apologize to the four of you. That wasn't fair of me."

"What did you do?" Jace asks what we all want to know, thankfully taking the attention away from us.

"I told them to kiss my lily-white poor ass, and if they didn't like me, we could go live in my little trailer and be perfectly happy without any of their money." She and Chuck laugh at the memories, and the tension disappears.

"Okay, if you excuse me, I need to make that call to Hope." Jacinta stands up and makes to leave, but I've got something I need to figure out with my sister before she wanders off.

"Hey, Jazzy, why don't we go outside for a walk before you do that? We need to talk." Her eyes cloud, but she gives a slight nod.

"How about I call Hope and fill her in?" Holden offers before helping her out of her chair. "I want to talk to her about Ninja Starfish and what the fallout was like. I haven't talked to her about it since we've been here. It's been a nice vacation, but I guess real life goes on."

She agrees, and the two of us step outside into the cooler New England air. I wrap an arm around her as we walk toward the converted stable block that Harlow calls home.

"Winter is coming; you can smell it in the air here," she says quietly. "I can't wait to see Aunt Mer at Christmas. As much as I love London, I'm so glad it's our turn this year. So much is happening, and I just want to be in my own space and surrounded by my own things while I come to terms with all of it. How are you doing?"

I think about the question for a moment before answering. "I'm okay, actually." I sound surprised even to my own ears. "This really doesn't change much except the fact that we finally have a name to put to a biological father. Biological roots, I guess, but it doesn't change anything else. I'm still a Summers. Dad is still our dad, the rest are still our siblings, and Harlow... Well, Harlow is my girl-friend. Everything else is insignificant."

"Ten billion dollars isn't really insignificant," she grumbles, then she bumps my hip with hers. "I feel the same way, except the girlfriend part, obvi-ously." I chuckle, which I think is what she was looking for. "But I'm super glad you guys are making that work. I think you're going to find yourself blissfully happy with this arrangement, and now that you're all working to make her dreams a reality, she will too."

"So, what do you want to do about the rest of the inheritance?"

"Do we need to do anything?"

"I think we need to decide whether we keep the properties or sell them. They'll be a monetary drain if we don't ever want to sell them. We could use them for holiday homes if we like them, but realistically, how often will we go abroad?" She bites her lip, her classic tell that she's thinking, so I wait her out. If I keep talking, she'll let me lead the conversation, but I need to let her get things out of her head.

"I know I said I didn't want anything to do with them, but it's our legacy, I guess. The count didn't sound like a nice man, but our biological father was Dad and Chuck's best friend. He can't have been all bad. We could hire a manager to oversee them, and we could turn them into Airbnbs. That way, they pay for themselves, so we don't really have to worry about them. Plus, if you want to surprise Harlow with a trip to the French Riviera, everything will be ready. I feel like that's a decision that lets us keep this connection to our biological family, and it would also make Dad proud too. I think he'll be glad that we're not severing all those ties, and we're still being purposeful. You know Dad taught us to always be smart with whatever we had."

"The castle in Romania and the property in Colombia, too?" I ask, mulling over her idea. It sounds pretty good to me. Neither of us needs any more work, and with the possibility of renovating the property for Harlow, I don't have time to flit around the world, looking over everything. "I think it's a good idea, but would you be opposed to dealing with all of it? Harlow's new venture will keep us busy, and I've possibly got a deal closing on that cruise line I wanted to purchase. If that goes ahead, I'll be rebranding and refurbishing the five ships in the fleet, plus the hotel in Hawaii. That's going to have its grand opening soon. I know it's a lot to ask, but you could take your designs with you, and Nana could oversee the day-to-day runnings for a few months if need be."

I thought she would blow up and rant about her job being just as important as mine, which has been her go-to argument in the past, but she's weirdly quiet.

"You know, I think I'd like that." Holy shit! What's going on with my sister? She's *never* given in that easily to anything that meant she'd lose time at Neighpalm Couture.

"Is everything okay at work?" I ask her, concern evident in my voice, but she waves her hand.

"Yes, yes. I love designing. Jace is an amazing designer and so easy to work with. Of course, Lindy and Rowena try to undermine me at every turn, and that's just bothersome, but it's a temporary problem. It's just that the whole industry is so superficial. Everything is based on looks and what one person decides is a trend, and you know I've never liked designing shit to follow a trend. The best thing about Neighpalm Couture is we design real clothes that people want to wear, not shit that's just for the shock factor on the runway. I'm just so tired of it all, Jax. I want to look into sustainability in the fashion industry and using natural fabrics. I don't want to deal with the day-to-day headache of it all anymore."

My mouth drops open, and I stop on the spot. "Never would I have thought the day would come when you got tired of playing with the superficial crowd."

"It used to be fun, but now it's a drag. I want real friends, and I want to make Neighpalm Couture a label that looks to future-proofing. We deserve to be a long-term name in fashion instead of a short blazing star that burns out within a couple of years. The hiatus that Dad and Nana forced on me was actually somewhat of a blessing in disguise. Although I thought I was dying to get back there when it happened, it made me realize how unhappy I had become. I'm all in favor of your idea. Design is where my heart lives, and the new arrangement will give me time to help take care of all the new responsibilities on our shoulders."

Honestly, I'm not sure I've ever been prouder of my sister. My family and I have always known that Jazzy had depth, that she had creativity and drive and what it takes to really shine. For so long, she's been content to let the world see her as a superficial girl because that was safer for her. If she never took risks, if she never showed her real passions, then she could hide from the world despite being front and center. This sounds like a real change for her, like my sister is ready to be the woman we all know her to be, and I can't fucking wait for her to take the world by storm. Of course, if I make a huge deal of this, it's just going to freak her out, so I've got to play it cool. *Deep breath, Jax, control the proud brother vibes.*

"Okay, sounds like you have a handle on everything, but make sure you say something if it becomes too much. Don't bottle it all away. I'll dump everything if I have to. In fact, I could probably find someone to temporarily take over at Resorts and Hotels, and we could do that together."

She leans closer and kisses my cheek. "It's fine; *I'm* fine. I promise. You've got Harlow as well, and I don't want to drag you away from her and everything you guys are doing for her."

She tucks her arm under mine and drags me over to DS and Jenny grazing in the day paddock. "The more I think about it, the more excited I am. If the house across the road has a secret vault, what's to say none of the other places do too? I'm looking forward to exploring them all. Maybe, if she has the time, Harlow and I could even do a girls trip when all of this dangerous stuff is all over. A sister bonding trip where she could show me what she likes to do in those abandoned buildings she loves."

A new set of worries starts to plague my mind. My sister, and possibly my girlfriend, too, in these foreign countries on her own. Yes, she's done this kind of thing before, but we don't know anything about the houses or the people who've been looking after them for the last twenty-odd years. Not to mention the count's less-than-savory reputation—another problem I need to worry about. I'll talk to Thomas and see what he thinks. Maybe I can convince her to take Jace with her. I would feel better if she had at least one person I knew with her, and he's a great guy. He's fit in perfectly with the family over the last week, just like he was always there, and Harlow already adores him like a brother.

"Come on, help me get these two inside for Harlow," she says, handing me Jenny's halter and bringing me back to the task at hand.

"Declan said that they're bringing the tiger back here. Do you think it's a good idea if they're near it?"

Her eyes widen, and she shakes her head. "No, not at all. Let's take them over to the other barn and see if Josh can find them a place over there. Wow, a tiger. I can't wait to see it."

"Do you think you could help me set up something special for Harlow? Maybe a picnic or something, so I can talk to her about everything. Shit, Jazzy. How the fuck do I do this?" I put the halter on Jenny's head, and we walk to the other stables to look for Josh. My nerves are already ramping up at the thought of asking Harlow to share her life with us and maybe move in together.

Jacinta is smirking at me, but not in nasty way, just that smug sister face. "Don't stress, bro. I'm sure you only have to ask, and she'll jump at it. She's already packed up to move out there, and with Melinda and Chuck and Max also making California their home, I think you've got this in the bag. I see how she looks at the six of you. Just be your charming self, and it will all fall into place."

The animals' hooves echo on the floor of the barn as we enter, matching the beating of my heart, but Jacinta's words have given me a little more confidence, and now I can't wait for Harlow to get home.

Chapter Eight

Harlow

At the sound of my voice, they all peek up from the corner of the room they're in. Really, room is a generous term. Quite honestly, the thing is a cage, a barebones one at that. The only thing in the enclosure is a bunch of old blankets, and that's where they were hiding, but now that they've heard me, five curious cubs come running over on unsteady legs until my feet are surrounded. Sinking down, I run a hand over them as they try to compete with each other for my attention. I pick one up by the scruff of the neck and bring it up to eye height. I examine his eyes, which look to be a bit runny, and there's discharge coming from his nose too. Black fleas are crawling all over his tummy, and it's raw from him scratching at the biting bastards.

"Aw, poor baby," I coo as he screeches at me plaintively. I put him down with his siblings and go back out to find Thomas squatting down next to Jim, closing his eyes. Jay shudders as he takes in the blood surrounding the body.

"The cops have to look at this; they'll need to call the coroner and tell his wife or whatever she is out there."

"Okay, will the two of you give me a hand carrying what I found, please? I don't want to separate them from their mom, but I'm pretty sure she'll have to be euthanized after attacking Jim. Being in a safe place is our best hope of training them. Plus, they all need checking over. I'm sure the doc will have a carrying cage or something we can put them in."

To their surprise, the tiger cubs have trailed behind me, but I was expecting a reaction like that. Leaning over, I grab two by the scruff, passing one to each of the men before handing Thomas a second and taking the last two myself. With a cub under each arm, I lead the men back around the front to the flurry of activity that's taking place. There's an Animal Control truck with a transport crate on the back of it, and Doc Davies has recruited Declan and one of the cops to assist him in rolling the tiger onto a sling. Together, they're going to shift her into the crate in the back of the truck.

We wait patiently while they do that, and in the

meantime, I can see the woman being questioned by the cops. When she sees the three of us with the cubs in our arms, she starts screaming, "They're mine, you thieves! Don't you dare take them!"

The cop leaves her with the paramedic in favor of approaching us. Can't say I blame him, given her piss-poor attitude. "She said her husband was back there. Did you find him?" We exchange a glance, and I can't hide my grimace.

"Ah… yeah, but he's not going to need a medic. You're going to have to call the coroner," Jay says, and the cop winces.

"Ok, I'll get on the phone then go have a look."

"Before you go, I need to ask her some questions about the animals. Is that okay?" I ask him. His eyes drop to the cubs in my arms, and a smile lights up his face as he scratches one of them on the head.

"Yup, no problem. Why don't you get them locked up? I'll check out the body and break the news to her, then you can ask what you need."

"Sounds good," I tell him, and Jay, Thomas, and I head over to Doc Davies' truck, where I know there's going to be an animal carrier of some kind; he's always got one tucked into the back. But when I get there, my hands are full.

"Here, let me help," Declan says from behind me, and I think he meant to open the door, but I spin and hand him the two cubs. His face is comical when he realizes what he has in his arms, but the big old softy, of course, melts as soon as he recovers, cooing like a schoolgirl to the bundles of fluff in his arms.

I chuckle with amusement, but there's a huge grin on my face as I let myself into the back of Doc's truck. Sure enough, there's a large dog cage in the back, so I grab it, placing it on the ground next to the vehicle. Jay hands me his cub before heading over to help with mama tiger and speak to his colleagues. Placing him in the cage, Thomas and Declan pass me their four cubs, so I add them to the cage and close the door before they can escape.

"Dec, can you watch over them while I ask the woman some questions about the other animals? When I'm done with her, we'll head home and get the enclosure sorted for when Animal Control bring the tiger."

Dec enthusiastically agrees, and with a smile, I leave him to it. Thomas and I walk over to the woman, who is now sobbing hysterically.

She looks up as I approach, her face a mess of snot and tears. "What do *you* want?" she snaps.

"I just want to ask where you got the animals from." She shrugs and wipes her nose on the back of her hand.

"I don't know."

"You did all of this on your own, just the two of you? How did you know she was pregnant?"

She rolls her eyes at me. "Well, it's just like a house cat, isn't it?"

"No, it really isn't. I can't believe you managed to have a successful birth, and she didn't kill any of her babies. Tigers often kill their babies if they're not comfortable in their surroundings, and let me tell you, that cage was inhumane."

The woman stares at me like she has no clue what I'm talking about. I guess she probably doesn't. Sighing, I ask another question. "So, do you know where he got them from, the tigers, I mean?" I can tell by the look in her eyes that she might have an idea, but she stubbornly shakes her head. "Okay, what can you tell me about the jaguar?"

The shrug she gives me in return makes me want to fucking strangle her. "Jim came home with it a couple of weeks ago. I think he had plans to do the same thing as he did for Shinto—find a male for her. I think she's about a year old. He said she was also house raised, but she grew too big, and the owners wanted her out. She was chewing on their furniture."

Fuck my life. The sheer stupidity of people. "So you didn't declaw her?" No doubt seeing the violence in my eyes, she shakes her head emphatically enough that I'm almost worried about it falling off.

"No, no, she came like that. I had her inside because she's a sweetie, and I missed Shinto, but Jim insisted she go out to the barn with the others."

"Does she have a name? And will I need to sedate her to get her into the cage?" As I ask the questions, the woman's eyes stray to the barn, where the paramedics are wheeling out a bodybag atop a gurney.

She breaks into tears again. "Nyx, and no, she had a collar and leash that's hanging on the wall of the shed." She sobs as the cop helps her to her feet and walks her over to the ambulance. They probably want her to ID Jim before taking her for medical care and to be booked into the police station.

She's their problem now; I just have to make sure that the animals don't suffer any more than they have.

They have Shinto on the back of the truck, with Doc listening to her chest, and the frown on his face says it's not good. When he looks up, my eyes meet his, and I know it's really bad. He shakes his head just enough, and a wave of sadness flows over me, followed by panic. Fuck, I didn't want to face this reality even though I saw it coming. I just became the mom of five tiger cubs. Or maybe Declan became the daddy because when I look over, he has them crawling all over him, and the laughter that reaches my ears contains complete joy and wonder.

Doc jumps down from the truck and strides over to me. "I'm sorry, Harlow. She just wasn't strong enough. That has nothing to do with you and everything to do with the fact that she's underweight and malnourished." He pulls me into a hug, and for a brief moment, I allow myself to accept his comfort. A small amount of guilt prickles at me, as well as sadness, but loss is one of the first things you have to get used to when deciding to become a vet. Much like a doctor, I guess you need to come to terms with the knowledge that you can't save everyone. If I hadn't tranq'd her, we'd all still be in danger. There was no other option.

"Shit, well, we've got two more cats and some snakes." I shudder, and he chuckles.

"I guess you want me to deal with the snakes."

"Please."

"Animal Control already told me that they can take care of them."

A huge sigh of relief leaves my mouth before I can stop it, and he chuckles again. "Come on, let's see what else we're working with."

We walk back to the barn in comfortable silence, and when we get back there, the male tiger is becoming aggressive, leaping at the cage and snarling as we enter. The wire rattles, and it pops away from the frame enough to spark the smallest bit of worry.

When his front paws hit the mesh, it becomes obvious that someone tried to declaw him too, and it was recent. His paws are a bloody mess, and nausea hits my stomach because I know how much pain he must be in.

"I'm not sad that Jim got eviscerated," I say to Doc quietly, and he murmurs his agreement.

"I think the best thing for him will be to be euthanized," he tells me. "Those paws are a mess, and you know declawing can cause long-term pain."

"I know, which is why I need you to look at the jag. It's been declawed, but it seems to be walking fine, so I'm assuming it was done when it was small —by someone who knew what they were doing."

"Ok, let's deal with this guy first. I'll check with the ACOs, but I doubt they'll have any arguments. His pain must be excruciating. We'll sedate him like we did Shinto, then I'll administer the drug to euthanize him. AC said they'll dispose of Shinto's remains after they check for rabies, so I'm sure they'll help us out with him too." Doc leaves me to get what he needs, so I lean against the opposite cage and watch the poor tiger pace back and forth.

Because of someone's greed, both of these magnificent creatures suffered needlessly. My sadness quickly becomes anger, though, and I want to punch the bitch in the nose. It makes me more determined to work with big cats and help educate people that they really aren't pets. If I can't get an internship, maybe I'll work on lobbying Congress to bring about stricter exotic animal laws. Try to get it made illegal in all states to own exotic animals as pets without a license. With Dad's name behind me, I'm bound to get some notice.

Doc returns, and we take care of the poor male tiger. His passing is peaceful, and he's finally no longer feeling any pain. Animal Control rolls him into a sling, taking his body to join Shinto.

"Okay, let's have a look at the jag." He sighs and moves over to her cage.

Sure enough, hanging on a hook is a collar and leash. Just as I'm about to open the cage and step in, Thomas enters the barn.

"Harlow, what the fuck are you doing?" He hurries over and grabs my arm, but Doc waves him off, showing him the tranq gun in his hand, which is filled with a fast-acting sedative.

"It's fine. We're pretty sure that this one is tame, and she has no claws. I can shoot her if she does anything aggressive, but I don't think she will. I'm surprised she's so calm, what with everything that's happened. She should be as agitated as he was, but she really doesn't seem to have any of the natural instincts that big cats have. Maybe we should bring the cage over so we don't have her uncontained for as long."

I can see in Thomas' eyes he really doesn't want me to do this, but treating animals is always a risk, even the domestic ones. Maybe it'll be good for him to see this. He's an expert at what he does, but I am too.

He reluctantly lets go of my hand, and I enter the cage. Nyx comes padding out of the shadowed corner, a chuffing sound rumbling in her chest, and butts her big head into my leg before trailing her body against it, then dropping to the ground and rolling onto her back for a tummy rub. "Oh my goodness, aren't you just the sweetest thing?" I whisper to her as I crouch down and give her what she wants, breathing a sigh of relief. At least the woman wasn't lying about her disposition. I give her a quick rub before strapping the collar around her neck and getting back to my feet.

"Harlow, the police and paramedics have left, so has the truck with the remains. The only one left here is the one with the cage. We're going to load Nyx in, then drive her to your place, so she can stay there overnight while I make arrangements. Animal Control will come back for them, but they won't be yours to deal with." He points to the snakes, and I'm grateful to not have to deal with them. They really give me the heebie-jeebies.

"Okay. Come on, Nyx." I start walking, and she jumps to her feet and follows after me, perfectly docile. Thomas starts to take a step back, but I hold my hand up. "Hold out your hand so she can sniff you," I tell him. She does exactly what she did to me, headbutting his hand, giving it a lick, then rubbing her body against his legs. His eyes widen in amazement, and I can't stop my smile. "It's pretty special, isn't it?" Given the way he's too busy petting her to respond, I'm thinking I might have two cat daddies on my hands.

"Come on, you two," Doc calls from the entrance. "Let's get moving."

When we leave the barn, he closes the door behind us and snaps a padlock on it. We make quick work of loading Nyx into the cage. She goes in happily and lays down, watching as I close the gate and shut the tailgate.

"Alright, we'll meet you at your place," Doc says, climbing back into his car as Declan loads the cage of tiger cubs into our SUV. How did I know he wouldn't be letting them out of his sight? Sure enough, he climbs into the back and passes Thomas the keys.

He reaches over and gives me a squeeze on the shoulder after I climb into the passenger side. "I'm sorry about the parents," he says quietly, and I shrug.

"Me too. Come on, let's get these ones home. I'm going to have to do some research on what three-week-old tiger cubs need. Do you think we can find a butcher that will deliver? Nyx is going to need some fresh meat. She's underweight as well." Declan pulls out his phone and starts to search while I contemplate what will happen to them all when we return to the West Coast tomorrow. Hopefully, Doc Davies can find somewhere for them to go, though I know it will be hard to say goodbye.

Chapter Nine

Harlow

When we get back to Chuck and Melinda's, a crowd comes pouring out of the house. We're the first ones to arrive, so I jump out and hurry into the barn to ready the cage for Nyx, leaving Declan to deal with his cubs. Poor Princess and her kittens, lucky they're not here to be jealous.

"Whoa, look at the baby danger zebras!" Oliver's voice carries to where I am, and I snort. Trust him to lighten the situation. I grab a broom and open the cage, giving it a sweep out, then I hurry to grab a bale of hay. As I'm carrying it to the cage, a hand on my shoulder stops me before Kai takes it.

"I got this." Happy to have the help, I grab another for myself. We set about spreading it out on the concrete floor of the cage. Then I scrub out the water bowl and fill it with clean water, flipping it to autofill for when it gets too low. By the time we're done, everyone else has joined us. Thankfully, it seems Declan and Thomas have brought them all up to speed.

Jacinta grabs me and gives me a hard hug. "I'm sorry about the parents."

Before I can answer, I hear the Animal Control truck arrive.

"Who's that?" Chuck starts toward the door, and I shoot a look at Thomas and Declan. They're way too smug, so I guess they didn't tell everyone about Nyx.

We follow Chuck out, and the stunned looks on all of their faces is enough to make me laugh. I can't stop the giggles from coming out, needing to put a hand against the truck to hold myself up once it starts to get a little hysterical.

"Harlow, are you okay?" Jaxon puts a hand on my arm, and when my eyes meet his, I can't hold it back any longer. The tears well up and cascade over, and I start to sob uncontrollably. He pulls me into his arms, his scent enveloping me as I purge all my sadness and frustration in a good bout of tears. He rubs my back and murmurs words that help despite me being totally unable to understand them right now. Like animals, people just enjoy the warmth and presence of someone they love when they're hurting.

"Back off, man. Give her a moment," Oli

growls, but I shake my head, pull myself together, and step out of Jaxon's arms. Pressing a kiss to his cheek, I wipe my face.

"It's okay, Oli. These guys have to go wrangle some snakes so I don't have to. Alright, Jay, let's get Nyx out, so you guys can be on your way. I've got it from here, and Doc is making some calls about permanent homes for them." Jaxon's hand on my arm tightens, but he lets me go, and I climb up into the tray.

Opening the gate, I lead Nyx out, and my family all take a big step back.

"Holy shit!" Kai's quiet exclamation sounds slightly awestruck, but there's no fear there. I should have figured the adrenaline junkie would have no problem being around a cat large enough to take him down as a snack if she wanted. I jump down from the bed, and she follows behind me, ears pricked, looking around and sniffing the air. She's still incredibly calm, and if it weren't for the rest of the animals that we're responsible for keeping safe, I'd be tempted to take her for a longer exploration of the grounds. Poor baby deserves it after being kept in that horrible barn.

"Ok, guys, just give me some room. I'm going to put her in the cage in my barn, then you can bombard me with all the questions." I wave goodbye to Jay as he closes the cage and slams the tailgate before climbing back in, heading out to deal with the snakes. Thank fuck I don't need to worry about them.

Nyx follows me into the barn, stopping to sniff at the aviary and the stable that DS and Jenny are usually kept in. I can see that they've been moved, and I'm thankful someone had the thought to do that before we got here. I'm pretty sure they would have freaked out if they smelled Nyx.

I lead her into her temporary home before removing the collar and stepping back out, closing the door behind me. She paces back and forth, exploring every inch of it before flopping down and rolling around on the hay. Happy little grunts fill the air, bringing me a sense of peace. I can't say that I expected to find a freaking *jaguar* today, but there's nothing like the peace of a safe, happy animal.

"That's a jaguar." The stunned words make me turn around, seeing Chuck and Melinda standing behind me. He has his arm wrapped around her, though I'm not sure if they're actually worried about the big cat or if they're just responding to that instinct that says a true predator is in their space. They're staring at Nyx like they're waiting for her to do something interesting, but the cat is really just doing… cat things. Honestly, there's not much to see right now.

"Yeah, from what I got out of the woman, she was bought to breed. She's only about a year old, and they don't mature sexually until they're between three and four. If they had tried breeding her too early, they could have gotten one or both cats killed because the female wouldn't be receptive to it. Honestly, I'm not sure she would have been receptive even if they waited until the proper age. She would have been living in those horrid conditions for a long time and probably would have been as feral as the two tigers by the time they got to that stage."

"Harlow, I've got a butcher delivering us a leg of deer for her. Is that okay?" Declan asks, looking up from his phone in his hand, a worried frown between his eyes. I hadn't even noticed that he'd joined us. "What do we need to do for the babies?" He has the cage at his feet, and they look to be napping.

"That's perfect, Declan. Come on, let's leave her in peace until the meat gets here. I need to check over the babies." He takes the cage into my clinic, which is helpful, but I have to stop in my tracks and hold out my hands to stop the parade of Bostons and Summers who try to join us. "Okay, I know you all want to help, but that's not going to work. Declan and Jacinta can stay, but the rest of you need to find something else to do. I want to give them a full workover, and I don't want them handled by a lot of people until we figure out what's going to happen to them. If they get too attached to you, it's going to make it harder for whoever takes over. "

I laugh out loud when everyone's faces scrunch

like they want to argue with me, but they bite their tongues and leave us be, making me love them all the more for it.

As they all depart the barn, I hear another car pull up, followed by Doc's voice. After the rumbles of some small talk, he joins us in the clinic in time for Declan to lift the cage onto the exam table.

"Sorry I took so long. I stopped to pick up some supplies for the cubs." He puts a shopping bag down on one of the benches.

Declan introduces him to Jacinta as he pulls various things out of the bag. "I have a friend who has experience with leopard cubs, and they messaged me a recipe they used. But I would like to see if we can get some electrolytes into them before they eat," he suggests. "He also said that we should name each of the cubs, put nail polish on their nails so we know who's who, and keep a separate record for each of them. Have you got any notebooks? You can write it all in there."

I scramble around in one of my drawers and pull out five notepads. "Will this work?"

"Yup, should be fine for now."

"Jacinta, can you ask Melinda for some nail polish? I know Max has plenty if she hasn't. Five different colors." She leaves to do as I ask.

While that's being taken care of, Doc Davies lines up five bottles on the bench, already mid-explanation to Declan about how to wash them.

When we packed up my clinic the other day, I

labeled all the boxes so I knew exactly where all the important basics were. I pull out electrolytes, wormers, flea treatments, and nail clippers, laying everything on the exam table. With a small set of scales and a plastic container the size of a shoebox, I'm almost ready. I fill the sink that Declan isn't using with warm water and add some pet shampoo to it. The cubs are all filthy, and I want to give them a wash to clean them all up.

When I turn back, Doc and Declan are waiting for me, and I know Jacinta should be back soon.

"Okay, I think the best thing to do would be one at a time." I point to the sink Declan just finished using. "I want to use that sink to wash their eyes, noses, and back ends, using this cotton wool and running water." I hand the cotton wool to Doc. "Can you do that bit? Then pass them to Declan. You can be in charge of washing them. Is that okay?" The big grin on his face says an eager yes.

"Once washed, Dec, we need to dry them because we don't want them getting cold." I pull a hair dryer out of a cupboard, and he raises his eyebrows. "You'd be surprised how handy this is." Jacinta arrives back, puffing, in time to hear the rest.

I plug it in and lay out a couple of towels, setting up a makeshift station drying area. "Jacinta, it will be your job to dry them. Towel off as much moisture as you can, then low heat and low fan until they're dry, okay?" She nods, her eyes bright with excitement as she goes to her station and puts down five bottles of polish.

"Once they're finally clean, I'll weigh them, give them their flea and worm treatments, and clip their nails as well as listen to their lungs and hearts. We need to make sure we have a record of all that stuff before Jacinta can paint their nails while someone feeds them a bottle of electrolytes. Once they've done all that..." I pull a baby play pen out of the cupboard, set it up, and throw some more blankets on the floor. "Then they can go in here while we do it all over again with the next one. Anything I've missed?" The last comment is directed at Doc, and once I have his approval, we're all good to go. Thankfully, his beaming smile says I've got it all right, so I settle myself in to work, ignoring the heat of my blushing cheeks.

Two hours later, the four of us emerge from my clinic a little worse for wear but smiling. All cubs are now fully treated, and none of them show signs of any sickness other than being slightly malnourished, which, in itself, is a miracle, considering the squalor they were being raised in. I was worried about an upper-respiratory infection, but these little guys are so much more resilient than I had thought.

I put a hand to my back and stretch, groaning

thanks to being bent over for a long period of time, and Declan steps up behind me. With just the right amount of pressure, he starts to rub my back, the little show of care unexpected but much appreciated.

"Doc, do you want to come up to the house and have something to eat? Melinda told me to ask you when we were finished," Jacinta offers.

"No, thank you. I need to make some calls to figure out homes for the cubs and Nyx." Just as he says that, a refrigerated truck pulls up.

"This must be the meat for Nyx," Declan says. "Why don't you take a shower? Doc and I can feed her before he leaves, and I'll meet you back at the house."

I bite my lip, looking between the truck and the barn.

"Come on, let them do it. You've had a big day, and a shower is just what you need." Jacinta grabs my arm and drags me away.

"I'll call you tomorrow and let you know what I've found out," Doc calls after me, and I wave my hand at him, Jacinta not allowing me to stop.

When we get to the house, the living room is full of laughter, a noise that stops when we enter.

"Wow, way to make a girl feel self-conscious," I grumble as I look down at myself. Of course, now that I have a full audience, I notice I'm covered in dirt and white fur and… Is that poop? Nope, not going to look too closely at that.

"We have two girls and three boys," Jacinta proudly announces to the group. "Daphne, Velma, Fred, Shaggy, and Scooby." You could hear a pin drop after her announcement as everyone tries to process that bombshell.

"Seriously?" Holden's the first to come to his senses, breaking the confused silence.

"Yup," she confirms while they all discuss much better names for 'our' cubs. She ignores them all in favor of pushing me in the direction of Max's room and her ensuite. "Go shower while I find you some clothes," she orders. I do as commanded, not wanting to think about how attached everyone has already gotten to the cubs, knowing how disappointed they'll be when Doc finds them a new home. Honestly, I don't want to face my own disappointment either, but I'll pretend that I'm mostly worried on everyone else's behalf.

My hot shower goes a long way in distracting me from my thoughts as I close my eyes and rest my head against the tiles while the water flows over me. I really don't want to give the tiger cubs up, but realistically, I could only raise them for a few months before they would need more space than I could provide them. Even if Dad let me build a cage, that wouldn't be fair on them. They need space to roam, a place to swim, and things to climb. No, it would be best if Doc found them a zoo or sanctuary, but there are many dodgy organizations out there, I just hope he can find a legit one.

After I shut off the water, it only takes a few minutes to dry off and tug on the pajamas Jacinta had laid out on Max's bed. My apartment is completely packed up, so I'm supposed to be sleeping here, but I think I'll climb in with one of the guys instead. I feel the need for some comfort tonight.

Hurrying downstairs to find some food, I feel a frown form when I get to the kitchen and discover no one is around. Murmuring voices come from the living room where Chuck and Melinda, Jace, and Jacinta are talking quietly. I move between the two couches.

"Where are all the guys?" I ask, looking around.

"Out at the riding arena. They asked if you could meet them down there when you were done with your shower." Melinda smiles at me, and I groan.

"God, I'm exhausted. Do they really need me?" I grumble, finding everyone way too amused for my liking.

"See what they want, then you can go to bed," Chuck cajoles me, a small smile on his lips.

"Fine. What are they all doing over there, anyway? They're not pretending to joust with the practice lances, are they?" The thought of the six sexy Summers brothers pretend jousting flicks into my mind, but they're not wearing shirts. They're sweaty, and they run at each other in slow motion, practice lances in hand, aggression on their faces, but before they can hit one another, Jacinta nudges me with her leg.

"Did you just fall asleep on the spot?" I can't offer anything but a shrug, and Jace's snickers build in the silence of Jacinta's incredulous stare.

"No. I don't think so. Okay, I'm off."

Grumbling, I make my way to the big indoor arena we train the horses in. Similar to Dad's but bigger, there's a permanent jousting fence on one side with enough room for two horses to practice. The rest is a wide open space, but when I pull one of the heavy doors open, that wide space isn't so empty. In the middle, the guys have set out a picnic blanket and surrounded it with battery-operated candles. The six of them are chatting, bottles of beer in hand, but they all stop when they see me.

Chapter Ten

Harlow

H ey." I wave kind of awkwardly, and Jaxon puts down his beer and gets up, coming over to greet me with a soft smile and a gentle kiss on the lips. I'm a little slow to respond because I can't believe they've done this for me. Never before has anyone gone out of the way to make me feel special like this—well, no potential suitors anyway. It's definitely a lot nicer when your boyfriends surprise you with a picnic.

"Hi, sweetheart. Come have a drink and something to eat. We have something we want to talk to you about."

He takes my hand and leads me over to the blankets. Everyone moves over so I have room, and Declan passes me a glass of champagne.

"Oh, fancy. What are we celebrating?" I ask as

he leans in to kiss me. When he pulls away, he's smiling.

"You and what you mean to us." His words make my heart skip a beat, and I feel all tingly inside.

"Here, you must be starving after your day. Declan and Thomas just told us everything." Kai passes me a bowl of fragrant stirfry, and my stomach rumbles.

"You're not wrong," I tell him, carefully placing my glass next to me before taking the offered bowl. I can see they all have one too, and we're quiet for a few moments while we all tuck into the delicious food.

"Oh my god," I mumble around a mouthful, throwing any manners out the window. "This is delicious."

"We would have cooked, but Thomas is the best at that, and he was busy helping you, so we ordered in instead. Melinda said it was your favorite Thai restaurant, and I've gotta say you have great taste. Everything is great," Oliver agrees.

"So… What is it you wanted to talk about?" I ask, not wanting to put it off. The suspense is killing me, and if it's bad news, then I really just want to get it out of the way.

Everyone looks to Jaxon, who finishes his mouthful and puts his bowl down next to himself. He takes a sip of his beer and clears his throat a little nervously.

"The guys and I have been talking," he starts, but Holden quickly interrupts.

"No, this was Jaxon's idea. We're fully on board, but he deserves the credit."

"As I was saying," Jaxon growls at Holden, who just grins. "And let me preempt this by saying we discussed this before today's happenings. I… *we* would like it if you would take the abandoned house and its run-down zoo and turn it into a sanctuary for animals, like Nyx and the babies. Maybe it could even be an education center for school groups, or… I don't know, whatever you want it to be, really. If it was alright with you, we thought we could all move in and live together. Just the seven of us."

My stomach is in my throat, and I don't know what to say. My mouth sort of opens and closes like a fish, but no words come out. Jaxon hurries on. "I mean, if you like the place. The keys were delivered to Dad, so we can go have a look as soon as we get home. He said that he's having a temporary enclosure built for the animals since he has a friend in construction. The crew's coming out to build it tonight. It won't be fancy, but it means that the cubs and Nyx can come home on the flight with us. They'll have somewhere to live until we can get the zoo up to scratch. Dad and Nana have already started working on getting a license and sourcing staff from other zoos to consult, and he's set aside an amount of start-up capital like he did for Oliver when he started Neighpalm Ink. He believes in you, Harlow. *We* believe in you, and we think that your dream—and most importantly, your happiness—are worth all of this."

Holy shit! Am I hearing him right? He's giving me his inheritance *and* telling me I can start up my own sanctuary *and* I can keep Nyx and the cubs? I blink a couple of times, and he starts to frown.

"Harlow, are you okay?"

I carefully place my bowl to the side and launch myself at him. He grunts as he catches me, and I start to pepper his face with kisses. Laughter fills my ears, but I'm too busy mauling Jaxon to pay attention to who it is.

"Yes, yes, yes, yes, YES!" My mouth finds his, and I try to pour everything I'm feeling into the kiss, not caring that the other five are watching.

"Fuck, lucky bastard," I hear Oli say, and then there's a thud. "Hey, fuck! That hurt."

"Don't be a jealous bastard; he deserves all of that and more. He's making her dreams come true," Kai scolds.

I pull away. "He sure is," I whisper. If I could look like an emoji at the moment, my eyes would be filled with alternating stars and hearts. Jaxon, and the rest of them, are giving me things that I never knew I needed. Well, okay, I definitely knew I needed them on some level because my dreams are what I've lived for for so long, but I guess I just never thought I'd ever get them.

"Is that a yes to us moving in as well?" Holden asks carefully, and I move away from Jaxon enough to see the others without losing my comfy lap spot.

I look around at the guys who have all wormed themselves into my heart despite our rocky start. I couldn't imagine my life without them anymore, and although it seems quick, I really don't want to go back to the way I was—guarding my heart like a dragon guards its hoard. I'm ready to allow myself to love and be loved by others, and hopefully, we can create a healthy and loving relationship that works for all of us.

"Are you sure about this? I don't want to stop any of you from walking away if this isn't what you want. There will be no hard feelings. I mean, there will be disappointment and sadness but nothing that I'm sure we can't all move past eventually. We'll all still be family." I don't want to put any kind of damper on the moment, but I have to voice my biggest concern. They all start talking at once, but Declan holds his hand up to silence the clamor. There's that smugness on his face that started off as kind of dickish, but now it's pretty damn attractive.

"Harlow, I think I can safely say we're all in. We all know that if there are problems, we need to bring them out in the open."

"Communication, the key to every good relationship," Holden says from Oliver's arms. The two of them are lying side by side, looking so cute together. I'm glad it's not weird for the other brothers; they accept it, no questions asked.

"Maybe we need a moment each week where we all touch base. A family meeting of sorts," Kai suggests, and the rest of the guys agree. I really like that idea, and I especially like how proactive they're being about making this work. For a bunch of men who probably aren't used to compromise, they sure are doing a good job.

"And if we're not physically capable of attending, then we can do it via FaceTime or whatever," Thomas adds in. "Dad has shown us that family takes time and effort, or it'll never work. We can and want to give our effort to you and this family that we're making with the seven of us."

"And I want to make sure that I'm spending equal time with you all, but I don't really want to keep a schedule because that's just weird. If you feel like you're missing out on time with me, speak up. Don't let it fester until there's nothing but resentment between us. Ok?"

They all agree, and I blow out a big breath. "Well, cool, I guess we're doing this then."

"Orgy time!" Oliver shouts, sitting up. Holden rolls his eyes and drags him back down while the others throw bottle caps and napkins at him. Staying in Jaxon's lap, I pick up my food and quietly finish the delicious curry while the others talk around me.

"You're making lists in your head, aren't you?"

Jaxon whispers in my ear, and I nod, swallowing my mouthful so I can speak.

"Yeah. I'm so happy we can take the cats with us. I need to let Doc know he doesn't need to find them a proper facility."

"Dec already did that when you went into the house."

I climb out of Jaxon's lap and crawl over to Declan's. He smiles as I get comfortable, and he wraps his arms around me, placing a kiss on my neck.

"Hey, baby, everything okay?"

"Declan Summers, you were so confident in Jaxon's plan that you told the doc not to bother looking for homes?" His green eyes sparkle with amusement as I grab his face between my two hands and smack a kiss to his lips.

"Yes, baby, I wasn't leaving those cubs behind even if it meant Princess needed to make room for them in her enclosure. I saw how devastated you were about the parents. There was no way we were leaving Nyx behind either. She's like a large version of Princess; who knows where she could have ended up? Nope, you are the best bet for those cats," he says with a stubborn set to his jaw.

Aww, my serious man has a severe cat addiction. It's so freaking sweet. I rest my head on his shoulder. "Thank you," I whisper to him, and he squeezes my leg where his finger has been drawing circles on my thigh.

"I know you've had a long day. How about we check on the cubs and Nyx and then head to bed?"

"Actually, I need to feed them now, and they're going to need a feed in the middle of the night, too. I'm wondering if it will make sense to sleep in my own room. I'll grab a sleeping bag, and..." Before I can finish anything, he shifts me off his lap and stands up, holding out a hand.

"Babe, I've already arranged everything. Doc told me they would need feeding during the night, so I grabbed some bed sheets from Melinda. Your bed is already made up."

Seriously, who is this man? Fucking hell, scoring points with every move he makes.

"Shit, why didn't we think of that?" I can hear Oli complain once more, and my heart rate picks up with my worry. I really need to check in with these two to make sure everything is okay. I've neglected them a little since we returned from Prague, and I just want to touch base, make sure everything is okay. I'm hoping that it's just a need to get home to our own things and back into our own routines more than any real jealousy.

"Stop, Oli, I know you're joking, but Harlow's going to think you're serious and start to worry we can't share." I hear Holden scold him, and he's not wrong. I turn, a frown on my face.

Before I can say anything, Oli jumps to his feet and pulls me into his arms. "No, don't worry, Holden is right. I'm only joking, but I'll stop being an ass. I don't want you to worry. It's fine. Go take care of your cubs, and I'll see you in the morning. Text us if you need anything."

They both kiss me before they gather the bowls, empty beer bottles, and my half-drunk glass of champagne into a basket. Jaxon, Thomas, and Kai gather the candles and blankets. They all wish me good luck and leave.

"I need someone else to help us, but I'm not sure who to ask. I know Oli was joking, but I really worry about it." I turn to Declan, who has a mischievous look on his face. I have a very strong feeling that both great and equally terrible things come to pass when that look is on his face.

"Did you know that Thomas is quite the voyeur? He likes to watch." Holy shit, is he suggesting what I think he is? I mean, it's fun when Den and Oli share me, but I hadn't quite realized it would be a possibility with any of the others... Which, now that I think about it, was kind of a stupid assumption considering the situation Kai and Thomas are in with Veronica. I grind my teeth at that thought. Now I'm determined to wipe that experience from his mind. Poor Tom was screwed over by yet another fucking woman.

"Tom," Declan calls just before he gets to the door, "would you be able to help us feed the cubs? It's easier with more than four hands. And hey, you might need the practice in case it comes back that you're Veronica's baby daddy." My mouth drops open, and I smack Declan in the stomach. A loud whoosh escapes his mouth, followed by what could only be called a cackle. Thomas' face gets dark like a thundercloud, and he flips him off.

"Fuck you, Dec." I hurry to his side and tuck my hand under his arm.

"He's just trying to wind you up. Ignore the asshole. We'll worry about all of that once the DNA results come back. I mean, the likelihood that she was successful in inseminating herself with your and Kai's junk has got to be slim, right?"

He runs his free hand through his hair and sighs as Dec catches up to us. "Actually, it's more common than you think. I did a search."

"Shit, man, I'm sorry. I was joking because I thought there was no way," Declan apologizes, looking all cut up for his brother. "Has Forrest had any news?"

"Veronica was put on suicide watch because she was making threats while she was being booked. They're pushing through a court order for an amniocentesis to test for DNA as soon as it's possible. Due to the circumstances, he says he doubts it will be denied. God, I just want to know one way or another. No matter what, she won't be able to keep the baby. There's a clear case against her and her poisoning attempt. She'll be going to jail for a long time. I just want to know if it's one of ours so we can plan for it. She was spouting about termination too, but I worked it out; she's got to be at least 14 weeks. It's too late to have one unless there's something wrong with the baby. Forrest also added another court order for immediate neonatal scans to make sure it's healthy." Poor Thomas sounds defeated; it must be terrible to have that hanging over his head. "And if it is mine or Kai's, where does that leave *us*?" I realize he's looking down at me when he asks that.

"Oh, well, huh. I haven't really thought about it because I didn't believe it could be true. I thought it was all a little *Days of our Lives*-ish."

His question does do one thing without a doubt. Now, I'm thinking about the future and what it could look like if Veronica's schemes prove true. How do I feel about Thomas or Kai having a baby? I guess it's no different than if they already had kids with another woman before we got together. In fact, there's a tiny part of me that's internally cooing with joy at the thought of a baby joining our family. You don't have to be biologically related to love someone like they're your own. Look at Melinda and Chuck, they gave me all the love and support that was sorely lacking from my blood relatives.

"Nope, I'm good. It doesn't change a thing," I assure him, and the tension in his body begins to ease. "Come on, let's check on these animals. Good practice for when we literally live in a zoo."

An excited thrill runs through me at the thought, and it's all I can do to stop myself from skipping to my barn. Luckily, Thomas has a hold of me; otherwise I might fly off into space in my excitement.

Declan pulls open the door to my barn, and I flick on the light switch in the stable area.

Nyx is happily chewing on her deer leg, so I leave her in peace and turn the light on in the clinic. When we left the cubs earlier, they were safe in the playpen, and I had put some heating pads under the blankets for warmth. They're all sleeping where I left them, so instead of disturbing them, I decide to set my phone for two hours. I'll come back to check on them then.

"Let's get some rest. I don't want to wake them up."

"What time do you want me to come back?" Thomas asks, pulling out his phone.

"Why? Where are you going?" Declan asks.

"Well, to bed, of course," he responds, sounding like he thinks Declan's an idiot for asking.

"I set up the pull-out sofa as well, thinking that Harlow was going to need help through the night. It's all yours."

Declan leads the way up the stairs, and another sort of excitement starts to build inside. Anticipation fills me, almost tingling; I cannot wait to be surprised.

Chapter Eleven

Declan

I can feel a smirk lifting my lips. Riling my brother up is the only way I'm going to get him to cross that last hurdle with Harlow. My brother holds so tight to his self-control and his issues with his ex, he's missing out on giving his commitment to Harlow that last big confirmation. He's ready to move in with her, but he's still clenching his hands on those reins. I'm hoping this might help him finally lose it just a little. He's right there on that edge, and if I can just tip him over it, maybe he'll dive headfirst into everything else.

I want to get them over this hurdle, and what better way to do it than by ravishing Harlow in front of him? Or within hearing range, anyway. If I know Tom, he won't be able to stop himself from watching.

The pull-out sofa is made up, and so is Harlow's bed, but if I have my way, the pull-out won't get used for very long.

"I'm sorry. I'd offer you a coffee or a tea, but I don't have any here anymore." She's standing in front of the empty fridge, a look on her face that's adorably distressed. "I should probably turn the power off on this." She reaches around and flicks the switch before turning back to us.

"Don't worry about us," I assure her. "Tom will be fine on the sofa, and we need to be up in a few hours to check on the cats."

We wave bye to Tom, who is already undoing his jeans and shucking off his shirt. Harlow bites her lip as she peeks back over her shoulder at him, and a grin curls my lips.

When we enter her room, I make sure not to latch the door all the way. I want Tom to hear everything I'm doing to Harlow, but it's certainly no bothersome task. My woman is gorgeous and kind. How could I not want her?

Before she can say anything, I pounce, taking her lips with mine. My hands run up the back of her shirt to stroke the smooth expanse of her skin, our tongues twisting and turning as we pour all of our feelings into this kiss. A small moan slips from her mouth as I pull away, and she chases after me.

Chuckling, I pull her t-shirt over her head, throwing it to the side while she slides her shoes off before helping her out of her jeans. She's helping me get rid of my clothes too, and before we know it, we're mostly naked. Gathering her in my arms, I lay her down on her bed, savoring the knowledge that her bra and panties and my boxer briefs are the only things between us.

Another quiet moan leaves her mouth as I explore her neck, sucking and licking a path down her chest as she runs her fingers through my hair, her body squirming under mine.

"Don't be quiet, Harlow. I want him to hear you," I order as I push back the lacy cup of her bra and circle her nipple with my tongue. She grinds against my hard cock while her legs part, and I settle between them like we were made to fit. Never before has anything felt as right as this moment. Since I laid eyes on her, I knew she would change our lives. I didn't think it would be like this, but I'm so glad it is.

She lifts up so I can take her bra off, then I get up on my knees and slide her panties down her legs. Sitting back, I admire the naked body before me. "God, you're gorgeous."

"I'm only gorgeous once I'm naked?" I push her back and take her mouth with mine once more.

"No, you look just as good in clothes as out, but this way is more fun."

I slide down her body, nipping and placing kisses as I go, and she squirms, making me feel like the king of the world. How can I affect her body so much while doing so little? She must be made for me; I've had partners before, and trust me, I always left them extremely fucking pleased, but there's something about Harlow that sinks into my bones. The way she reacts makes me think that she feels it too, and that's so fucking intoxicating.

Her fingers find my hair as my tongue delves into her hot center. Her musky but sweet taste fills my mouth as I lick my fill before circling her clit. She's panting now, with her eyes closed, fingers tangled in my hair like she's not sure if she wants to push me away or tug me closer. Each breath feels like it should be something quiet, an intimacy only between us, but that's not the game this evening. No, I want those pants to become gasps, moans, anything that will travel the short distance to my brother's ears and entice him to cut those tethers binding him further from Harlow.

I continue to lick and suck her pretty pink, glistening folds while I slide two fingers into her warm heat. It ripples around them as she moans, the sound loud and throaty, and I can't stop my smug smile. There's nothing more heady than hearing your woman express her pleasure. I continue to work my fingers in and out, flicking my tongue around her clit, and her cunt starts to tighten around my fingers.

"God yes, Declan, just like that. Don't stop," she begs, but a noise behind me has me pushing away to face my brother. I don't bother to hide the evidence of her arousal that I can feel on my face. I want him to see it and know what he's missing out on.

Thomas is standing in the doorway, his hand down his briefs, stroking himself. All he needs is one more tiny push, then my brother will be one step closer to having everything he deserves.

"Are you going to stand there with your hand on your dick, or are you going to help me?" His eyes narrow at my words, then he pulls his hand out and stalks over to the bed. When I look back at Harlow, her wide eyes are glassy with lust, and she licks her lips as she takes in my brother's mostly naked body. Thomas is cut, with long, lean muscles, but it's the tattoo in the middle of his chest that's drawing her attention. Jesus on the cross is front and center—a testament to my brother's past and his fixation with thinking he needs to pay for his supposed sins.

"Touch her, Tom. Look at those nipples, they're practically crying for your attention." As he leans in, I return to what I was doing. I know the exact moment my brother wraps his lips around one of those nipples and begins to suck because her pussy clenches around my fingers again. She cries out, so I guess Thomas may have used his teeth just a little. I smirk against her clit as her tight cunt pulses on the brink of an orgasm. I pull away to deny her, knowing this moment needs to reach the next level, and she issues another cry, this time in disappointment.

"Harlow, get on your knees," I growl, and she

quickly does as I ask. She's now facing Tom, with him towering above her. "How about you show Tom how much you appreciate him looking after you?" Her body quivers at my order, and she slides her hands under the band of his boxers and pulls them down his thighs, letting them go until he can step out of them. Tom's cock juts out, long and thick and dripping with pre cum. Almost immediately, Harlow's tongue flicks out to lap at the drops, and my own erection pulses at the sight.

When my eyes meet my brother's, I gesture for him to kneel on the bed, forcing Harlow to bend over to keep teasing him with that sinful mouth of hers. I am more than happy to enjoy the beautiful sight in front of me; it puts her perfect pink pussy just where I need it. I lean in, grabbing her hair and yanking her head back so I can whisper in her ear.

"I'm going to fuck you while Thomas fucks your face. Be a good girl, and when you swallow him all down, I'll let you cum." Harlow pants and nods her head in agreement as much as she can with my tight grip. I kiss her hard on the lips and let her go, and she doesn't waste a second. The moment she's free, she starts working over Thomas' length. I can see his hands fist in an attempt to keep from grabbing her. "It's okay, Thomas. Grab her hair. She likes it rough. Our Harlow is a little bit of a freak in bed. You couldn't tell just by looking at her. It's always the quiet ones."

Harlow growls at me, the sound made significantly less intimidating by the way it's muffled by Thomas' cock. She's not going to deny it because she knows it's true, but she doesn't like that I called her out on it. I caress the soft rounded globes of her ass. The sound of her gagging as Thomas thrusts a little too deep is the only noise in the room.

"That's a good girl," Thomas praises her, his Irish accent thick with his desire. "Fuck, that feels amazing." His eyes are closed and his head thrown back as he works his hips back and forth. Harlow takes everything he gives her, eager noises spilling from her busy lips.

"She's a good little cum slut." I thrust two fingers into her pussy with my words, and I hear her grunt around Tom's dick before the sound ends in a muffled moan. Removing my fingers, I trail them up to her asshole and work them in. She helpfully pushes back, and they slide in easily. "Oh yeah, you like it, don't you? I'm going to put my thick dick in your ass, and you're going to love it." The other night, I noticed that Harlow gets off on dirty talk, and I absolutely aim to please. I've always been a little dark and dirty in the bedroom—must stem from having to be so polite as the face of Neigh-palm Productions. This is my way of letting go, and the pleasure it brings her is a serious bonus.

"I'm going to fuck your ass hard while my brother fucks your face. We're going to use you, leaving you *covered* with our cum, and you're going to love it."

She pulls off Thomas' cock and twists around to face me, tears streaming down her cheeks from the face fucking. "Please," she begs, and it's all I can do to stop from coming there and then.

"Have you got any lube, Harlow?" Thomas grips her hair to steal back her attention as I continue to prep her ass, scissoring my fingers to stretch her.

"In the bedside drawer," she sobs with need. He leans down and kisses her, wiping her face.

"Shhh. Such a good girl. Be patient, and Dec and I will give you what you need." He pushes her hair away from her face, stroking her back, his softness countering all the depraved things we're doing to her. I open the drawer, delighted by what I find. She must not have packed up any of her sex toys because it's filled with all sorts of things. One immediately catches my eye, so I grab it and the lube before moving back to the bed. I pour a decent amount of lube over my dick and down her crack before rubbing it all over my length and working it into her with two fingers.

Pulling away, my hand cracks down on Harlow's ass, and she jolts forward, squealing, before taking Tom's length again. "You're such a naughty little slut, aren't you? Do you know what I found in that drawer, Tom?" I ask him conversationally as I hold it up. It's a dildo with a loop on the end—for double penetration when you only have one partner. "Looks like Harlow here loves to have all her holes filled, and we are going to indulge her tonight." His eyebrows raise the slightest bit as I slide the ring over my cock and loop it around my balls. I reposition it until it sits underneath my dick so that when I fuck her ass, it will fuck her pussy at the same time.

"Ready?" I ask her, running my hands over her smooth, round cheeks again before parting them.

She nods emphatically, and I slide my cock to the entrance of her puckered hole, lining the dildo up with her dripping pussy. Just barely pushing inside her, I grit my teeth and grip her hips, sliding into the tight heat while the dildo makes its way in at the same time. Gently, I pulse back and forth to ease my way in, but she must get sick of that because she forces herself back, impaling my dick to the hilt. "Holy shit." I can't help the words that escape my mouth, and she looks back at me, giving me a cheeky wink.

"Oh no, baby, you've done it now." I look up, and Tom gives me a nod. He holds her head still and starts to thrust as I do the same, alternating to his rhythm. Harlow is trapped between us, unable to move, only capable of luxuriating in everything we're doing to her. The room fills with the sounds of grunting and gagging and the slick slaps of bodies against one another. I can feel everything tightening around me, her body clamping down on the verge of orgasm. It's all I can do to continue to thrust as I can feel my impending orgasm. Leaning over her, I slide one hand to her clit and lower my mouth to her ear.

"I like seeing you wear my mark." I move my mouth to her shoulder and slap her clit as I sink my teeth in. Harlow's orgasm rips through her as my brother and I continue to work her body over, and her muffled scream echoes throughout the room as her ass clenches on my dick. Her body becomes heavy, and I can see she's struggling to keep herself upright. So I finally give in to the need, thrusting two more times before emptying myself into her tight channel. Thomas pulls out and pushes her back before finishing all over her pretty titties.

Her body wrung out of everything, she collapses to the bed. Tom is already in the bathroom, running the shower, when I pull myself free from her body and watch my cum dribble from her ass hole. After I remove the strap-on and gather Harlow into my arms, I carry her to the shower and pass her to Tom, who's already standing under the water, a soft, expectant look on his face. Have I seen my brother make that expression before? Certainly never with his ex, which means it's highly likely this is the first time he's ever appeared that way. He lets Harlow's feet slide to the ground and wraps his arms around her, kissing her gently.

"Such a good girl, taking everything we gave you." He continues to praise her as he lets the water flow over her exhausted body. Leaving him to take care of her, I go back and strip the bed down, getting it clean and ready for when we're done in the bathroom.

'

Stepping back in to join them, I find myself growing hard again at the memory of what just happened and how perfect Harlow is for all of us. I can see that my brother has got her worked up again. He's lifting her up, her legs automatically wrapping around his waist, and without words, he slides into her tight, ready pussy.

I'm a little jealous—not in a true way, where it would turn into resentment or bitterness toward my brother. Instead, I'm simply wishing that I could join them even though I know now is not the time. I'm completely satiated, but there's a greedy part of me that says we can always make room for more Harlow time, especially *naked* Harlow time. Unfortunately for my dick, the better part of my nature knows that Thomas needs this moment, so, for my girl and my brother, I'll leave them alone and shower when they're done. They deserve some time alone.

I'll just put on some sweats and check on the cubs. As I go down the steps of Harlow's apartment, I realize that I'm whistling. It's amazing what a good woman and a great relationship will do for someone. I've never been unhappy in this family, but I didn't realize I was missing something until right this moment.

Chapter Twelve

Harlow

I got up twice during the night to check on the cubs with Declan and Thomas both coming along for feeding assistance. Then we all fell back into my bed until our alarm woke us in the morning.

We had to delay the flight by one more day while the Summers greased some wheels to get my exotic cat license sorted for California, which also gave Dad some extra time to have the enclosure built. That day was blissfully spent—hanging around, feeding cats, letting the cubs play out in the open on a grassy area next to my barn. I took Nyx for a walk on the leash too, the two of us strolling down the driveway and back, and she seemed to enjoy stopping to sniff things along the way. When we got back, we napped in the sun for half an hour, with Nyx content to lay down next to me, her back touching my legs as she closed her eyes and savored her freedom. The night was a little less pleasant, needing to wake up for feedings again, and all of us are dragging the next morning when we're finally ready to finish our preparations.

I yawn as we wait for the shipping company Doc Davies contacted to load Nyx onto the plane. The hold is climate-controlled, which should help with keeping her comfortable, but we also slipped her a mild sedative wrapped in a piece of chicken, and that will hopefully keep her nice and relaxed for the trip. She's in much better condition than the two tigers were, probably because of how recently they purchased her and her regular stays in the house. That makes it much safer to treat her than it was Shinto. Plus, the guys assured me they would have Jilly show me to the hold so I can check on her through the flight. Thankfully, this one isn't as long as the last.

With the cubs needing to be fed during the flight, they have to be kept with us. Declan's fascination with them means that he's the one who claims the responsibility of getting them all safely packed away, and before I know it, they're cozily snuggled into the large dog cage.

"Well, I can say this is definitely a first for me," James comments as the crate is loaded onto the plane. "I've never transported animals before."

"I doubt it's going to be the last time you do

either," Declan tells him, smiling wildly. "We have the capability to rescue animals from all over the country, so we might as well use it."

"Rescuing animals?" He looks a little confused.

"Come on, I want Jilly to show me how to get into the cargo area from inside the plane. Walk with me, and I'll explain it all." I tuck my arm in his and blow kisses to the two guys, hoping I can convince them to join me for a nap later. Declan's been commenting about a few business calls he needs to make, but I'll gladly take at least Tom if I can have him.

"Who is that?" I ask James, pointing to a uniformed man talking to Kai.

"That's Jack; he's brought the smaller plane we took to Hawaii. The police asked if we could transport Veronica back to California with an escort since she needs to be tried over there. That way we can limit the amount of public knowledge about her baby claim without putting all of you through the pain of having her on the same flight."

"That's *much* appreciated, thank you. I don't think I could have controlled myself, pregnant or not, if she opened her mouth."

"No, I don't blame you. Now, tell me about rescuing animals."

I tell him all about what happened in the last forty-eight hours, and then I have to tell it again when I find Jilly, but I don't care. I'm so excited about all of it that I'd probably tell anyone who asked. Finally, after everyone is settled and debriefed, we're in the air and on our way home. The flight is delightfully uneventful, and once we feed the cubs, they sleep for the whole trip. Which is what I do too, wrapped up between Thomas and Jaxon, who beat everyone else to claim the extra spaces in my bed.

"Goddamn it," Oli mumbles when he tries to sneak in. "I'm getting us a custom-made bed for the new house, one that will fit all of us." When I raise my head to look at him, he's already tapping away at his phone.

"Deal," I tell him, "as long as there's a room that it will fit in."

"We'll find out tomorrow," Jaxon sleepily says from next to me, and I wriggle as a wave of excitement runs through me. When Oliver leaves, I can't stop moving, my brain running through everything we're going to do tomorrow. We have to see what enclosures need to be updated and whether they're going to provide the kind of enrichment the animals need. We need to look at hiring assistants, cleaners, maintenance staff, keepers... Gosh, I hope there are some records inside the house of what animals he used to keep. I really want to know what was in the big pool. I asked Nana, but she couldn't remember ever seeing it since it was the count's private collection, and he didn't really show it off very often.

The proper authorities have to be called in California; if we're doing this for real, I want to make sure others know that we'll take animals that are seized and in need of rehoming. My body is twitchy as I have a silent meltdown, feeling like all of these developments are great, but they're also a lot to handle all at once. I haven't even been able to get my foot in the door with an internship. Where can I start with half the things these animals really need? The Summers say they'll all help, but will that be enough? I can't help but think we'll need all the help we can get.

We'll have to start advertising for job openings, though maybe we could get some high school students who are interested in vet studies to come clean cages and do weekend internships or something. I wonder if any of the students I went to school with would be interested. I'm trying to think about whether any of them had an interest in exotic animals when a conversation I had when I first arrived in California pops into my brain.

On that very first shopping trip with Alex, he talked about how he volunteered at an animal shelter in between modeling gigs. Maybe I can still do that, just do it from the zoo. Maybe once or twice a month, we could have the shelter bring by animals that need to be sterilized.

"Harlow, be still," Tom grumbles as he throws an arm over me in an attempt to stop me from moving. "How can you still be awake?" He's wrapped around my back, so his breath tickles my ear, moving my hair when he talks.

Jaxon's back is to me, the little spoon to my middle spoon to Thomas' big spoon, but I'm suddenly full of energy. Before I can convince them to make me the filling in a Summers sandwich, I hear the rumble of snores coming from both of them. Jaxon had been up half the night making to-do lists, scouring the internet for contractors, finding out more information on the MacGinty Sanctuary staff, and Googling top vets in the field of exotic animals. Why he did all that last night is anyone's guess, but I can only hope that he's as excited and restless about this whole thing as I am.

Carefully crawling out of the bed, I leave the two of them to sleep. Before I make any decisions about anything, I want to see the house. I'm sure all the decor and furniture will be dated, so some Pinterest research might not be a bad idea.

Wandering out into the lounge, I find Kai talking to Jacinta and Jace.

"Where's everyone else?" I ask as I sit down next to Kai and snuggle into his side.

"Holden and Oli claimed one of the bedrooms down the back, and Declan is working in one of the offices," Kai says as he places his arm around me and gives me a kiss on the head.

"What are you doing? Why aren't you napping?" Jacinta asks, looking relaxed and comfortable in her seat next to Jace. I don't know if they realize they're touching or if they subconsciously gravitated toward one another. I can't wait to see how the dynamic between the four of them unfolds. Alex is as dramatic and flamboyant as she is, and I can see the potential for them to clash, but I bet it'll be hot when they do. Shane is his silent and steady self, and Jace has that country-boy-next-door thing going on to balance out the other two perfectly. I just have to be patient because I have no doubt they'll wear her down eventually.

"Oh, I can't sleep. I'm so excited about seeing our house tomorrow." I bite my lip as something occurs to me. "Are you okay with what they did? I didn't even think to ask. That's so fucking rude of me. I'm so sorry," I ramble. I was so fucking thoughtless by not thinking about Jacinta. It's half her home after all. With the progress we've made to get us here, I don't want to hurt our relationship.

She waves her hand at me. "Don't even think about it. I'm so fucking thrilled that my brother wanted to do this for you and that you're all taking a leap of faith. Plus, I love the house I live in. I've said all along that when I have a family, I'm going to kick my brothers out so we can live in our wing. We're going to have the papers drawn up and put it in your name. That way there's no questioning who it belongs to, and you won't have to worry about it being taken away from you."

Tears prickle in my eyes until I have to wipe them away so that they don't fall. I just can't even with these people. I mean, Chuck and Melinda were always wonderful, but I grew up being the outsider from the wrong side of the tracks, and to experience all that I am now after such a rocky start, I just don't know whether to pinch myself to make sure I'm not actually asleep and dreaming or if it was me that got shot. Maybe I'm trapped in a wonderful coma created by my own subconscious.

She must be able to see what's going through my mind because she holds her hands out. "Show me your Pinterest page! We need to start adding things that you like. Something that doesn't scream illicit 90s drug den. I wonder what it looks like inside. I'm just as excited as you to check it out tomorrow."

We spend the rest of the flight oohing and ahhing over interior decorating and paint samples. When we touch down in California, there's another truck waiting to receive Nyx and take her to Dad's. The other surprise as I step out onto the tarmac comes in the form of Alex and Shane, both wearing big grins as they greet Jace with smoking hot kisses. Phew! Jacinta and I receive kisses on the cheek, and if they linger a little longer over hers, then I'm not upset.

"Hey, this is a nice surprise," I say to them when they finish greeting Holden, Oliver, and Jaxon. I'm not sure where the others are, but I bet Declan is with the tigers.

"Yeah, Jace called us to come pick him up.

Lucky dog, going to Prague with you. I wish I had gone with him when he brought over those dresses," Alex says, pouting prettily.

"Well, you've been overseas before, Jace and Harlow hadn't. Stop being such a baby," Shane gently scolds before turning back to us. "Did you have a great time?" I feel a blush heat my cheeks as I think about my date with Thomas in Prague, which was definitely a highlight.

"It was a blast," Jace answers before I can. "The thought of going into work and dealing with Lindy and Rowena makes me want to climb back on that plane and jet off into the horizon."

Jacinta groans and bumps him with her hip. "God, me too. Why did you have to mention it?"

I don't miss the pleased look that softens Jaxon's face at the interaction between the two of them. With him making plans for the next steps forward in our relationship, it makes sense that it's even more important to him that his sister have her own happiness too.

"Sorry to interrupt." Kai appears from somewhere, deceptively sneaky for a guy who's usually hard to miss. "But the chopper is ready. Shall we get moving? All the luggage is loaded, and I want to get us home so that Harlow has time to get Nyx situated comfortably."

"Nyx? Who's Nyx?" With the way Alex is looking around, Jace seems way too pleased. I'm guessing he's left some details out of any updates he's given his boyfriends.

"I didn't tell them. I knew they were coming to get me, and I wanted them to be surprised."

Just as he says that, the crate gets unloaded from the plane, the forklift placing it on a truck not far from us. I hurry over to check on her even though I know she was fine when we landed.

"Shut the front door," Alex gasps as I climb up to see her. Her big yellow eyes blink sleepily at me, and a big yawn has her showing us all her big teeth. "Harlow, that's a jaguar."

"Yes, Alex, it is." I chuckle, then he helps me back down, maintaining his grip on my hips to hold me in place.

"Girl, you've got some explaining to do."

"It's going to have to wait." Declan's words have us turning to him. He has his cage full of tigers at his feet, and he's looking at his watch.

"Aghhh!" Alex squeals. He bends down, quickly followed by Shane, and they push their fingers through the cage to pet the little creatures.

"I'm driving back with these guys since I'm not sure if they would be upset with the sound of the helicopter. I'll see you soon, okay?" He leans in and gives me a kiss before waving goodbye to the others. He picks up his cage and heads for Thomas' bullet-proof tank, which is parked just beyond the truck.

"Jace can tell you everything. I was surprised he hasn't already."

"I wasn't sure how Jacinta and Jaxon would feel about me sharing their news," he mumbles, and I see Jacinta practically melt.

"Thanks, man, I appreciate it." Jaxon slaps him on the shoulder. "It's fine if you tell them, though if you would keep it to yourselves until we're ready to go public, I'd appreciate it." He takes my hand, and I wave to the guys and Jacinta while Jaxon, Oliver, Holden, and I hurry to the waiting helicopter which has Thomas in the pilot seat and Kai in the passenger.

"God, I can't wait to get home," I sigh once we've strapped in and donned headsets. When I glance up, all three of them are watching me with varying degrees of affection.

"What?" I ask, not sure what I did to deserve the looks.

"You called our place home," Holden says as he puts his arm around me and tucks me into his side.

"I guess I did." I smile as Jacinta climbs in and pulls the big door closed behind her.

"You heard her, Tom. Take us home," Oli orders, and before I know it, we're in the air and winging our way across the sky.

Chapter Thirteen

Harlow

The property is a bustle of activity as Thomas lands the helicopter on the wide expanse of lawn. Dad comes racing out from the house while the blades wind down, the whining sound loud in the peaceful yard. In typical fashion, Nana and Poppy are keeping pace with him, refusing to miss any of the action. Honestly, I'm surprised Nana wasn't leading the charge.

I let the others get out of the helicopter first, and as soon as my feet touch the ground, I'm swept up in my dad's arms and hugged tight. There's no stopping the smile that breaks out as my arms come up around him. I can't find the words to explain this feeling, but there's just something about being held so tightly by my actual dad, having him clutch me to him like I'm precious, that slots something into place. *This*. This is what I'd yearned for so many times throughout my childhood, and my soul celebrates every time I have a hit of that warmth and love.

"Hey, Dad. I missed you too." He pulls away and looks me in the eye, his so much like the ones I stare at in the mirror every day.

"Harlow, honey, I'm sorry about Luke." Poppy and Nana sweep me up into their own hugs next, so I don't have time to answer.

"That poor boy. He may have been unbalanced, but nobody deserves to die like that." Nana shudders, and Poppy puts his arm around her, pulling her closer.

"Rubbish! He got what was coming to him. How dare he stalk my Hally and frighten her like he did. Good riddance." Nana scowls at him, but he ignores her, refusing to let her win this one. God knows that, more than anything, is a perfect indicator of how strongly he feels about this. Nana is his queen, and it's not often that he isn't swayed to see things her way. "Brad, can we show Harlow the thing now?" His eyes sparkle with excitement, so much so that I don't even mind the change in subject.

With the boys having taken over the whole luggage process, I'm free to follow Dad and Poppy. Declan has the cubs, and I know they're perfectly safe with him, even if they're going to take a little longer to get here. He talked about setting up a playpen in the conservatory for them since they won't be able to go out into the cage until they're a little older. I'd like to see if I could put them in with Nyx. Maybe I'll keep them side by side for a few days and see if she creates a bond with them. I'll need to be careful because it could go the other way, but maybe the experts Dad was hiring could help me do this safely.

Nana links her arm with mine as we walk. "So much has happened in the last week. How are you doing, sweetheart? Are you okay with everything? The boys aren't rushing you or pushing you to make choices you don't want to?" Her worried questions are asked in almost a whisper, like she's preparing herself to be the keeper of some dramatic secret. Fortunately for her, I have nothing of the deep, dark sort to share.

"No, Nana, everything is perfect. I'm happy, *really* happy, and I'm looking forward to everything. Did you hear that they're giving me the property next door so I can run my own animal sanctuary?" She squeezes my arm in hers.

"Yes, I know. What a brilliant idea. Sometimes those boys really outdo themselves. It just takes them a little while to get warmed up, but then they show you why they're worth the wait, don't they?"

"And I have my first rescue animals! You should see Declan. Those tiger cubs already have him wrapped around their tiny little paws. Poor Princess." Nana chuckles with me.

"Declan's capacity for love is never ending. You know he was Brad's first child, which could have resulted in some jealousy issues, but he never had a bad or angry word or action when the rest of them came along. He took them under his wing and loved them unconditionally. At his core, our Declan is warmhearted; it's just not in his nature to resist someone or something who could genuinely use him in their lives. He certainly has enough love to go around for all of the baby animals."

I think about Declan's actions since I've known him, and although I will never agree on the Summers' initial methods, everything has been about protecting his family from hurt and harm. It must be why he was such a stuck-up ass to start with. That wall, a defense mechanism to keep anyone from getting too close, must be exhausting to keep up. I'm so glad he's allowed me to scale it.

"Now, are you excited to see the work?" Nana pulls me out of my musing, and I practically start to vibrate with anticipation.

"I sure am. How did Dad find someone to do this so quickly, anyway?"

"Well, dear, when you've got enough money, you can make anything happen. Us Summers just like to use those powers for good… for the most part." Nana pats my hand and gives me one of those teasing winks of hers. "But Hope actually recommended this company—someone she knows from when she was younger. She said that they did good work but were struggling because one of the owners has a police record. Such a sad story, one of those situations where he did something stupid as a teenager, and now it's impacting the rest of his life. You might have realized this about your father, perhaps not, but Brad loves supporting the under-dog, so he hired them on the spot. They've been working relentlessly since they got an idea of what needed to be done."

"And how did they know what to build?" My curiosity has been overwhelming me, my brain whirling when I think about inspectors and permits and safety standards that will all need to be signed off on. From my perspective, it's this daunting mountain to climb, with my dream right there, balancing on the peak so far out of reach.

"Do you remember that zoo that rejected you?" she asks as we continue around the other side of the house away from all the horse yards.

"The MacGinty Sanctuary?"

"Yes. Turns out we've actually donated to it on a regular basis, so Brad called and asked to speak to their head veterinarian and zoologist. He offered them both jobs at the new soon-to-be open Neigh-palm Sanctuary, and they jumped on it. Apparently, the director is hard to work for, so they both wanted out. It was perfect timing. Of course, it will all be subject to your approval. Right now, we have them on a three-month contract to start, like all of our new staff, so if you don't like them, we can reassess.

I'm pretty sure the place across the road is going to need some major maintenance before it's ready to reopen anyway."

I really have no idea what to say at this point. Growing up with the Bostons put me on the fringes of seeing what life was like when you were wealthy, but this is nuts. I mean, I can't say I'm not happy to benefit from it right now, but it's still kind of mind-blowing to see the power of wealth when you come from a world where the things you want take time.

"Close your mouth, dear. You'll catch a fly that way. Anyway, the head zoologist sat down and created a rough sketch of what we needed. The guys worked hard for the last day and two nights to do it for you. They are lovely young men. A little like my boys, in that all four of them grew up together in the same foster home. In fact, Brad is really impressed with their work. I daresay he's been inspired by them, really, and he's already looking at the option to make them a business offer. Right now, the rough idea would be to put their business under the Neighpalm banner. They'd get to control everything, including what business to take on and such, while retaining all earnings, but they'd get the Neighpalm name to help them. The only stipulation is that they prioritize the construction of the zoo first."

We round the final corner of the house, and I stumble to a stop. The area is filled with the noise of hammers banging, nail guns firing, and some kind of power tool squealing. Men are everywhere, attaching steel mesh to the structure in front of me. It looks like it's sixty feet by sixty feet, the back third covered by a roof, and there's a wall sectioning it off from the outside area. There's a release door in the wall, so I'm assuming that's for access to night quarters.

"Holy shit!" The words slip out, and Nana laughs as we catch up to Dad and Poppy.

"Yeah, they've done amazing work, haven't they? They were a real find. I'm not sure why Hope hasn't suggested them in the past. Come on, I'll introduce you to the boys." Dad leads the way over to a group of men standing around an open truck bed not far from the construction.

"Guys, this is my daughter Harlow. Harlow, this is Miles, Wyatt, Ethan, and Parker." He points to each one individually so we can shake hands and exchange greetings. Miles is tall, with close-cropped black hair, dark eyes. He's swarthy and exotic-looking, with broad shoulders and nicely defined arms that are shown off by his *McCallister Construction* t-shirt. Wyatt and Ethan are blond-haired, blue-eyed identical twins that have made an effort to look different. Ethan's hair is curly and tousled, while Wyatt has a crew cut. Ethan is also smiling at me despite Wyatt's more serious, closed-off expression. I recognize the look, having had my own issues socializing with strangers, so I respect it, giving him a simple nod as opposed to returning Ethan's enthusiastic handshake. The last one, Parker, has chocolate-brown hair that falls to just above his shoulders and green eyes. There's a smattering of freckles across his cheeks. He's taller and leaner than the other three, but he's not lacking in the muscle department either. They just look like they could be from swimming or running as opposed to lifting. My guess is they're all around my age.

The rest of them are waiting on Dad to say something else, but Parker is studying me like he's trying to figure something out. "Are you really in a relationship with all of the Summers boys, or was that a load of shit the media made up?" The words blurt out quickly, like he's trying to finish the question before someone slaps their hand across his mouth. For a second, I'm not sure what to do, but there was no judgment in his question, simply curiosity. That noted, I go with the amusement that's threatening to make me laugh.

When the other brothers stare at him with disbelief, Ethan smacking him on the back of the head, I can't hold back a snort. "What the hell, man? You don't ask those kinds of questions."

Nana, Poppy, and Dad are all having their own issues with laughter, but Parker's starting to look like he's worried. Poor guy probably thinks he's just jeopardized their job security. Wanting the men to calm down, I wave a hand at them all.

"Don't stress about it. I'd prefer people ask rather than talk shit behind my back. You'll find all of us are like that, and it's the right way to go about dealing with the Summers. Yes, I am."

"And that works?" Miles asks thoughtfully, and there's something in his eyes that makes me think this is important. He's going to put some kind of weight behind my answer even though it makes absolutely zero sense to me.

"It sure does. It's a work in progress, obviously, but none of us have any complaints at the moment."

"I'm sure there won't be either," Nana chimes in, her eyes narrowed at the brothers. Oh, I know that look. They better watch out because Grace Summers has her scheming hat on. Yep, they're definitely on her list of victims. Maybe I can at least delay the torture if I distract her.

"I can't believe how much you guys have done in forty-eight hours." Is it the most foolproof change of subject? Oh, god no. Nana is a dog with a bone when she gets an idea in her head. But right now, it's the best I can do.

"Shall we take the tour?" Miles hands me a hard hat before offering them to the others. Dad takes one, but Poppy and Nana decline.

"I'll look once it's all finished. I'm going to head back into the house. I want to talk to Jacinta about some of the things that have been happening at Neighpalm Couture this week. Then, when Declan gets back, I want tiger cub snuggles," Nana tells me before dropping a kiss on the cheek.

"And I've got a meeting to finalize a few arrangements for the fundraising gala that's in two weeks," Poppy explains. "So I'll catch up with you a little later."

I watch with a small smile on my face as the two of them stroll away hand in hand. "That right there is relationship goals 101," I tell Dad while Miles directs us to the enclosure.

"It sure is. Though I might have done some meddling and invited an extra guest to the gala that neither of them know about—Dad's best friend from before they were married."

I think back to the story Nana told me on our first plane trip, and a grin spreads across my face. "Damn, Dad, I didn't know you had any of Nana's meddling genes. Good for you. I can't wait to see their faces! Does this stem from your own newfound happiness? Are you officially part of a throuple?" I keep my voice down, not wanting to share anything he may want to keep private for now.

Dad wraps an arm around my shoulder and squeezes. "You worry about your relationship, and I'll worry about mine. Though I will say it's a relief that all of you are happy and accepting of it."

"Dad, you deserve all the happiness you can get, and if Molly and Emma can give that to you, I'm all for it."

By the time we finish that exchange, we've reached the back of the enclosure. There's a man installing a security camera at the back door. He nods as we pass him and enter the enclosure.

"So, as you can see, this is the back area." Miles takes charge and gestures around the space. We're standing in a corridor, and against the far wall, there's a stainless steel bench with a sink, some cupboards above and below, and a door next to it. "We followed the layout that the zoologist gave us fairly closely since this is something none of us have ever done before."

"Yeah, the thought of fucking up has been in the back of my mind the whole time. I've been a bit of a perfectionist, riding the workers' asses to get it right," grumbles Wyatt—the first words he's said since we were introduced. "Nothing like the threat of a jaguar escaping to keep you from fucking up."

"He's not wrong. I don't think he's slept much in the last forty-eight hours. He hasn't wanted anything to be unsupervised," Ethan chimes in, smiling affectionately at his twin.

"He suggested we put in two den areas." Parker takes over, pointing to the wall separating the two spaces. "We put in a solid wall there because he suggested it would be better in case you were housing different species. Both den areas connect to the exercise/outdoor area through gates which are controlled there." He indicates a lever system on the wall that separates the dens. "There are levers for these food doors too." He points to two small hatches in the wire mesh walls that allow me to see into each habitat.

"That's fantastic. I can put the cubs out here when they get a little bigger. I'm not sure how long construction is going to take on the zoo renovations, and they're going to grow heaps."

Dad smiles, and there's a little bit of mischief in it. "We were hoping, if you were happy with the work they've done, to contract the guys and their crew to do the renovations."

I don't miss the hopeful look on Ethan and Parker's faces. Miles and Wyatt have better poker faces than their brothers, but their stiff body language gives away that they're waiting for rejection.

"As far as I'm concerned, it's a done deal. This is fantastic, and we haven't even gotten outside yet." I can see them all relax, and Parker doesn't hide his relieved sigh. Nana might have downplayed the roughness of their financial situation. "Show me the rest."

Miles opens the door to one of the dens, and we all step in. "Both are set up the same, with drains in the floor for hosing down waste, as well as automatic water troughs, and the food bins are removable for easy cleaning."

"I talked to Doug, the zoologist your dad contracted to advise on the reconstruction across the road, and he suggested that the animals need stimulation, so I hung this tire and sourced those big logs there." Ethan points out each item as he speaks. "In the storage room next to the sink, we've put a couple of big chest freezers for food and an area for straw bales if you want them for animal bedding. One of the chest freezers is large enough that a big bucket can be placed in it. I thought you could make them big ice blocks with treats in them during the summer."

My eyes widen in surprise. "Wow, Ethan, you really did your research, thank you." His smile is bright and shiny, and with his upbeat energy and that blond hair, he looks like the quintessential California surfer boy.

"Come on, let's show you the outside." Parker opens the human access door, and when we step out, it's even more amazing than I had hoped.

The terrain has been transformed. The space is still grassy, but there's now multi-level landscaping, including a rock cave built under one of the slopes. In another corner, they've planted bamboo, leaving space between the shoots for hiding. Smack bang in the middle of the enclosure is what looks like an oversized scratching post/climbing tree. It has platforms at different levels, and the bottom of it is covered by carpet for clawing. I feel a little sad that Nyx won't be able to make full use of that, but the cubs will love it.

"Do you like it?" Parker asks hopefully before hurrying on. "My cat has one he loves, and he spends most of his days there. When I asked Doug, he said it was a great idea for the big cats too. We couldn't put trees in, but he said jaguars like to climb, so this was the next best idea."

I grab him by the hand and squeeze it tight. "Parker, it's fantastic. Nyx is going to love it. Everything is amazing. I can't thank you all enough."

"Doug also says that jaguars like water. We didn't have time to build a pool, but we rigged misting sprinklers through the whole structure." Wyatt points up to the roof of the enclosure. "You can put them on a timer or manually turn them on and off in the back area." Even when talking about his work, his voice is gruff and no nonsense. At this point, I don't think it's just me; he's probably like that with everyone except his brothers.

"That is brilliant. I can't wait to see what you guys do with the place across the road."

"Well, now that it's decided, shall we set up a meeting in a day or two to go over the contracts, Miles?" Dad asks.

"Yeah, that would be good." He sounds enthused, which he should be. Working with Dad is a great opportunity for them, and I know that he'll take care of the guys and their company.

"Are you guys from LA?" I ask as we make our way back out of the enclosure.

"No, we're from a small coastal town a little south of San Francisco," Parker tells me. "We drove up when your dad offered us the gig."

"So, where are you staying at the moment?

Have you got families you need to return to? I'm sure Dad would be happy to come to you, or we could talk over video chat."

"Nope, it's fine. None of us are married. Wyatt has a son, but he lives with his mother at the moment. Our adopted parents still live in town, but none of us have lived at home for a few years. We're staying at a B and B not far from here, but we haven't really used it because we wanted to get the job finished for you." Ethan shrugs, and I look to Dad in horror. He stares back at me, a confused crinkle in his nose, until I raise my eyebrows and give him the most subtle nod that I can. Well, everyone did say that Dad's brilliant at business but not so great at people-ing.

"You guys must be exhausted! Look, we have plenty of room over at the house. The four of you are welcome to make it your home base for as long as you need to."

"Oh no, Mr. Summers, we couldn't possibly impose." Miles shakes his head, running a hand through his short hair.

"You're not imposing. I'd feel better if we could help make this a more comfortable experience for you guys since you're doing such hard work for us. Though I guess I should warn you, Harlow has had a few… safety issues lately—just some hiccups with a stalker. Thomas, one of my sons, will probably need to do background checks on you all just to be safe. Is this going to be a problem?"

The four of them exchange glances. "No, there's nothing I haven't already talked to you about," Miles says, looking Dad in the eye.

"Well then, it should be fine. All of that is in the past. It's not like every one of my children hasn't been arrested before…" He gives me a look filled with barely veiled humor, and I feel my cheeks pink up before I redirect my gaze to the ground.

"Ah, babe, we've all been there." Ethan throws an arm around my shoulder and gives it a squeeze. "Builds character."

He walks me out of the building, his arm still on my shoulder, but I don't think he's being sleazy. I think he could see I was uncomfortable and is trying to distract me, which is awfully considerate of him. There's something about him that exudes comfort, and I can appreciate a friendly guy who's just that —friendly. Parker pulls the door closed behind him after everyone exits, and thankfully, a truck pulls up right as we step outside.

"She's here. Perfect timing."

Chapter Fourteen

Harlow

The rest of the workers are packing away all their tools as the truck pulls to a stop. Like excited children, they drop what they're doing and crowd around the vehicle until Miles puts his fingers in his mouth and blasts out a loud whistle.

"Get back to work, you lot. They can't unload the cat if you don't tidy up all your shit."

The driver hops out and comes around, brandishing a clipboard. "If you could sign to say it arrived, I'll get to unloading it."

I take it from him, and he goes around to the back and starts loosening all the tie-down straps. Dad jumps up and gives him a hand as I scribble a signature across the page.

With the truck's hydraulic ramp, they maneuver

the cage onto the ground and wheel it onto the grass.

As the driver goes about closing his truck back up, Wyatt steps closer. "That's not going to be easy to wheel across to the enclosure."

I smile at him and hand him the clipboard. "That's okay. If you could ask your men to all move to one side and keep the noise down for a moment, I've got this."

His eyebrows raise, but he does as I've asked. Grabbing the leash off the side of the travel cage, I reach through and clip it onto Nyx's collar. Like the overgrown house cat she is, she's standing up, looking around with curiosity but no aggression. I can't wait for her to explore her structure. In the seconds that I've been interacting with her, the noise of men talking and tools clanking has completely dropped off; the air is so silent the drop of a pin could be heard. I want to torture them a little more with the suspense, but the poor girl deserves to go inside and see her new home. I open the cage, and she immediately steps out, rubbing against me in greeting.

"Holy shit." I hear the whisper from somewhere around me as I rub behind her ears.

"Hey, baby girl," I croon to her. "You've been such a good girl. Ready to see your temporary home?" Her temporary home is a million times better than her last one and will do nicely until we can get the zoo up and running.

We walk past the group of men whose expressions range from awestruck to terrified, and she doesn't stray except to stop and sniff at Wyatt's feet. He eyes me, waiting for permission.

"Can I touch her?" he asks quietly, his tone of voice softer than I've heard it so far.

"Sure. Let her come to you, then hold your hand out so she can sniff you first." He does as instructed, and his face lights up with a huge smile as she head butts his hand and rubs against him like she did to me. It transforms his whole face, going from grumpy but hot to laughing and gorgeous. Now he really looks like his brother.

"What's her name?"

"Her name is Nyx, and she's, from what we can work out, about a year old. Unfortunately, one of her previous owners had her declawed. It's incredibly cruel to declaw a cat since it often leads to permanent issues. She looks to be fine at this stage, but I want to take some x-rays and have someone more experienced than me assess it."

"Why is it cruel?" someone asks from behind me. The question is understandable, really, since it's been such a common practice with house cats that people assume it has to be okay to do.

"When you declaw a cat, it's not just a matter of cutting off the claws. They grow from the bone itself, so you have to remove that bone up to the last joint in the toe. Then you need to reattach the tendons. It's *incredibly* involved. That's why it can easily go drastically wrong."

The guy looks a little green once I finish explaining, but that's probably for the best. Tugging on Nyx's leash, I pull her away from her new best friend and bring her through the back door into the corridor. A quick walk later, we're in the nighttime den. Closing the double door behind me, I unclip the leash and remove her collar before leaving the enclosure. I pull the handle to open the door to the outside section, but she explores her current surroundings first, cautiously sniffing at the tree stumps the guys have left her.

Leaving her be, I exit the back area and walk around to the front where everyone has gathered. "I'm not sure if she'll venture out or not," I explain, seeing the way they're expectantly waiting in front of the cage.

"Alright, you heard the lady. Get your stuff packed up and get out of here. You can't wait all night," Miles orders, which I'm grateful for. Nyx may be acting like a house cat, but I want her to be free to figure out that she's in a safe space where her other instincts could come out. She's already learned a lot of behavior from her owners, but with some freedom, she might also remember the instincts they tried to train out of her.

The crew grumbles, but Miles seems to have gained their respect. Quickly, they snap back into business mode. "Are these all your workers?" I ask him as we watch them all pack away.

"No, our company consists of only the four of us at the moment. I put out a call to an old colleague in the LA area, and with what Brad was offering to pay them, it was easy to find skilled workers." There's a hint of something in his voice that wasn't there before, almost a little bite of aggression, which has me wondering. Before I can ask any other questions, he sighs and physically gives himself a shake. "Sorry, I'm a little defensive. We had a crew, but circumstances changed. We're… Well, we're from a small-minded community, and when they decide something, there's often no changing their minds despite the reality not being what they think it is." That's just vague enough that I really don't have much of a clue about what he could mean, but what I *am* familiar with is being judged by people whose minds are a lot smaller than I ever care to deal with again.

His body language starts to stiffen with each passing moment of silence, and I can see his expression becoming more guarded. Well, shit. Dad's not the only one with poor social skills sometimes. Nice job, Harlow, just freak the guy out, why don't you?

"Miles, let me tell you something. Small towns aren't the only ones who jump to conclusions and judge people on perceived truths. As long as you've disclosed anything of importance and relevance to Dad, I have no problems with you guys taking the job. I only asked because you'll need a much bigger crew than four for the next job we have for you."

He visibly relaxes once more, and I give myself a mental pat on the back for remembering how to actually people. He shoves his hands into the pockets of his jeans and nods. "Let's work out the particulars before I advertise. I also know one or two guys from back home who would probably relocate for the job too."

"I'll speak to Nana about arranging accommodations. I know they usually put people up at the Neighpalm Hotel in LA, but that's not going to work for this project. I'm sure she can find somewhere close by even if we have to rent a house." He looks like he's going to argue with me, but I hold up a hand. "It's not charity. It's usually included as part of the package of employment, and, in case you haven't noticed yet, my grandparents and dad aren't shy about using their resources when they want a job to be done. Really, you're the ones doing them a favor by providing such dedicated labor."

The rest of his crew joins us after waving off the other guys. Dad had disappeared after I unloaded Nyx, so I'm assuming he went back to the house to talk to Thomas about the background checks and catch up with the others. I can see one of the security guards out of the corner of my eye. He's being discreet, but he can see me from where he is and quickly get to me if need be.

With no one else around, I decide to have a quick

conversation with the four brothers. "Look, I don't know your circumstances, and I don't really care, but let me give you a little piece of advice. The Summers family really is like no other out there. They're willing to take a chance on you guys, and you need to grab this by the hand and run with it. Dad is going to offer you the chance to name yourselves Neighpalm Construction, or whatever you want to call it, and allow you to retain all rights and earnings, in exchange for you doing this job for me." The guys look so shocked I could knock them down with a feather. Wyatt, of course, already has a firm set to his lips that promises an argument, so I rush to cut him off. "You'll also be paid *extremely* well for this job, as will your crew. You would be nuts not to take this."

"Why are you telling us this now?" Ethan asks, his face masked with a level of seriousness that seems much more suited to his brother.

"I don't want you blindsided when you go into the meeting in a couple of days. I think you deserve a chance to discuss it. Having the Neighpalm name behind you will open doors everywhere."

Miles looks thoughtful. "Harlow, do you know how your dad got our name to begin with? He didn't tell us, and we were so glad to have a job that we didn't think to ask."

I startle, surprised by his words. "I thought you knew?" They all shake their heads.

"Hope Green is the Vice President of Neighpalm Records, and she suggested you. Hope is practically family, so of course Dad trusted her opinion." If I thought they were shocked at the last bit of news, then this one renders them mute.

"Harlow! Harlow!"

"Speak of the devil," I mutter under my breath. My friend is rounding the corner of the house. In an almost comical fashion, she freezes, basically tripping over her own feet when her eyes register the men standing around me.

"Hope?" Parker's voice cracks on the word before he runs over, grabs her, and hugs her, spinning her around. I can see her slapping at his arm to put her down, though he doesn't oblige until he smacks a big kiss on her cheek.

"Sorry, Brad had said everyone was gone, so I was coming to get you for lunch. Hi, guys." She waves kind of awkwardly at the other three who are still staring at her like they've seen a ghost.

"Fuck this, I'm going back to the B and B. I need some sleep." With that eloquent goodbye, Wyatt heads back to one of the remaining trucks, starts it up, and tears out of the area.

My mouth drops open, and Ethan looks at me with worry. "I'm sorry about that. He's an asshole most of the time, but when he's had no sleep, he's practically unbearable." He steps up to Hope and gives her a hug and a gentle kiss on the cheek. "It was nice to see you, Hope. We should get back and clean up." He waves goodbye and heads over to the other truck.

"Tell Mr. Summers I'll call him tomorrow to set up an appointment," Miles says before following Ethan. His goodbye hits the middle ground between Wyatt's cold exit and Ethan's kind one. Hope isn't ignored, but she receives only the same simple nod that I do. "Let's go, Parker," he calls back, but Parker looks torn.

"Go," Hope urges him. "I'll see you again soon. I promise."

He hugs her hard again and follows after his brothers. Before she notices me watching her, Hope looks after them with obvious sadness and longing in her eyes.

"What was that?" I ask, but she shrugs.

"*That* is a long story—one that requires copious amounts of wine. One day, I'll share it with you."

She links her arm with mine, and we walk back to the house, her lost in contemplation and me leaving her be for now like a good friend. There's plenty of time for me to get Jazzy up to speed so we can come up with a plan.

A body cuts through the water of the pool as Hope and I turn the corner of the house, approaching the back entertainment area. Holden and Oliver are lounging on lounge chairs, sunglasses on, and I'm assuming they're both asleep because neither of them look up when we approach. It's Jaxon's dark head I can see swimming furiously like he's trying to outrun his demons. I leave him be and follow Hope into the house. Nana is placing platters of sandwiches on the table, then Jacinta pushes open the swinging door to the kitchen, carrying a jug of what looks like iced tea in each hand.

"Perfect timing, girls." Nana smiles as she greets us. "I thought a late lunch/early dinner would be a good idea after all your traveling today. Did the jaguar get settled in ok?"

"Sure did. I'll go back to check on her later. Do you know if the guys gave Dad a key to lock that back entrance door?"

"I think so, dear. He and Howard disappeared into the office. Can one of you tell them supper is ready? Declan is back too. I think he might have broken every speed limit to get here so fast."

"Can you? I want to check on the cubs," I ask Hope, and she smiles.

"Sure, but I want cuddles with one of those adorable creatures as soon as I can." She disappears down the corridor leading to the front of the house.

"Hey, Harlow," Jacinta calls before I can head toward the conservatory. "That basket came for you." She points to an extravagant thing on the coffee table in front of the huge sectional. It's a big brightly wrapped basket, packaged in pink and red cellophane.

My hands clench into fists as I eye it like it could explode at any moment. My stalker experiences have put a bit of a damper on the idea of surprise presents even though I know my family would never let me open something that hadn't been checked for danger. A set of hands on my shoulder has me jumping, a small squeal coming out before I can stop it.

"Oh my god." Jacinta buckles over with laughter. "I'm so sorry, but you should have seen your face. You were looking at it like it might bite you!"

"Ah, yeah. You probably would too if the last package had the mutilated bodies of two of your boyfriends in doll form," I snap at her, and she sobers immediately.

"Oh shit, I forgot about that. I'm sorry." She wraps her arms around me and gives me a big hug. "That package has been checked by security. I'll definitely lead with that next time so you don't worry about it. It's from Aunt Merideth. That's her signature wrapping, and there's a card." She points out the card stuck into the pretty wrapping on top. "Go on."

I pull out the small envelope and open it up. The writing is pretty, with loopy feminine lettering.

Dear Harlow,

Welcome to the family. I am so very excited to meet you at Christmas time. I have heard so much about you from my brother and nephew. I saw that you have decided to be brave and attempt a relationship with all six of my great-nephews. Good for you, sweetheart. I have enclosed a few gifts from our collection that will probably come in handy with 6 men to keep sexually happy.

See you soon.

Aunt Merideth

Frowning, I put down the card and reach for the wrapping. I can feel Jacinta peering over my shoulder, and her giggles immediately fill my ears when I peel back the layers of cellophane. Fuck my life. I shake my head as I take in everything that my great-aunt has gifted me. There are too many condoms to count, but I pick one up and admire the Sugar and Spice logo on it before tossing it back in the basket. There are five different bottles of lube, a number of vibrators and toys that I will probably need to read instructions to so I know what to do with them, then there seems to be an array of bondage equipment—handcuffs, a whip, a paddle, rope, blindfolds, nipple clamps, and just to round it out, a maid's outfit.

Jacinta must see the disbelief in my eyes when I face her because her giggles dissolve into outright laughter as she collapses onto the sofa, hands over her stomach. "She did it for all of us when we hit eighteen. I guess she didn't want to leave you out of the mortification of having your great-aunt gift you sex toys."

Nana comes back out of the kitchen. "Oh good, you got Merideth's gift. So thoughtful, isn't she? She's really looking forward to meeting you."

I'm pretty sure I look like I've been hit over the head with a two-by-four as my stare ping pongs between my sister and my grandma. I shake my head, not sure exactly what to say. Jacinta gets herself under control and stands up. "Just go with it. Send her a polite thank you card and some flowers. She'll love it. But beware. She does *not* shy away from any talk about sex, and she will be asking you all sorts of questions when she comes to visit. Best to prepare yourself now."

"Did you check on the cubs, Harlow?" Nana asks, and I shake my head, still speechless. "Well, do that so you can sit down. Tell Declan the food is ready. Jacinta, go find Tom and Kai, will you? I think they went upstairs. I'll tell the others out at the pool."

Nana and Jacinta both bustle off, and I head to the conservatory, considering whether to hide there with my cubs for the rest of the night. I'm desperately hoping no one brings the sex basket up at dinner, but if I know my sister—and I'm definitely starting to—I'm sure I'm not going to be so lucky.

Chapter Fifteen

Jaxon

I've always found comfort in swimming. It blocks out everything surrounding you, all the background noise and movement, allowing you to be one with your thoughts. Sometimes I plow through the water, letting my mind focus on the repetitive movement of arm over arm, keeping my legs kicking, up and back, over and over again. And sometimes I use the time to go over the problems in my life with no outside interference. I just like to pretend the world doesn't exist outside my bubble, but this is one of those former times. It's a blessing to allow all my worries to float away in the wake of my body. All I'm responsible for is concentrating on my heartbeat and breathing—nothing else. At least until something hits me in the back of the head.

"Nana! Did you just throw a pool noodle at

me?" I gasp out as I tread water. She's standing on the side of the pool, hands on hips, looking slightly miffed.

"Goodness, Jaxon, I'd been calling you so loudly Prada could probably hear me in the stables."

"Sorry, Nana, I was kinda zoned out." Her face softens, and she drops her hands.

"Nevermind, dry off and come have something to eat."

"Has Harlow finished with the cat?" I ask her as I swim over to the side of the pool and pull myself out.

"Yes, Hope retrieved her, and they're back now. I'm pretty sure she would have stayed there all night if we let her." Nana smiles affectionately as I hurry over to my towel and dry myself off. I spoke to Emma as soon as I had dumped my luggage, and we're going to check out the house tomorrow.

"Excellent, I can't wait to tell her my news." She reaches up and ruffles my hair like she's been doing since I was very small, her eyes shining with emotion.

"I am so very happy for you and the boys. You know I had always wanted to introduce her to you in the hope she might catch your eye. Such a sensible solution to share one wonderful woman. Poppy and I always thought she would be perfect for you. Wouldn't put up with any of your shit, which is of course very necessary with all of my darling boys."

We walk side by side through the glass doors. During the summer, they're usually thrown open to let in any afternoon breeze, but now that it's cooling down, they're kept shut.

"You're going to have to start using the indoor pool again. It's starting to get too chilly to continue using the one out there. I don't want you to get sick. I'll get the pool company to winterize it next week."

"Sounds like a good idea. I'm just going to run upstairs for a hot shower and a change of clothes," I tell her, giving her a kiss on the cheek. Holden and Oliver are already sitting at the table with Jacinta, but the others haven't arrived yet, so I'm sure I have time.

"Be quick," she warns as I hurry away.

Racing through a shower, I stay under the water just long enough to chase away the chill on my skin, then I throw on some sweats, a t-shirt, and sneakers. By the time I get back to the table, everyone is seated and waiting.

"Sorry," I apologize as I grab the seat next to Hope, giving her a kiss on the cheek as I do. "Hi, I didn't know you were here."

"That's because you dumped your luggage, made some phone call that had you grinning from ear to ear, then disappeared into the pool," she explains, and I raise my eyebrows in surprise.

"You saw all that?" I ask, surprised, and she snorts while a couple of my brothers chuckle.

"She was sitting on the sofa the whole time, but

you were off in your own little world," my sister points out, and she's not wrong.

"Sorry," I apologize, and she waves me off as we all start to help ourselves to the food.

"What was it that had you smiling so madly?" Kai asks before taking a bite of the sandwich in his hand.

I look to Harlow, taking a second to drink in the smile on her face. She looks so happy, and I'm glad that we can make her feel that way. I don't think I've ever cared so much about making my partner truly happy—emotionally happy, not just happy materialistically or sexually. It's really a whole new experience for me, but I don't hate it at all.

"I spoke to Emma, and we're going to meet her at the house first thing tomorrow morning for a tour. All of us." I eye my brothers, not wanting to leave them out, before moving on to Hope and the rest of my family. "Cancel anything you had planned because I want this to be a full family thing."

"Even me?" Hope asks from next to me, and I nudge her in the side with my elbow.

"Come on, you know you're an honorary Summers. I'm sure Dad would even adopt you if you wanted to take the name."

Her eyes widen as they fly to my dad. He's smiling brightly, his eyes creased with joy.

"Of course I can make it official if you want. What's one more child in my brood? It's not like we don't have enough of everything to go around." He chuckles, but Hope wriggles in her chair a little uncomfortably. I know she grew up in foster homes, having never been formally adopted. She doesn't have any biological family, and she's spent Thanksgiving and Christmas with us since she met Holden in college, so I guess she's not close to any of her foster families.

"Think about it, dear. It may seem like it's come up in a joking manner, but we're serious. You know how closely my grandchildren guard their family. None of them would have offered if your place with us wasn't genuine. We would love to make you an official part of the family, even if you are an adult. Hope Summers would have such a nice ring to it, wouldn't it?" On her other side, Nana pats her hand before putting her attention on me. A meddlesome woman she may be, she's also got a big heart. Having dealt with all of her grandchildren's baggage, she realizes all too well what this kind of offer means to someone who has Hope's background.

"That sounds wonderful. I haven't been in that house for years, not since Brad was a child. The count stopped having as many parties once Dragos was born and he lost his wife. He turned slightly reclusive. It will be interesting to see if things have changed since then."

"I can't wait." Harlow is practically bouncing up and down in her chair. "I also want to do a walk-through of the zoo and make notes about what needs to be done in there." She turns to Dad. "Can you invite the vet and zoologist you poached from the MacGinty Sanctuary? I'd love to have them visit the property after we've gotten our first look."

"Sure can." Dad pulls out his phone to make a note.

"Not at the table, Brad," Nana chides, sounding exasperated. "You know the rules." He sheepishly shoves it back into his pocket.

"That sounds good, but I really have to get back to work after that. You'll have to do the zoo walk-through without me. Not that I really have any knowledge to add to that." Declan takes a sip of his drink and screws up his face. "Anyone want a beer?" All five of my brothers, Dad, and Poppy put their hands up. Nana huffs as Declan gets up and heads to the kitchen to grab us all one.

"Declan's right. We all need to get back to work too." Holden looks apologetically at Harlow. "Thomas will be with you though. You still need protection until we can work out what the two attacks in Hawaii were about."

"I'm going to bring my tablet so we can make notes as we walk through the house. I know you'll want to concentrate on the outside renovations, so I'd like to help out with the interior if you're okay with it," Jacinta offers, and Harlow nods enthusias-tically.

"God yes! This is such a big project. So as long

as it's not going to take time away from your work, I would love your help." That exchange only makes me feel more settled. Having my sister and the woman I'm in love with actually have a relationship is more than I ever hoped for. I love my sister, but I like to think that I'm usually pretty honest with myself about what she's like. The odds that I would find someone who clicked with me *and* her were astronomically tiny. With Harlow at my side, I get to keep my family and explore a real relationship that I actually care about. If a zoo and a house is the least I can do to repay the gift she's given me, I'm overjoyed to give them to her.

"Actually, I spoke to Nana when she came back up to the house. I'm going to be stepping back from a full-time role at Neighpalm Couture. I love my company, but my forced hiatus made me realize I much prefer working in the design capabilities. I'll still be CEO, but we're going to advertise for someone to take over the management side while I stick to the creative side. It will free up a lot more of my time, and I can design wherever I am. Jaxon and I even talked about me flying out to assess the properties we inherited because he wants to stay here with you. It's a big step, but I think that it's actually going to be the right one for me."

Harlow's head swings to me, and her eyes are filled with an emotion, one I'm pretty sure mirrors what I feel for her. "You don't want to check out all those amazing places?" Her voice cracks.

"I mean, sure, one day, but you don't have the time at the moment, and I want you to come too. Not to mention my hotel in Hawaii is planning its opening weekend, and I'm wrapping up negotiations on another business. I don't really have the time either, so I thought we could all go together once Jacinta makes decisions about them and everything has settled down here."

"What are you going to do with them all?" Kai asks, and she shrugs.

"Maybe Airbnb, or we could keep them as holiday homes and allow Neighpalm employees to use them as bonuses. I'm not sure yet, but we definitely need to take an inventory of them."

"Do you think we might find the mysterious vault tomorrow?" Oliver asks, his brown eyes sparkling behind his black-framed glasses. The blue in his hair has just about faded, so he's ready for a new color. I overheard him and Holden talking about it on the flight home.

I shrug. "Who knows, but Emma did say she has something she wants to talk to us about before we start the walk-through. Maybe she has more insight into it than we know."

"That would be awesome." Holden and Oli look at each other, their eyes lit up. "What do you think the count kept in there?"

"Who knows, but he became more reclusive and secretive the older he got. Thought everyone was out to get him. He had a small security force that surrounded him constantly," Poppy says, looking serious. "That vault could contain just about anything."

The table is quiet for a moment as we all concentrate on our food and contemplate Poppy's words, but it doesn't last for long.

It's now that Thomas, ever the quiet one, chooses to speak up. "I'm running background checks on the McCallister brothers." At this news, Hope's face pales just enough for me to notice. "I thought it was a good idea to get that done as soon as possible. But apart from what they've already disclosed to us, they look clean. I didn't think they had any connection to this second stalker, but it's better to be safe than sorry. I mean, the four of them have never even left California, so it couldn't have been any of them in Hawaii. When you have your meeting with them, you need to inform them that any crew they hire will have to go through background checks too. If any of the guys they want have some kind of record, we can still give them a chance, pending what the circumstances were."

Dad clears his throat, causing all of us to look over at him next. "How do you all feel about me offering them the Neighpalm name to work under?" he asks, and I can see the surprise on my siblings' faces. Hell, I'm feeling the same way. This is news to most of us, considering Harlow, Nana, and Poppy are the only ones who appear totally at ease. Dad sighs. "Hope suggested them to me, which obviously goes a long way toward vouching for their character and whether they would honor the connection to our family name." Hope hunches in on herself, trying to avoid our open attention now that everyone's focused on her.

"Anyway, her recommendation aside, I did my due diligence. They do excellent work, but something happened to one of the boys. No, I won't tell you; that's their business, not ours, and he was cleared of all charges. However, these things stick like glue in the kind of community they're from. What was a bustling, thriving business dwindled off to basically nothing. Two of the brothers picked up second jobs to keep the business afloat, but really, they belong in the construction business. You should see what they accomplished so far for Harlow."

"Guys, it's amazing," Harlow gushes, "and they seem like nice guys."

"I wouldn't be offering them this chance if I didn't think it was worth it. It's our family name on the line, after all. Regardless of what happens with them long-term, I've offered them rooms here at the house for the duration of the zoo rebuild. They need to live close by, and who knows how long this construction could take. There's room in our wing, not to mention there will be plenty of space once you all move out." He looks sad at this, but he shakes it off.

Holden is looking at Hope quizzically, which

surprises me. I thought he knew everything about his best friend. "Who are these guys to you, Hope?" he asks gently, and she breathes out a deep sigh before looking him in the eye.

"They were my foster brothers in the last home I was in before I came to LA."

Holden's brow crinkles a little in confusion, but with a little nod, he turns to Dad. "They get my vote since Hope recommended them." Obviously, Holden trusts Hope, and we trust him, and Hope's personal life is just that—personal. I'm sure she would share it with us if she thought we needed to know. "I trust Hope and Holden, and you seem to have done your research, so I'm fine with it."

Each of my siblings is quick to agree, and we finish dinner by discussing more mundane topics, most business-related, but it's a pleasant way to pass the evening.

We're all early to retire after the long day, and I'm first to whisper in Harlow's ear, inviting her to my bed. She's just as quick to agree, making her way to my room after she's had a shower. There's a curious look on her face as she studies the inside of my room while I watch her from my spot on the bed. I had been reading over some reports on my tablet while I waited for her, but they can't sustain an ounce of my attention now that she's here.

"I wasn't in here for long the other day, so I didn't get a good look," she says as she picks up one of my swimming trophies. Her eyes lock on it, probably reading the inscription, before she puts it down. My motorcycle helmet is hanging on one wall next to my horse riding helmet, and she grabs that next. "You ride a bike?"

"Yeah, whenever I can, but since you've been here, I haven't really got it out. I've been so busy, it was easier to get a lift to the office with one of the others. Do you ride?"

"I haven't had the opportunity before, but I'd really like to," she says, hanging it back on the hook.

"Jacinta has a helmet. I'll grab it for you in the morning. How about we get up a little earlier, and I'll take you for one before we go over to the house?"

Her face lights up with a grin. "That would be great."

She leaves her perusal to climb onto the bed. She smells like her shower gel, something fruity, and her hair is damp from washing it. There's nothing special about how she looks right now, but I think that's why I'm so drawn to it. I've had all kinds of women, but I've never really had one stick around long enough for me to get this, that post-shower nighttime comfort that says someone is comfortable with me.

Wrapping her arms around me, she pulls my head down for a kiss. It starts off soft and gentle but quickly moves into sensuous and seductive, her tongue tangling with mine as I wrap my arms around her and pull her in until her body is flush with mine. One of her hands continues to run through my hair, but the other drifts lower until she's cupping my ass cheek and tugging me impossibly tighter against her body.

She pulls away, her eyes a little dazed as she licks her lips like she's trying to chase the taste of me. "God, you're so sexy. It was all I could do to keep my tongue in my mouth when you came to dinner with those gray sweats on. Don't you know they're catnip to women?" She's all breathy and flushed, so I just wink at her. Did I think of it when I got dressed? Definitely not. Will I think about that in the future? Fuck yes. Jaxon Summers, master of seduction right here.

"Of course I do. With six men for you to choose from, I've got to do everything I can to stack the odds in my favor."

Her laughter is music to my ears. "You don't play fair," she whines jokingly, then she takes the bottom of my shirt, peels it over my head, and tosses it to the side. She runs her hands all over my torso, her nails creating just the tiniest bite of pressure against my skin. "God, this body." She takes a nipple into her mouth, and I grunt as she bites down on it, trying to adjust my rapidly hardening dick which is straining against my sweatpants. She pushes my hand away and grabs hold of it herself. "I can't wait to have this inside of me."

That's enough to break my fragile restraint, and

I pounce, rolling so I'm on top of her. She squeaks in surprise, but that turns into a moan as I grind my dick into her pussy.

"Well, you're going to have to wait because I want to taste you first." It's my turn to remove her top, tossing the tiny tank in the same direction she threw mine before I wriggle my way down her body, pulling her sleep shorts off at the same time. Leaning back, I take in her naked body beneath mine. "I didn't get dessert earlier, and now I'm starving for it."

Chapter Sixteen

Harlow

Jaxon's tongue worships my pussy like it's his last meal on earth, and I come twice as he uses his fingers and mouth to drive me crazy. I'm a sweaty, panting mess when he finally climbs up my body and kisses me. He tastes like me, but I don't care. Our mouths are still fused, tongues rolling against one another, as he lines himself up and slowly enters me, his thick length stretching me until he fills me up. I pull away and moan my pleasure, unable to hold it in.

His mouth finds one of my nipples as he starts a slow rolling glide in and out. He's in no hurry, his body worshiping mine. My hands roam up and down his back as he hitches one of my legs over his hip so he can get deeper. I say a prayer to Poseidon, the god of the ocean, because I'm pretty sure he blessed Jaxon with some mad swimming skills. They're paying off in bed with some super amazing rolling action. Fuck, the man can move, and he easily works my body to the precipice of orgasm again. Unlike his brothers, Jaxon doesn't talk dirty, but he does mutter words of praise. "It feels so good. You're so tight and hot." It gets me going just as much as the dirty talk does because I know he's lost in this moment with me.

"Harder, Jaxon," I demand as my hands find his tight ass, and I squeeze. He picks up the pace, and my toes start to curl as my pussy flutters madly until we hit that peak together. As one, we fall off that cliff. Jaxon keeps pumping through my orgasm, but his teeth are gritted and his neck muscles strained. Finally, he starts to slow, his dick not losing any of its hardness, so he stays right where he is, propped up on his arms, kissing me as we both come down from our orgasms.

"Wow, that was…" I break off, slightly breathless.

"Amazing, fantastic, the best ever?" he prompts, and I chuckle. He groans when my pussy clenches as I laugh, then he slowly pulls out. He rolls off the bed and disappears into the bathroom, returning with a warm washcloth, one he refuses to relinquish when I try to take it from him. He cleans me up before running it over his deflating dick and throwing it into a hamper in the corner.

"Well?" he prompts, and I realize he's actually

waiting for an answer. Another laugh breaks free, and I feel something dribble down my thigh. Groaning, I roll off the bed.

"Unbelievably incredible," I tell him, kissing him as I go past.

"Where are you going? Want to watch a movie?" he asks.

"Yup, just going to pee and clean myself up a little bit more. Your future kids are running down my leg." He pales when I point to the cum that's dribbled out. "Relax, I'm kidding. I'm protected, remember? I wouldn't mess with any of our futures like that." I think there may be a slight flash of disappointment in his eyes before he smirks.

When I come back, he's got a movie playing on his tv, and I climb in next to him. Snuggling into his side, I try to work out what movie he has on, but he feels kind of rigid next to me, not the good kind. What could have happened while I was gone?

"Do you want kids, Harlow?" he quietly asks after a moment, and I turn my head to look at him. He's staring at me like my answer could make or break him.

"Yeah, I would, though I wouldn't care if they were biologically mine or if we decided to do what Dad did and adopt a hockey team."

He chuckles at that. "Hockey, hey?"

"Yeah, huge hockey fan. I can't wait to see if Kai ends up buying the Colorado Grizzlies," I tell him, giving him a little tangent to cling to in case he's not ready to pursue a conversation. I'm not really sure why he seemed upset, but I don't want to push him too much, too fast.

He seems to relax, all the tension leaving his body, which seems like a safe enough indicator that I can ask him the question too. "What about you? How do you feel about kids? With our... untraditional relationship, there's also the factor that any kids I have might not be yours—biologically, at least. Does that bother you?" It's a lot, but if we're taking this situation seriously, then I guess there really isn't too soon of a time to think about this. Protection isn't foolproof, and god forbid something happens, I don't want that to be the first time he shares his feelings with me.

He pulls me up a little so my head is resting on his chest, and I can hear his heartbeat beneath my ear.

"With my awful start in life, you would think I wouldn't want them, but Mom wasn't really bad to me. I was her golden boy, and when she was sober, she smothered me with love and attention. Or that's what I remember. But anyway, yeah, I want a whole bunch of them. I don't care if they're mine biologically or one of my brother's or kids we can give a safe and happy home to. I just think with the kind of money we have, we can at least rescue some like Dad did for us. I mean, look at him, offering to adopt Hope. I think he would probably adopt more. He was so thrilled when he heard about you, but it easily could have been another child he rescued and brought into the house. The McCallister brothers, for example. That's a classic Dad move, trying to help out people less fortunate than him. I might not have had a good parent model with my mom, but Dad, Nana, and Poppy are pretty damn good examples of what I'd like to be as a parent."

He rests his chin on my head before slipping down again to nuzzle into my neck, his hand resting on my stomach. "I can't think of anything sexier than you rounded with one of our babies in your belly." His words are a hot whisper across my ear as he nips at my neck, and my whole body clenches with desire. Holy fuck, that's hot. Why is that so hot?

"For what it's worth, I think you're going to be an amazing daddy one day. And practicing wouldn't hurt, would it?" With that, I pounce on him. I plan on riding this man hard and putting him to bed exhausted, and with the grin on his face, he doesn't look like he's upset at all.

The next morning, the wind rushes past my body as I hold on tight around Jaxon's waist. Safety first, of course, and the whole part about clutching his body and pressing against him is an unspoken bonus. His bike, a sleek black number, flies over the asphalt like it has wings, and my blood rushes through my veins.

Jaxon had taken me to breakfast at a cute little café about half an hour from the house, where we had coffee and enough food to last me all day, before riding back for our meeting with Emma and the rest of the crew.

Thomas' face is a thundercloud as we drive across the wooden bridge of the moat, the click clack sounds making me grip Jaxon harder in fright. When we get closer, any excitement I had been feeling just moments before turns to guilt. The rest of my boyfriends don't look happy either; in fact, none of the crowd does.

""Oh, fuck. I think I'm in deep trouble. I forgot to tell people we were going out. Did you tell anyone?" I mutter to Jaxon through the microphone in the helmet.

"Shit, only Jazzy when I grabbed the helmet, but she was half asleep. Thomas is going to kill me," he groans as he pulls the bike to a stop and switches it off, dropping the kickstand.

I climb off and pull off my helmet. "Oh god. I'm so sorry, everyone. I didn't think. It was nice to be able to just live in the moment, but that doesn't mean it's worth any of the worry it caused you guys," I apologize as I approach the group, my eyes on Thomas. His arms are crossed, mouth firmly set in a frown, and if his body weren't so tense, I'm sure his foot would be tapping away. "It was a spur of the moment thing; nobody knew we were going to do it." Yep, that certainly didn't help. If anything, he's somehow standing even more rigidly than before.

"What if someone had been watching the house, Harlow? What if they saw you leave and followed you? How could you be so irresponsible after everything we've done to try to keep you safe!" His words hit the target, and I can feel my shoulders hunch in as tears prick my eyes.

"Whoa, man. Hey, this is my fault. I should have told one of you. I didn't think either." Jaxon steps between us, holding his hand up.

"Damn right, it's your fault. It would have been on your head if something had happened to her. How could you be so selfish?" Declan spits angrily, and I huddle against Jaxon's back. The reappearance of this Declan has me cowering like I would with my mother when I was small. What did he say to trigger this? I think about his words. *How could you be so selfish?* My mother used to say that to me all the time, referring to just about anything I did, or said, once I started living with Chuck and Melinda. Therapy helped me see that she was the selfish one, not me, but those words still awaken something small and hurtful inside me.

"Whoa, whoa." Jacinta steps up. "Like you guys have never done anything without thinking first. Lay off the two of them. They apologized. Let's not ruin what's supposed to be a momentous occasion."

Declan turns away from us, and if he were a girl, I would say he flounced toward the front of the house. I have no idea what other word fits this melodramatic storming off that he's seemingly perfected. How the hell does he do that?

Thomas, at least, sticks around, uncrossing his arms before he growls at the two of us. "Don't do it again. I could have easily gotten up, taken one of the spare bikes, and come with you." He sighs, closing his eyes like he's silently counting to ten in his head, then places a kiss on my cheek. "You look hot in those riding leathers, though." He looks me up and down and winks before following his brother.

"Holy shit. I thought that would go a lot worse," I say to Jaxon with relief, and he sighs.

"Don't worry, Declan will make us pay for a day or two." I grab his hand and squeeze it.

"Not if he wants to be on cub duty." A snort of laughter behind me has me whirling around. Kai's standing there with a smile on his face.

"Let me take that." He grabs the helmet from my hands. "You sure know how to manipulate our biggest brother already." He walks back to the bike with Jaxon, and they put the helmets on the ground next to it as Holden and Oliver approach me. They must see my face fall at Kai's words. I don't like being accused of manipulations; that's not what I had intended.

"Don't worry, babe. It's not really manipulation,

more a workaround. You've got to use what you can. Dec holds grudges, and he's likely to sulk for a day or two, so use what you can to get him to come around. Lord knows we all would if we had the chance." Holden kisses me on the cheek and squeezes my arm reassuringly.

"Just make sure not to do it again. Dec is protective of all of us, and he sees what you did as a failure on his behalf. He failed to predict something like that would happen, but he thinks he should have," Oliver explains, grabbing my hand and towing me after the rest of the group. I can see that Dad, Nana, and Poppy were worried, but none of them are going to scold me like a child, which is how Thomas and Declan made me feel. At least Thomas came around without a dramatic production.

Jacinta drags Jaxon over and shoves him into my side before walking around me and linking her arm with mine. "Come on, let's do this together." There's a smile on her face that screams she's doing her best to give a stiff upper lip, and that reminds me that this isn't about me. This is just as much about the two of them. Maybe using me as a distraction is a way for them to get through this, but if it makes it easier for them, I'll let them do it every time.

"Are you sure it's okay that I'm here?" Hope steps up on the other side of Jacinta, and the former waves her off with a hum and links her arm too. "You heard everyone last night. You're being adopted, and even if you don't want that, you're still one of the family." The four of us must look like the characters from the *Wizard of Oz* as we mount the steps and enter through the big double doors. I mean, this *is* a little like Dorothy going to see the wizard and stepping behind the curtain, isn't it? We finally get to see everything behind the legend.

Emma greets us warmly as we step into a foyer that looks like it's out of a gothic novel. Dad gives her a kiss as he looks around. "No Molly?" he asks, and Emma shakes her head, looking a little guilty.

"No, I asked Molly to stay home today because I have things I need to tell you. You may decide you don't want anyone outside of your family knowing the information."

I exchange a look with the twins. *Now that doesn't sound ominous at all.* What other possible life-altering shit could Emma have to tell us now? But everyone else is so distracted by the house that it seems I'm the only one who stops to think.

"Holy wow!" Oliver lets out a loud whistle as he looks around the room.

Nana, Poppy, and Dad don't seem so surprised, but the younger generation of Summers looks around in awe.

The entrance foyer is large, with dark porcelain tiles covering the floor and burgundy runners decorating the middle of the room to the bottom of a set of steps. There's a mezzanine level that the steps lead up to, overlooking the foyer. Decorative arches and columns line the length of the space, each arch leading to a closed door. The room is lit by a big wrought-iron candelabra that hangs above us, and there are wall sconces that look like they could have been used for candles. There are also two candelabras either side of the staircase, both with lit candles in them.

Nana sees me studying them. "The count liked to say the candles created an elegant ambience even though they would make a mess and drip wax all over the floor, not to mention burn down. He had an employee whose only job was to keep them all lit and clean up the wax in the mornings." She points to the roof, and of course my eyes naturally follow. "That one used to be candles too, but someone got hurt lighting them, so he switched to electricity." The ceiling is cathedral-style, with gothic cornices and frescoes painted on its surface. I'm trying to get a better look at what's actually painted there when Hope claps a hand over her mouth. I frown and look at her, raising an eyebrow.

"It's porn," she whispers, and my eyes fly back up to the ceiling. Sure enough, I can now make it out. There's an orgy on the ceiling, but it's not just a human orgy. There are all sorts of creatures painted there, defiling one another.

"That stays," Oliver chuckles, and even though Holden elbows him, he can't hide his smile. Tablet in hand, Jacinta turns to me. I feel my cheeks grow pink, but I quickly nod. It certainly is a talking piece, and unless you look up, no one will notice. Jacinta raises an eyebrow but smirks and makes a note.

"Hey, let's go in here first." Emma walks across to the first door on the left, and we all follow. When we enter, it looks like an office. There's a huge gothic-looking desk taking up a good portion of the room, and it looks out over the moat and the draw-bridge at the front. There's a mismatched array of chairs taking up the rest of the room, and Emma gestures to them. "Take a seat. I stole chairs from all over the house, so we would have enough. I know it's a squeeze, but there are some things we need to talk about."

We do as she asks, and as we get comfortable, I see Emma sort of brace herself like what she has to tell us isn't going to be good. There's something about the gesture that puts me on high alert, and I grab a twin's hand in each of mine.

Emma sighs. "I'm afraid I haven't been completely honest with you all."

Chapter Seventeen

Harlow

"My father wasn't just the caretaker for the place; he'd worked for the count since before I was born. I guess he was his manservant or butler or whatever you would call it these days. Simply put, my father was a jack of all trades. He'd been working for the count for a few years when he'd met my mom. She thought he was a catch because he was handsome, and had a well paying job and quickly agreed to marry him. My father wasn't a stupid man and he kept his relationship with my mom very separate, I don't think my mom had even met him before the wedding. And she certainly hadn't realized what a deviant the count actually was until after she had married my father. Dad kept her well clear of all the orgies and drugs. She told me it only got worse once Dragos was born and his mother died in childbirth."

Nana nods. "Yes, Adelina and I got pregnant at the same time, and with her pregnancy, she started to see things in a different light. Their lifestyle was fun when we had no responsibilities, but once she found out she was pregnant, she begged the count to stop, to change, but he wasn't interested. By then, he liked his lifestyle and the power. After Adelina passed away, we barely saw the count, and Dragos was raised by nannies." Nana smiles gently at Emma. "I didn't realize your father was Vincent and that he had become the caretaker when the count had disappeared."

"My mother begged my father to quit, but he wouldn't. He chose the count over the two of us, so my mother divorced him, and we moved away. Looking back now, I think Dad knew too much, and him pushing Mom away was his attempt to keep us safe. I still had a relationship with him, but he would come to me. I never stepped foot on the property again until after Dragos and Count Bucătaru had disappeared. My dad called me about five years ago. He'd been diagnosed with stomach cancer and only been given a few months to live. He said it was imperative that I take over as caretaker because he trusted no one else. What was I supposed to do? I didn't want to drop my whole life, but my father had limited time left, and this had been *his* entire life. So I left Molly to run the boutique we own, then moved in with him here. In the few months before his death, he told me things that made my toes curl. He said that he had known about Carmen being pregnant and that she had given her children up. He was adamant that they would reappear one day and would need to know things."

My dad is staring at Emma with hurt in his eyes, and I want to reach out and hold his hand, but I'm not close enough to without getting up. She must see the hurt because she quickly reassures him.

"He had no idea that it was the twins or that you had them. She had come to him when she was heavily pregnant, begging for his help, but his hands were tied. He couldn't access any of the accounts because they'd been frozen by the police when Dragos and his father went missing. Once the Bucătaru wealth was handed over to the trust, he was only able to get them to pay for things that were needed around the property. He was also suspicious of Carmen. He knew her history and didn't necessarily believe that her child was Dragos'. She was furious with him and made vile threats before eventually leaving once again, and he never saw her again. He made me promise that DNA tests would be run to make sure that the heirs were really of the count's line."

"Why would he be so insistent on this? It seems a little bit paranoid," Poppy muses.

"Not really. I know you look for the good in

everyone, but in reality people are assholes. Plus, there were other measures that made it important to verify the biological connection. The vault is secured with a biometric lock that can only be activated by someone with the same genetic signature of the count, and it needs a code which only one other person knew."

"Your father?" Thomas guesses.

"Yes. With his last dying breath, he told me the location of the vault and the code. That wasn't even the last of the secrets he shared; contained in the vault are maps detailing the secret tunnels within the estate. Tunnels which make it easy for people to move around undetected."

"Holy fuck! Why did you never tell the trust about this?" Holden asks her, and she shrugs.

"My dad told me not to. He was suspicious of one of the lawyers—Patricia. She was always coming around to inspect the house, stopping by at least once a month. By the time she began to grow really bold, Dad had been diagnosed with cancer, so he obviously had other things on his mind. He called the firm to ask why this was happening, but they were just as confused as he was. Apparently, she'd been given no orders to spend any time on the property, let alone the amount that she was. He started to refuse her after that, and I think she must have gotten a reprimand too because she stopped coming. Once he passed, she tried to do the same thing with me, but I put a stop to it immediately.

She was definitely looking for something, though how she would have any idea what to look for, I have no clue."

Thomas pulls out his phone, already on his way out as he says, "I'm going to call Jake and ask him to do a background check on her."

"So that's it. I have the code you need to get into the vault. Nobody else would have been able to even if they had found it. Even if they had your blood."

Jacinta gasps, her hand slapped over her mouth, as Jaxon starts to swear a blue streak.

"What's wrong?" Declan growls, though I don't know if he's freshly upset because his siblings are upset or if this is still part of his anger over our unannounced ride.

"In the month before Mom took us to Brad, a woman came and took a vile of our blood; she came back once every week." He turns to look at me. "Actually, it was the friend who I thought looked a little like your mom. After the blood was drawn, they would usually go out, leaving us alone, only for Mom to return the next day, angry as shit again. But on the last visit, something happened. She and Mom argued the whole time she was there, and Mom made her leave just as soon as she was done with the blood draw."

"It was the only time I really remember Mom being kind to me. The woman wasn't gentle. It was like she didn't know what she was doing. It always took her a couple of goes to get the needle in." Jacinta's eyes glaze over like she's lost in the memory. "Mom would hold my hand and tell me I was such a good girl, that our lives would be so much better if I did this for her. But it never lasted. Mom was even more manic and twitchy after that last blood draw. The day after, we were on Dad's doorstep."

"Do you think she was looking for the vault?" Oliver leans forward, his elbows on his knees, like he's completely enthralled by the story.

Jacinta shrugs, the motion nonchalant even though the look in her eyes is anything but. "Well, what else would she need our blood for?"

"Maybe they found it and realized that there was another measure needed to open it up," Dad speculates.

"But she didn't have access to the house. How would she have found it? Surely, Dad would have known," Emma points out, but Kai shakes his head.

"You said it yourself; there are secret passage-ways all over the estate. Carmen was one of the count's working girls. Who's to say that she didn't know a different way into the house?"

"Kai's not wrong." Thomas has returned in time to hear the last bit of the conversation. "We need that map so we can make sure all the access points are closed off."

Emma stands up and brushes her hands on her jeans. "Do you want to go straight to the vault, or do you want to wander through the house first?" she asks Jacinta and Jaxon, but they exchange a glance before looking at me.

"You decide. This was all for you, so it's only right we do what you want," Jaxon says, and my heart skips a beat.

"Jesus, it has to be the vault, no questions asked. I would hate to be kept waiting, and there's no way I'm going to make you guys wait."

Oliver sighs with relief. "Thank fuck. If you had said you wanted to tour the house and leave us in suspense, I probably would have died." He's so fucking dramatic, but I can see everyone feels the same way.

"Okay, let's go then." There's a commotion as we all stand up and move after her. She heads back into the wondrous foyer and straight up the carpeted stairs that lead to the second-level mezzanine. Directly in front of the stairs, overlooking the whole area like a king surveying his kingdom, is a large painting of a man.

"Fuck me, that could be you in a few years, Jax." Kai's whispered words only echo what surely has to be on everyone's minds. We've all stopped as one, gaping at the likeness on the wall.

Except for the ridiculous mustache and soulless eyes, he's a dead ringer for Jaxon. The similarities between them would have been enough to make anyone stop and do a double take, but it's the differences that are making the goosebumps rise. Those eyes… There's just something about them that's haunting. They're like an empty void, causing a shiver to run down my spine. This isn't just a normal portrait, no, this is one where it feels like he's staring directly into my soul.

Nana speaks next, something thoughtful and hushed about her voice. "I had forgotten about that. You know, it never occurred to me to put two and two together. It's so obvious now. I feel like such a fool." Poppy wraps his arms around her and sighs.

"If you were a fool, so was I. When we cut him out of our life, I didn't really think about him anymore. Even when he disappeared, it had been years since we had seen him. Not since you were pregnant with Brad. That's over forty-seven years ago. Don't be down on yourself." The soft sound of Poppy's voice is a comfort to more than just Nana, chasing away the chill brought on by the count's stare.

Looking around the mezzanine level, I notice it matches downstairs, with all the arches leading to more doors and the same style wall sconces. Opposite us is a staircase to another mezzanine level.

"I bet you can really see the porn from up on that level," Oliver whispers in my ear, and my nipples pucker at the sensation. I smack him on the arm as I stifle the chuckle that wants to escape because now is not the time, but I tuck the idea away for later.

"The house is riddled with secret passageways.

Essentially, the count wanted his help to be invisible. Each room has a secret entrance. Dad made me memorize them all, so I'm probably the only remaining person who knows about them. Most of the former servants were elderly, and I think most of them would have passed on by now," Emma explains.

"Well? Where's the secret vault?" Jacinta asks breathlessly. For someone who wanted to have nothing to do with the house, she sure is excited. Has she changed her mind?

"Don't worry. She's just caught up in the drama of it all." I spin to where Jaxon is behind me, surprised.

"How did you know?" I ask him.

"Babe, you got all tense and clenched your hands. I took a guess."

I don't get to respond before Emma answers Jacinta. "There's only one way into the vault from the house." She reaches up and pulls down on the wall sconce. There's a click and a mechanical whirring sound, then the painting of Count Bucătaru swings away from the wall. A false wall pops back and slides to the side, exposing a set of elevator doors.

Holden looks up at the elevator, then back down at Emma before saying, "That's all well and good, but how the hell do we get up there?" Almost as though the house itself was listening, a false wall opens below the painting, and a set of steps rolls out, leading directly to the doors.

"Wow, that was cool," Hope whispers quietly, the words carrying in the silence of our collective amazement.

"The elevator goes down to the vault which is below the main structure. We can't all fit in, so we'll have to go in turns. Thankfully, the elevator doesn't require blood to activate it. I'll go with the first lot so I can put the lights on down there."

"How about Jaxon, Jacinta, and Harlow go first? We can follow after in a couple of trips," Dad suggests, and everyone agrees.

"That sounds good. There's a button in the elevator that will make everything close up. The count didn't want anyone else knowing it was there, so he couldn't leave it hanging open when he was going to be down there for a long time. The last group to come down can press it. You can't miss it; it's got *Close* written on it."

We all shuffle around, with Emma being the first up the steps and in the elevator. She pushes a button, making the doors close, before turning to face us.

"This elevator only goes down to the vault. There's another hidden elevator, which I will show you later, that goes into one of the turrets."

"What's up there?" Jacinta asks before either Jaxon or I can. Emma looks uncomfortable but answers anyway.

"The count's sex room. Apparently, that's where the sex parties took place. You had to be invited up there and had to agree to be blindfolded if you said yes. Again, it's the only room the elevator goes to, but there is another hidden passage from that room to a room directly below it, which is where the count moved his master bedroom after his wife died. It has full safe room capabilities."

"A safe room up there is dangerous. What if the house was set on fire?" Jaxon asks.

"I said the same thing, but Dad said the house is made of stone. That would prevent or at least slow down any major fires, and there's an exit in case of any emergency. There's a slide that winds down and into a subterranean room. I think it's on the same level as the vault."

"Wow, this house just keeps piling up the secrets."

Emma shakes her head, looking a lot less impressed than I am. "You have no idea. Wait until you see it. Assuming you don't mind if your family all knows about it, we'll go there next."

"No, that's fine. They all know how to keep a secret," Jacinta assures her as the door slides open. The room in front of us is pitch black, so Emma pulls a phone out her pocket and turns the flashlight function on.

"Give me a second." She disappears into the darkness, and within seconds, the room is flooded with light. Just like the foyer above, this room has sconces on the stone walls, and to the left of us is a giant vault complete with old-fashioned wheels. Next to it, flashing on and off, is some kind of scanner. "If you step out, the elevator will return to get the others."

So we hurry out into the cold dank room, assaulted by the smells of must and mold, and my nose wrinkles. There's dust on the floors, like nobody has been in the room for a while. Jaxon wanders around the room as Jacinta steps up to the vault to get a closer look.

"Hey, there's a door back here, and it's cracked open. Is it supposed to be like that?" His voice kind of echoes throughout the room, and Emma's frown tells me that she doesn't like what he's telling her.

"No, it's not. It should be sealed tight."

Chapter Eighteen

Oliver

I watch the doors close on my girlfriend, brother, and sister before surveying the rest of this house. "This is really something," I say to nobody in particular. My eyes run over the paintings, and I inwardly cringe at all of them. Yes, they might be classed as masterpieces, and I recognize a few from my art history class, but they are really not gelling with me. I'm thinking we sell them or store them downstairs in the vault. I've got some of my own art I'd like to display, and Kai's friend Madeline has some amazing nature prints that I think would look great in this house. She has a whole series on animals. If I could get them blown up and framed, I could gift them to Harlow for her birthday.

What I really envision for this house is that it

comes to be a reflection of us, something where you can think about the people you love simply by looking around you because there are hints of them everywhere. I know I'll be thinking about them when they're not around, Den and Harlow the most, of course, and I'd love for this to really become a *home*. It sounds like some cheesy daydream, but what can I say? Dad, Nana, and Poppy always made us all feel loved, and through them, I learned that home is the people you care about and the spaces that are filled with their presence.

Looking down, my mind continuing to catalog changes, I grimace at the carpet beneath our feet. The mosaic monstrosity has to go. I wonder if the floors are wooden underneath or if we'll have to recarpet. If we do neutral, I'm voting we leave behind the patterns or prints. I'm loving the gothic feel the place has, but it just needs a few touches to modernize it the tiniest bit. I don't want to lose its ambiance, but this dark, gloomy, and oversexed castle vibe isn't quite feeling like us. I take out my phone and write down my suggestions while everyone is still walking along the landing looking at the paintings.

"I'll add it to the list," Jacinta promises after she gets my message and looks it over.

"You know, now that I think about it, we didn't really see much of the house apart from the ball-room. It's downstairs and has a lovely view of the lake between the house and the zoo. When he had parties, he would set up floating pyres that would burn through the night, and it always looked so magical. But unless you were invited to his private party within the party, there was always security to stop you from wandering. So I can't say I'm not excited to see the rest." Nana ambles along the mezzanine level, looking at the paintings that line the walls. She stops in front of one and gasps. "Look at this!"

"What's wrong, Nana?" Declan asks, stepping up next to her.

"This is the *Nativity with St. Francis and St. Lawrence* by the Italian Baroque master Caravaggio. The original used to hang in a church in Palermo, Sicily, but it was stolen in the sixties. I remember studying it in one of my art classes at college. It certainly is a fantastic copy."

I exchange a glance with Holden, who looks as skeptical as I feel. "What do you want to bet that it's not a copy?" I whisper out the side of my mouth, and he shakes his head.

"I'm not that stupid, no bet."

"I don't blame you," Kai says from close behind us. "I wonder what else in this house is stolen. What a pain in the ass. The media is going to have a field day with this."

Nana steps further along and gasps again. "Oh!"

I move over to where she's standing, and my

eyes widen in surprise. Much like the porn fresco on the ceiling, this is explicit too. "Oh, well, the count really was a bit freaky."

She waves her hand at it. "These were considered the first printed pornography. They were done by the Renaissance master Marcantonio Raimondi, and most of these were destroyed by the Catholic church in the fifteen hundreds. Though there were rumors that some had survived. I wonder if this is a copy or the real deal." She steps closer to get a better look, but the elevator returns, and the doors silently open, drawing our attention.

"Dibs," I call and hurry toward the stairs. I'm dying to know what's in the vault. Plus, it's been a little bit trying to have less of Harlow's time over the last few days. I'll soak up any moments that I can get with her.

"Hey, did you see that?" Thomas calls, and I stop to see what he's talking about. He's leaning over the railing, peering at the front door. There's no direct line of sight from the front door to where the elevator is, but he's further around from us. "I thought I saw a shadow through the door glazing, but it's gone now."

"Alright, let's get moving then. I don't think there's any way to see what we're doing up here, but better to be safe than sorry." Dad waves at the steps, and I continue on my way. Dec, Holden, and Kai join me.

"I'll do the last trip. I want to keep an eye on the

front door. Did we lock it after we came inside?" Thomas must decide to check because he heads down the stairs as the elevator doors close in front of me.

"I think we need to brace ourselves for the worst case scenario. The twins aren't really thinking clearly, and Harlow is all caught up in the excitement, but realistically, that vault could be empty," Declan warns us, and I feel my excitement dull.

"Judging by the art he had hanging on his walls, it could also be full of stolen artifacts," Kai says dryly.

"Yeah, and we need to decide what direction to go if it is. Do we leave it there, or do we call the police in. If there's anything of real value in there, I'm sure they'll seize it. It could end up being a media debacle, and I'm not really sure we need more attention from the media at the moment."

"There's nothing we can do about it if it is. We'll make a decision as a group and go from there. Let's wait and see what happens." Holden's the voice of calm reason that we need, bringing down the tension that was filling the small space.

The doors open quietly, and the musty smell of damp and mold hits my nose, causing it to wrinkle. "Well, that's not pleasant. I guess the count didn't think he needed any kind of ventilation down here."

My brothers and I get off, and it returns for the last trip and the rest of my family.

Looking around the room, I see only Jacinta and Emma. "Where are Harlow and Jaxon?" Jacinta rolls her eyes hard and points to the wall opposite the vault. It's a bit far away, and there doesn't seem to be as much light over there as there is on this side, but I can just make out an open door.

"That's one of the secret tunnels. They've gone to see where it leads to."

Shit, that's not good. I exchange a look with my brothers. The four of us hurry over, but when we get there, Jaxon and Harlow are just exiting.

Harlow is brushing off cobwebs, totally unperturbed by the whole thing. "We didn't get far. We didn't want to keep you waiting, and it looks like it goes quite a distance. If the cobwebs are any indication, it doesn't seem like anyone's been down there for a while."

There's a dusty smudge on her arm where it looks like she might have brushed against the wall. And hey, perfect opportunity to get a little bit closer to her. I move over and brush it off before plucking a stray cobweb from her head. Her smile is bright as she leans forward and gives me a kiss.

"Thanks, pumpkin," she teases. Before she can move away, I grab her and press forward until her back is to the wall, caging her between my arms.

"No problem, teddy bear. When we're done here, want to make out under the porn frescoes?"

"I can do you one better," she says, with a cheeky grin that pricks my curiosity.

"Oh?" She mimes zipping her lips.

"I'll show you when we're done here. Be patient." With that, she slides under my arm and hurries over to where everyone else is now waiting. Grumbling, I join the group just as Emma shows Jaxon and Jacinta how to activate the biometric scanner.

"If you prick your finger on the spike and allow the blood to drip onto the panel, it will take a moment to read it. Once it lights up green, you put the code into the keypad."

Jaxon and Jacinta give each other a look, holding the other's hand as Jaxon reaches out his other. The suspense is killing me, but I keep my mouth shut. I know when my commentary isn't needed, and Jacinta has a wicked tongue and a pretty strong punch if you piss her off enough.

Jaxon rests the fleshy bit of his thumb on the scanner, flinching when we hear a click a second later. He holds his thumb in place as the scanner reads the sample. It feels like it takes minutes, and all I can hear is the breathing of the rest of my family; the tension in the room is beyond prickly. Finally, the scanner flicks to green, and Emma lets out the breath she was holding.

"Okay, the code is 5318008." She types it in, and I stare at it, finding the number somewhat familiar. What the fuck is it? I've never been one for math, so there's no reason it should mean anything to me. It's not anyone's birthday, or a holiday, or… Oh shit.

"No fucking way!" I blurt the words before I can stop them. Everyone turns to look at me just as the screen lights up.

Emma quickly turns the handle of the huge metal door, and there's a click as it pops open just enough to tease us.

"What, Oli?" Jacinta asks, slightly annoyed. We're not in punching territory yet, but the last time she sounded like that, she "accidentally" bumped into my newest, still sore tattoo.

"The count really was a strange one," I tell them, and Jacinta rolls her eyes while everyone else frowns at me, waiting for an explanation. "The code. Remember when you were a kid at school and you had to start using calculators?" Everyone nods, not knowing where I'm going. "Well, those numbers spell something out on the calculator if you turn it upside down."

"Boobies!" Kai shouts, a crazy grin on his face. Of course he would recognize it. He and I were always trying to come up with new and interesting ones once we figured out we could. Unfortunately, there are only so many words you can make out of numbers, so we didn't get very far.

"Exactly." I reach over and put my fist out for my brother to pound it, which of course he does. The rest of the group shake their heads and turn back to the vault. I mean, Harlow's smiling, so at least there's that. I'll gladly take a punch from Jacinta if it gets me a smile from my girl.

"Go on." Emma points to the heavy door. "It has to be the two of you first. Apparently, the lights are motion activated, so they should turn on when you step in. We'll wait out here and give you a moment."

As much as I want to push past them and yank open the door myself, I allow my brother and sister to do it. It's only right that they get the first glance at their inheritance, even if it turns out to be nothing but air. For better or worse, I'll be here to commiserate with them.

The door is huge, so we all shuffle backward, giving the twins room to move. Together, they pull on the big wheel until the door starts to swing. It's on a roller that allows it to move a little smoother, but it's been twenty-something years, so the hinge is stiff. They give up after they get it wide enough to slip past, which prevents the rest of us from having a full view.

My hand comes up to my mouth, and I start to chew on my fingernail. It's a dirty habit, one I've mostly broken, but the suspense is killing me.

"Stop that." Holden smacks my hand.

"Gah, distract me—something, anything. This is beyond excruciating," I whine, but he simply chuckles.

"You're *such* a drama queen. Do you want to go

back and make out in those dark tunnels? You might miss out on the big reveal." My gaze goes from the vault to the tunnels, contemplating my choices, then a bloodcurdling scream comes from inside the vault.

Holden and I leap toward the door and pull, Kai and Declan joining us as Dad and Thomas, his gun pulled, move Emma, Harlow, Hope, Nana, and Poppy out of the way before rushing into the vault.

Agonizingly slowly, the door rolls outward. "We need to get some oil on those hinges ASAP," Poppy says from behind us.

"I don't think it would be a good idea to let others down here. I think we should keep this in-house," Nana says. Thomas steps back out just as the door opens wide enough for us all to see.

"Keeping it in-house is *not* going to be possible," he says as the rest of us see the vault's contents.

"Fucking hell," Holden swears, taking the words right out of my mouth. The space is huge and goes back a long way, but directly in front of us is a pallet piled waist-high with what I'm guessing is cocaine or heroin. Lining the walls are crates, and Dad has one of them open, lifting up an AK47, a cloth between his hand and the gun.

"This is full of these," he says, putting it back down, which should be enough of a mindfuck, but the most shocking thing is the skeleton that's leaning against the pallet. Its clothes are ragged and dusty, and he looks like he laid down to take a nap and never got up. Or he would if it weren't for the bullet hole in the middle of his forehead.

Jaxon has his arms wrapped around Jacinta, who's crying into his shirt. Harlow and Hope are holding each other's hands, both pale and a little shaky. Emma has a hand over her mouth and tears rolling down her cheeks, Nana's arm wrapped around her, comforting her. The rest of my family just looks resigned. There's no way we can keep this a secret now. A murder has taken place, even if it's a mystery that's over twenty years old.

"Does anyone want to make a bet that that's the count?" Declan's words echo through the silent vault.

"No way am I going to take that bet," Kai says, about to poke at something, but Thomas slaps his hand away.

"Stop it. They'll want to fingerprint everything. The thing I want to know is, there's only one body, but two went missing. That's either the count or his son, but no matter which it is, where's the other one?"

Again, the room is silent as we consider what he said.

"Alright, let's all step out and head back upstairs. I'll call Jake and see if we can do this a little more discreetly than just calling local law enforcement. Let's keep it out of the media as long as possible."

"Wait!" Nana shouts. "What about the rest?

Everything will be sealed. Do we want to go through the contents to see if there's anything we want to keep?"

"Mom!" Dad exclaims in surprise, and the rest of us range from looking amused (yes, that's me), to surprised, to downright shocked (only Dad).

She shrugs. "What? I don't care if they take the drugs and the guns, but I'd like to see what else is down here."

My family exchanges glances. I can see in their eyes that they're all kinds of curious as well, but no one wants to admit it first. "I say we have a look and take some photos on our phones, just to make sure that nothing mysteriously goes *missing* during the investigation."

Nana's eyes light up, and she gives me a thumbs up, which causes Thomas to sigh and run his hands through his hair with frustration. "Fine, for record-keeping purposes only. Don't touch anything if you can avoid it, and if you have to, use a cloth to pick it up with. Let's not leave our fingerprints everywhere; that'll make us look like suspects."

"Oh," Emma cries and hurries to a shelf at the entrance of the vault. She pulls out a box of gloves and starts handing them out. "Dad told me the count used to make everyone wear them before anyone could enter the vault."

We all take a pair and pull them on. "I thought you said he didn't allow anyone to come down here?" Harlow asks as she grabs pairs for both her and Hope.

"He didn't let them come down in the elevator. The only people who knew that was there was the count, his son, and my father. Others came through the access tunnel. You might notice the tunnels are big enough for a golf cart. They used one with a trailer attached to bring big things in and out. That's how these crates and the pallet would have gotten here."

"Did you know the drugs would be here?" Poppy asks her, though he's just curious rather than accusatory.

"No, Dad hadn't been down to the vault for a few weeks prior to the count's disappearance, and something as undeniably illegal as that, well, he wouldn't want to put me at risk. Though that doesn't get rid of the possibility that the count snuck these things in without my dad noticing. In fact, he was visiting me in San Francisco when the count went missing. He always blamed himself; he thought maybe he could have prevented it. Dad was always of the thought that the count would never just run away, but the drugs and guns might add a layer of complication to the mystery of his disappearance." Her sigh has an obvious hint of melancholy that has Dad putting his arm around her.

"Looks like he was right, but had he been here, we could have been looking at two bodies, not one. Come on, let's go upstairs. We'll go over to your cottage and have a cup of tea. The others can handle this, and when the authorities arrive, we can come back." He looks to Thomas for his okay, receiving a tip of his head in answer.

"Okay. When you need to leave, the call button will activate the elevator. I don't know if you noticed, but there's a security feed on the wall over there." We all swing around as she points it out. "It will show you if anyone is around or not so that you can activate the painting to open. Not that anyone should be, but just in case."

"Do you think we could find out where the tunnels lead to and bring the police in that way? I don't like the idea of everyone knowing about the painting. If we use the tunnels, they don't have to know there's an access point through the main house." Jacinta is chewing on her nail much like I did earlier. We're all going to need damn manicures at this rate.

Thomas nods. "That's actually a smart idea. Let's find the map and bring them in a different way. We can always collapse that tunnel once they've left, so no one can get back in."

"Okay, let's do this." Nana holds up her gloved fingers like they're jazz hands. "Shall we team up, so we're all not tripping over each other?"

"That map is the priority." Thomas goes to say more, but I stop him, hurrying forward.

"Yes, yes, we know. Be careful not to damage anything, and for god's sake, stay away from the guns, the drugs, and the dead body." Nana giggles and hurries deeper into the vault, and I feel a little guilty at being so excited and eager to trail after her. I mean, that could be the twins' dad or grandfather lying there, but I feel like a pirate with his treasure or a dragon exploring its hoard. The fever has hit me, and there's no stopping me now. I'll apologize to the twins once it dies down a little.

Right as I think this, Jacinta shoves me out of the way and runs after Nana, so I guess the guilt isn't really necessary.

Chapter Nineteen

Harlow

The sheer scope of the vault's contents is staggering. Paintings, jewels, antiques, and artifacts are thrown together. There are three small stacks of gold bars, all of them evenly stacked except for one which is missing a few. Everything is kind of haphazardly placed except for the bars. It's like someone was searching for something, and when they couldn't find it, they sort of shoved everything back in. But what could they have been looking for that wasn't any of this treasure trove? There's so much valuable shit in here, I'm clueless as to what else someone might have wanted.

"I'm pretty sure this is a real Fabergé egg." Jacinta holds up a clear case containing said egg, a glazed look on her face that's usually only seen when she finds a beautiful piece of couture.

"And this is a Picasso," Declan calls out, pointing at a painting that's stacked against a whole heap of others.

Nana walks over, carefully holding up a pretty blue and white vase. "There is no mistaking this for anything other than a Ming."

"These jewels are flawless and priceless; who knows where they came from." Thomas' voice comes from the side of the vault where he's standing beside an honest-to-goodness chest. It looks like something you'd find in a pirate ship, and it's over-flowing with gems. Who the fuck was this guy?

"The only thing that can't be found is the map of the grounds," Kai comments, coughing a bit from the dust cloud that just blew up from the rug he was examining.

"How is it so dusty in here?" Holden asks, a curious look on his face. "Isn't the vault sealed airtight?"

"Well, someone else has obviously had access to it. First step, we need to figure out who that body is over there. That will rule out one suspect, and then I guess the remaining one has to be whoever is not dead. Didn't Emma say that only her dad, the count, and Dragos had the code to get in? Only the count and Dragos had the right blood," Oliver points out, and my heart sinks.

"Plus Jaxon's mom and her friend," I quietly add. There's so much information running through my head, not to mention questions.

"Fuck, I had forgotten about that, but they wouldn't have gotten in without the code. Why did they keep taking blood if there was another security measure stopping them anyway?" Jaxon asks.

"Assuming that they used one of the passages to get in, my guess is they kept coming back to try different number combinations. With unlimited blood, they could have tried indefinitely," Thomas muses.

"So why did our mom give us to Brad then? Without us, they were out of luck," Jacinta says.

"Maybe she was protecting you," Hope suggests, though even she sounds a little skeptical. "You said that she had argued with the lady the day before she went to Brad. What if her friend wanted more blood or wanted to take you from your mom, so she always had it on hand. Maybe by giving you to Brad she was actually doing right by you for the first time ever?"

Maybe I'm a pessimist, but I don't know if I'm believing that. Okay, maybe it's my own mommy issues getting in the way of Hope's glass-half-full situation, but I'll just silently reserve my judgment until we learn more. If there's even a chance that the twins could come out with something positive about their mom at the end of this, I don't want to rain on that parade.

Jacinta and Jaxon exchange a glance, both of them with raised eyebrows, as they think about this new theory.

"Why come back when I was a teenager and kill the handyman?" Jacinta asks, and Hope shrugs.

"I don't have those answers, sorry."

"It's actually not a bad theory," Thomas says as he rubs his chin. "But for now we need to get out of here and call the police. We're going to have to follow one of these tunnels all the way along until we find an exit. Without the map, there's no other option."

"And how are we going to explain to the authorities about finding the vault?" Declan asks.

"Emma showed it to us. Same story as what actually happened, but we exchange the elevator for the tunnel. It's easy enough. I'll go find an exit, and we can call them as soon as I do."

"What if you get lost? Maybe you need some chalk or a piece of string to find your way back," I ask, biting my lip with worry, and he smiles, pushing a lock of hair behind my ear.

"I'll be fine, sweetheart. I'll take Kai with me. I'm sure it won't be too hard. They wouldn't have wanted to risk getting lost with the drugs."

"Okay. Is there cell reception down here?" I ask, and everyone holds out their phones to check.

"Nope, doesn't look like it." Poppy shakes his silver hair and shoves his phone back into his pocket. "We need to do something about that. Find a way to communicate down here and in the tunnels just to be safe."

"How do people in mines communicate?" I ask him, and his eyes light up.

"Good thinking, Hally. CB radio may be just the thing we need. I'll have to look into it."

"Okay, let's close up here and let Thomas and Kai find an exit. Once they get to the surface, they can call us and let us know where they came out. I'm sure Emma won't mind if we do a tour of the house without her while we're waiting. We'll call in the authorities once the boys are back with us." Nana pulls off her gloves and shoves them into her pockets. "Bring the gloves with you until we will find somewhere to stash them. I'd rather the police not know we didn't call them right away."

We file out of the vault and close the thing behind us. It's a matter of pushing the big door closed, which a couple of the boys do, and then spinning the wheel to re-engage the lock. The bioscanner blinks red once it's sealed. The police need to know we discovered the body, but they don't need to know we explored before we tried to do anything about it.

While they do that, Hope, Jacinta, Nana, and Poppy head back up in the elevator, leaving me down here with just the boys.

"Here." My eyebrows jump as Declan pulls a gun out of the back of his jeans and hands it to Kai. "You never know what you might find in the tunnels. So far we've been able to keep this secret from the media, but once the authorities are involved, that's not going to stay quiet. Someone out there knows about these tunnels even if they haven't used them recently, and we don't know if this is the only vault. It seems to me that it would have been silly for the count to keep everything in one place. Until we can find that map and physically check *all* the tunnels, we are going to be careful."

"When we get back, we have to talk to Emma about other possible places the map could be. We don't want anyone else getting their hands on that," Jaxon agrees.

"Could it be hidden somewhere in the house? Emma did mention the other room. Who's to say there aren't other secret rooms that she doesn't know about?"

"What other room?" Oliver jumps on the information. He's got this tangible energy about him, something my kindred spirit recognizes. He's got that explorer's high going on, where you're pumped up and ready to go headfirst into the next adventure as soon as you've got a location. It's not the biggest reason that I love exploring abandoned places, but it's definitely a benefit. There's just something almost intoxicating about running after a secret, not sure what you'll find on the other end. Will it be trash or treasure? You never know, but that's half the fun.

"I told you I would show you after. Be patient."
He mutters something under his breath that I can't
hear, but Kai slaps him on the back of the head. The
elevator returns, and I move over to Thomas and
give him a lingering kiss. Although we've come a
long way, I'm not feeling as secure with him as I am
with the others. It might seem a little silly, but that
moment between the two of us gives me enough
comfort that I can step back with a smile. "Be careful
and look after each other." He nods as I turn to Kai.

"You, too. Watch his back and come back to
me." I kiss him like he's going off to war, and he
looks a little dazed but smug as fuck when he pulls
back.

"Wow, I need to volunteer for these kinds of
things more often." I roll my eyes, but warmth fills
me up nonetheless.

Thomas studies the door closely. "This has a
lock on it." He takes a step and peers around the
tunnel side of the doorframe. "And there's a keypad
here. This door must have been left cracked open
since the body was disposed of. If they had closed it,
they wouldn't be able to get back in."

"What are the odds that it's the same code as
the vault?" Holden asks, and Thomas shrugs.

"Do we really want to risk that it's not?" Jaxon
points out, and we all shake our heads.

"Nope. Let's leave it as is, and we can work out
if we need to reprogram it later. Emma may know

of the codes, or they may be written on the map. While you're having the tour, keep an eye out for where it could be."

Thomas and Kai wave goodbye and leave down the tunnel. The light from their phones bounces off the walls, and their voices echo for a short way before abruptly cutting off.

"Guys?" My worried question echoes down the dark tunnel, and when the don't answer, I take a couple of steps to follow before Declan jumps in front of me.

"Stop. They probably just went around a corner."

"But what if something happened to them?" I try to step around him, but his arms wrap around me, holding me back.

"Babe, it's okay." Holden steps up and cups my cheeks in his hands. "Declan is right. They'll be okay."

I sigh and stop struggling, sagging in Declan's arms. "I'm sorry. I was just worried. So much has been going on, and I guess it's a little irrational, but…" Declan's arms loosen, and he presses a kiss to the back of my head.

"It's okay. I get it."

"Come on. Hurry up," Oliver calls out, already in the elevator. "Let's get the rest of the tour back on the road."

"You all know the suspense of not knowing

about the other room is killing him, right?" Holden laughs.

"Of course, why do you think we won't tell him more about it?" Jaxon takes my hand and places a kiss in the middle of my palm before tugging me to my impatient boyfriend.

The other two join us, and the doors close. With a single press of a button, the elevator begins its silent ascent.

"You guys are no fun." Oliver's pouting in the corner, making full use of that lower lip until Holden wraps an arm around his shoulder.

"Come on, you love surprises. Just think of it like that," he reassures the sulking man. It doesn't seem to help much, but his lip isn't as pouty when the doors finally open, allowing us to exit.

Two hours later, we've toured the whole house… except for the other secret room, and we've gotten some good news. Kai and Thomas found an exit from the tunnels. Apparently, it's in the zoo, inside one of the old animal enclosures.

"Well, that's certainly one way of ensuring that nobody accidentally finds the entrance," Holden points out after Declan hangs up and fills us all in.

"You're not wrong. I'm sure that's why it's located there. He said the rest of the tunnels branched off toward the boundaries, but they didn't bother searching. They figured this entrance will be safe enough to tell someone about. Once the zoo is up and running, we'll have some security to protect the entrance, and that will discourage treasure hunters. He also said he spoke to Jake, who got in touch with an FBI agent he trusts. They're on their way now."

"They're probably going to want to talk to Emma, Jaxon, and Jacinta. The rest of you can go back to the house," Dad says as he sits down on an ornate couch in the fancy sitting room we've gathered in. It looks like something out of the Palace of Versailles, which doesn't spare it from Jacinta's extreme home makeover. She might have underlined that particular note about gutting it. The whole house is a mishmash of styles, like whoever decorated it couldn't decide what they wanted, so they tried a little of everything. The bathrooms are very art deco, and a lot of the bedrooms have a 70s pornstar feel, with round beds that vibrate and turn and mirrors lining the walls. There's a lot to be done, and Jacinta took copious notes as we went, but it's mostly cosmetic, thankfully. Structurally, the house looks good.

"Alright, I'll head back and see about an early dinner. It's too late for lunch now, and who knows how long you'll be. You'll all be starving by the time you return." Nana and Poppy wave their goodbyes and take off.

I clutch the record of the zoo in my hands. Emma had located it and left it for me in the library before they had gone to her place. Now, that's one room that's staying the same. It looks like it was yanked right out of *Beauty and the Beast*. Jacinta and I had squealed madly when we saw it, the two of us trading off with Hope to slide atop the ladder, Belle-style.

I really want to go back there, sit down on the sumptuous couch, and read through all the information about the former zoo, but Oliver's fidgeting tells me he's not going to be put off for any longer.

"Alright, I'm going to go do that thing now." I wave to Oliver, wanting to get the two of us out of the way before the police come. I think he'll spontaneously combust if he has to wait and sit through questioning before he gets to see the secret. "Come on. I'll show you the surprise." Jaxon gets it right away and chuckles, but the others look a little clueless.

"Let them go. It will keep Oliver out of our hair for now at least," he tells them.

"But I want to know what the secret is!" Holden looks a little put out, and Declan has a big frown on his face. God, they're far too adorable when they pout.

"I'd really like it if a couple of you were here when the police arrive. Thomas said they'll come up to the house first, then we'll need to bring them down to the zoo. Forrest is coming, too," Jaxon says.

Declan and Holden instantly lose their disgruntled look, puffing out their chests like they're getting ready to protect their younger brother. It's so freaking cute that I have to hide my grin.

"I swear I'll show all of you, but I promised Oliver this, okay? Holden, can you hang on to this for me?" I hold out the zoo records, and he takes them from me. "I want to take that with us, so I can read it tonight."

They reluctantly give in, and I wave goodbye, tugging Oli out of the sitting room and into the foyer. We head up the stairs, passing the secret entrance behind Count Bucătaru, and ambling around the mezzanine. We slowly trudge up the next set of stairs until we reach the top, finding another painting at the top of this landing. This one is a floor-to-ceiling painting of a naked woman being pleasured by three men. Her head is thrown back in ecstasy, and I can't say I'm not jealous. There's a thrilling reality that this could be me. I stop, and Oliver stops next to me. He reaches for the wall sconce to the side of it, but I shake my head and push a finger into the ass cheek of one of the naked men. The button sinks in, and the painting parts, revealing the elevator behind it.

Oliver's eyes just about boggle out of his head. "That, that… You couldn't tell that it wasn't one piece. It was flawlessly sealed."

I giggle, enjoying the fun of surprising Oliver; he reacts so deliciously. "Come on." I tug him into the elevator, and it closes behind us. "Emma says it will go back to looking like one painting again after it closes, but that's as much as she really knows. She never came up here. Promised her dad she wouldn't," I explain, pressing the button she told me to look for. Thank god, it starts to move.

"And she never did? She's good. I totally would have." I shake my head at his confession, though I'm not surprised. I admit I probably would too.

"Anyway, this is where the count's 'private' parties took place," I tell him, wiggling my eyebrows.

"Private?" The door slides open, letting us look around the room. "Holy fuck!" Oliver gasps.

Chapter Twenty

Harlow

"**A** sex room!" he exclaims as we step out.

This was *not* what I was expecting, though I suppose I should have. I had pictured a giant bed with lots of pillows and maybe some seating for people to watch, but nope, this is a BDSM fantasy dungeon. It's a large open space; the walls are raw stone, and the ceiling is covered in a velvet-like material, making it look like the roof of a tent. Familiar wall sconces are evenly spaced around the room, and they must be motion activated because they light up as we move further from the elevator. It's low lighting, but we can still see clearly. There are no visible windows, but Emma did say there was a balcony, so I'm guessing it's behind the velvet curtains across the room. Thanks to the room being inside the turret, the space is circular. I'd love to see a schematic of this place because it's not obvious from the outside.

"This also definitely stays," Oliver says as he wanders around the room. I can't see his face, but he's practically turning in a circle, his head bobbing here and there like he's trying to drink all of it in as quickly as possible.

"Oh really? Should I start calling you Mr. Gray?" I snicker and then screw up my nose. "I don't know how I feel about using all the equipment. Who knows who and what has happened on it. Jaxon's grandaddy could have defiled any number of women, or men, in this room."

Oli's expression instantly changes to disgust as he yanks himself away from the bench he had been running his hand over. "Gross, Harlow. Now I have *that* in my mind."

To the left is a large sunken pit filled with pillows and cushions, probably for group activities. Beyond that are two doors, and in front of us is enough equipment to furnish a BDSM club in nothing but dark wood and red leather. There are stocks, benches, and a St. Andrew's cross, all with chains and cuffs hanging on and around them. There are also a couple of sex swings hanging from the ceiling and a bunch of other instruments neatly racked along the wall—whips and paddles and feather-tipped wands as well as more extreme-looking things like a cat of nine tails with metal tips and a metal-studded paddle. Next to that is a glass-doored cabinet holding a brow-raising amount of packaged sex toys.

"Oh look, these are all still closed! We can keep them." Oliver opens the doors and pulls out a large jewel-tipped butt plug, its packaging glinting in the light. Well, I won't argue with that. Some of those things look like they'd be fun to use.

To the very right of us is a cage. It resembles an ornate bird cage, though it's big enough for at least two people, and there's a comfy-looking bed inside. Almost without thinking, I move closer, a tingle in my core as I think about role-playing with my boyfriends. The cuffs and chains open up so many possibilities… I run my hand over the bars before stopping at the door built into the wall behind the cage. I turn to look at Oli.

"First things first, all the sheets, cushions, and fabrics can be burned. Now, the leather, I guess we can just wipe over with sanitizer. I'll leave it to you to decide what you want to keep or get rid of, and we can get a big dumpster to collect all the trash. All I know is that we're not using this room ourselves until it could pass a blacklight test. We can explore the rest of the room later, but first, come on. I have more to show you."

After I put in the same code that opened the vault, the door behind the cage clicks open, revealing a dark interior. I pull out my phone, clicking on the light and shining it into the darkness. Lucky I did because it's not a room, but a set of spiral stairs leading down. "Come on." I grab Oli by the hand, and we carefully make our way downstairs.

At the other end of the steps is another door. What strikes me as most odd is that this one looks like it could be made from reinforced steel or something. There's another keypad. "Apparently, this is a safe room as well as the count's master bedroom. His paranoia had gotten so bad he didn't feel comfortable unless he slept within these walls. Or that's what Emma told me, at least."

When the door clicks open, we step into another dark and dungeon-like room. Honestly, I'm expecting to see a lot of metal and chains, but the bed is a pleasant surprise. It looks like something out of a fairy tale and is most definitely custom-made. Or at least I assume it's a bed. Taking up a big chunk of the space is a large box with sliding doors on the end. Carved panels enclose all sides, with creatures of myth and fable practically leaping out of the wood. Much like the frescoes on the ceiling of the foyer, these animals are wickedly indulgent. Small air vents are cut into the top of the panels, and the enclosure appears big enough for five or six adults.

"Oh wow. I love it!" I can't stop the words from escaping me as I take it in. Stepping up, I slide the doors open, squealing as a family of mice run out of a hole in the middle of the mattress. "Well, that's going to need replacing." They disappear behind it, and I wrinkle my nose when the smell hits me. "Hopefully that's just the mattress. Do you think it will fit in the elevator?" I ask Oliver, and he shrugs.

"They got it in here somehow. It was either through the elevator or maybe a crane over the balcony. I'm just surprised they got it down the spiral staircase. Don't worry, we'll figure it out." I close the doors and look around a little more.

On the side, like the room above, are two more doors. We didn't look at the ones upstairs, but I'm not skipping these. I leave Oliver and walk over to them. Pushing open the one on the left, I step into a *huge* bathroom. There's a big sunken Roman bath in the middle, with a large vanity on the wall and a shower big enough for an orgy. Behind a half wall is the toilet. The room is done in white and gold. I'm not complaining about the break from the rest of the house's dark decor, but I have no idea how this is what he settled on.

"The count must have been super paranoid to lock himself in here. There's no way out except the way we came in. What if the house was on fire?" Oliver sounds perplexed, and a smile touches my lips.

Pulling the door closed, I open the next one. It's a huge walk-in closet, exactly what I was looking for. "Oli, come here," I call as I push all the clothes to one side. Dust flies up, filling the room, and I start to cough.

"Shit, I guess the cleaning service wasn't

allowed up here." Oli waves his hand in front of his face as he stands at the entrance while I continue to cough.

Wiping my eyes, I seek out the panel I was looking for, and a circular piece of the wall drops away after I quickly tap out another code.

"What the fuck is that?" Oli asks, finally braving the dust to stand behind me.

"*That* is the way out," I tell him smugly, and he steps closer, shining his phone's flashlight into the hole.

"It's a slide!" he gasps as the light drops away from him.

"Yeah, it goes down into a room next to the vault room."

"We should do it!" Oli is practically vibrating with the urge to go flying down that slide, but I'm unsure.

"I was thinking that we should search for the map first. This was the only other secure place I thought it might be. I'm really worried that someone else knows the ins and outs of the tunnels, and I don't want them to have access to anything."

I can see him struggle with the want to ride the slide and the need to do the right thing, but good Oli wins. He sighs and steps away from the slide. "I promise you can slide your little heart out as soon as we find the map." I give him a kiss and press the button on the panel to close it up. There's a time delay—likely to allow you to climb onto the slide—but it eventually whooshes closed again.

Oliver gropes for a light switch in the side of the closet door, and a moment later, the space lights up. "Okay, if you were the count, where would you hide an important document like the map?" he asks, and we begin to search the room.

Drawers are opened and shelves are searched. Pulling back another section of hanging clothes on the back wall, I discover a smaller version of the vault. "Oli, look."

"What are the odds that the code to that is the same as all the others?"

"Only one way to find out." He reaches over me, his front pressed to mine, and plugs in the code. Sure enough, the panel lights up. He spins the small wheel, and the safe pops open.

Inside is some paperwork, a hand gun, a passport, some stacks of cash, and what looks like a diary or maybe a book of contacts. I reach in and pull everything out, handing them back to Oli so I can get at the paperwork under it all. He opens the passport. "This is the count's, so does that mean it *is* his body downstairs? His son lived with him. Would they have kept their passports together, or would they have kept them separately?"

"You all keep your passports together on the plane," I point out, and he purses his lips.

"Yes, but we all get along. From what I understand, Dragos and his father did not have a great relationship. He spent more time at our place than he did at home. I mean, the twins' father is looking like the perfect suspect. You heard how many properties they had overseas. I wonder if any of them are in countries that don't have extradition treaties with the US…"

"You think Dragos killed his dad?" The thought hadn't occurred to me before, though I guess maybe it's not so surprising when I think about it. It's not like Dragos had a great relationship with his father.

"Sure, why not? People can go to extremes to escape an unwanted situation." He mutters the last bit, and a wave of guilt hits me. I wrap my arms around him, the passport jammed between us.

"Oh god, Oli, I'm not judging. I promise. Of course they do. It just hadn't occurred to me." He shudders in my arms, his childhood memories likely flooding his mind. I hold him tight for a few moments, letting him soak in all my love. "God, I love you," he whispers.

"I love you too." He pulls back, and I kiss him softly on the mouth before wiping a stray tear from his face. "Come on, let's check out these papers. Once we go over those, we can go back upstairs and see what's through those other doors in the sex room."

He breathes out a big sigh and nods, putting the passport and diary on a nearby chest of drawers. I grab the paperwork out and scan it. There's the deed and title to the land and house, a birth certificate for Dragos Bucătaru, and the last will and testament of Count Radicus Bucătaru.

"Holy shit, that might change a few things," Oliver says, eyes locked on the will. "Especially if that body downstairs is the count." I pass it all off to him and reach for the last thing in the safe, a stack of laminated schematics. When I flip through them, there's a layout of the house. Each floor is diagrammed, showing where all the secret passages are located and how to activate them in each room. The next one is an aerial view of the estate, including the house, lake, the little house on the island in the middle of the lake, and the zoo. Over the top of it is a clear overlay showing the layout of all the tunnels, where they lead to, and notations on how to activate them.

"Jackpot!" I angle it so Oliver can see, and he whistles, the sound sharp in the quiet between us.

"Yup, we wouldn't want anyone else finding that. We'll have to be careful that it doesn't fall into the wrong hands. Let's take it with us, and we can put it in one of the safes at home."

"What about the will? Should we bring it?" I ask him as I pack the other items back into the safe.

"If we present this and it turns out to be different than the one the trust has on file, then Jax and Jazzy could lose it all. At this stage, maybe we should let sleeping dogs lie. Let's put it back and not tell anyone for now."

"We could just open it and read it." I gesture to the wax seal, my fingers itching to crack it open.

"Do you want to have to lie to them?" he asks, and I shrug.

"Aren't we already lying by not telling anyone about it?" I'm worried about what they'll do if they find out that we lied to them. Do I really want to start one of my relationships with a lie? Not to mention Jazzy and I are finally in a good spot. This could ruin everything.

"Okay, we'll let them decide. Just shove it back in there for now. Once the police have left, we'll tell them about it."

I do as he says and slam the safe closed, engaging the wheel, and it clicks as it rearms.

Oliver is looking through the count's hanging clothes. "I really can't work this man out. He has some really nice suits hanging here, but he's also got some pimp outfits that put Hugh Hefner to shame." He holds out an elaborate brocade robe in one hand, and in the other, he's got a raspberry velvet morning coat. "And then he's got things that would make him look like Willy Wonka."

Smiling, I flick through them myself. "Or Rocky from *The Rocky Horror Picture Show*." I hold out a hanger with a pair of gold lamé speedo hanging on them.

"Don't forget Elton John." Oli's now holding a coat with pink and yellow ostrich feathers lining the neckline. "Who was this man?"

I put back the hanger with the swim shorts, and the next choice I pull out has a black leather pair teamed with a gimp mask.

"I'm not sure, but from the look of his clothes, I'm not sure if he wasn't a number of different men."

"What, like a spilt personality?" Oliver hangs the things up, and we walk out of the closet, closing it behind us.

"Yeah, maybe? I think he definitely had at least two sides to him—Nana said as much. Maybe his wife's death really did fracture his psyche."

We leave the room behind and trudge back up the spiral staircase. Sure enough, the two doors hold a bathroom and another closet. This closet is just as interesting as the one downstairs, stocked with a wide variety of costumes in different sizes. Sexy nurse, sexy cop, sexy schoolgirl. Then there are the leather things that are more straps than anything else, and the most strange… the furries. Heads, tails, gloves, and accessories, including sheaths that I'm pretty sure go over the man's cock to make them look more animal-like. There's a panda, dog, cat, and more, and when you look closer at the tails, you realize they're *insertable*.

"Gross, I think I need brain bleach after all this," I say as Oliver strokes the head of one of the animals.

"I don't know. Maybe it could be fun. You could be the zoo keeper, and Holden and I could be the naughty zoo animals. You'd have to punish us for our behavior. " He waggles his eyebrows in a playful manner, but I can see in his eyes that he's serious. And to be honest, the way his voice dropped as he described that scene made my stomach lurch and toes curl in a very good way. I never thought I'd be into dress up and role play, but these guys are really pushing my limits, and I can't deny I love it. I sigh, not wanting to let on that I'm actually turned on as fuck.

"Fine, who am I to kink shame? I'll give anything a go once, but can we please get new things? Who knows how many people have used all of this." I gag a little at the thought of sharing sex toys. I guess if you're coked out of your mind or flying high on ecstasy, none of it matters, but I'm frighteningly sober right now.

This wardrobe also contains a safe, and when I put the now familiar combination in, it pops open, revealing the party drugs. Bottles and bottles of pills and a few blocks of white powder. "Fucking hell! Is this house going to be a never ending supply of illegal substances?" I slam that door shut and walk away. I don't want anyone up here and don't plan on telling anyone about it so I can't very well hand it over to the police. "Come on, I've had about as much as I can take today. Let's take that map and head downstairs. We need to hide it so that nobody sees it. The house will be turned upside down, but we don't need to give away any secrets the police can't find for themselves. As far as they're concerned, the tunnel they'll come in is the only one."

I stomp back to the elevator and press the button. Oli wraps his arms around me from behind and he snuggles into my neck.

"I love rebel Harlow. She's so fucking sexy." He nips at my ear and grinds his erection into my ass.

"I don't know about rebel. It's really selfishness. I just want to start renovating my house and zoo and my future with you guys. An ongoing police investigation is going to hamper that."

He kisses my cheek then steps back as the elevator opens. "Yeah, you're not wrong. I think we're doing the right thing. It's not like we're hurting anyone. The drugs and guns will be gone, and if the twins end up with a little less because everything else gets seized, I'm sure it's not going to bother them too much. Nana might be another story. I think she'll cry if all that art turns out to be stolen."

We're both chuckling as we step in, the doors closing behind us. Turning on the camera, I check that the area is clear before I press the special button which should open the painting downstairs.

As we feel the elevator move, Oli gasps. "Oh, I just realized what it reminded me of—Harry Potter! The painting of the fat lady, except that woman looks to be a lot... happier."

Chapter Twenty-One

Holden

Harlow and Oliver disappear as longing builds in my chest. Everything is so new with both of them that I want to be around them all the time. I know Oli isn't *actually* new, but this version of us where we don't have to hide or worry, this second chance where I can hold him, kiss him, love him openly, that's a new addictive taste of life. And Harlow is just more than I ever really hoped for. Having the two of them is undeniably one of the brightest turns my life has taken, and I have this clawing desire to bask in their glow whenever possible.

I want to join them, but I know it's important to be here to support Jaxon and Jacinta when the police arrive. Dad was going to keep Emma company, so I know my siblings will need all the backup they can get.

"We stick to the truth. Emma only told us about the vault today. She was sworn to secrecy by her dad. That's the only entrance. Thomas said the rest of the tunnels are very cleverly hidden, so if you're not looking for them, you can't see them. Hopefully, the police take us at our word that it's the only one and don't actively look for more," Declan says as I place the zoo records on a table next to the couch and take a seat.

Jacinta suddenly shouts, her voice easy to hear from the other side of the room. While Declan ran through our plan, she was creeping through the cupboards, the two of them both trying to keep busy in their own ways.

"Huh, look what I found." She pulls out a crystal decanter filled with an amber liquid. "This has got to be the good stuff. It's at least twenty-five years old now." She puts it on the table, grabs five tumblers, and sloshes a couple of fingers in each. Before I can think about whether I even want one, she's handed them out. "Cheers." She tosses back the entire contents of her glass before wiping her mouth with the back of her hand. "God, I needed that. It's not every day you find a dead body in a secret vault." Her eyes are a little wild, but is that really any surprise? Like she said, today has definitely got to be one for the record books.

I sip my whiskey a little slower than Jacinta,

enjoying the smoky liquid as it goes down smooth as silk. "That's really good," I say to no one in particular, and both Jaxon and Declan grunt their agreement.

Hope coughs after taking a sip. "Strong."

"Pussy," I tease her, and she flips me off.

"What's that book?" She points at the one on the table. I guess she didn't hear Emma when she handed it to Harlow. Though I'm not really surprised since we were in the library to beat all libraries. I swear the girls just about melted into puddles of goo. Jaxon really knew what he was doing by putting a secret library in his hotel in Hawaii. What is it they say? Bitches love a library.

Before I can answer, a loud boom from outside has the furniture in the room shaking.

"What the fuck was that?" Declan shouts as we all put our glasses down and hurry into the foyer.

In the lead, Jaxon throws open the front door and hurries down the steps toward his now flaming motorcycle. "My bike!" he shouts, but I grab him before he can lunge for it.

"No, man, there's nothing that can be done. You'll just get hurt." I wrap my arms around him, squeezing tightly, until he sags with defeat.

"Dad!" Jacinta cries, causing us to both turn. Leaning against the side of the house is Dad, his body shielding Emma from what must have been an explosion if the pieces strewn across the front of the house have anything to say.

"We're okay." He waves and pulls himself off Emma, wrapping his arm around her as they slowly join us. "We're not hurt," he says rather loudly as he gets to us, pulling on his ear. A trickle of blood is running down his cheek. My heart races with adrenaline and fear at seeing my dad injured. Never before have I had to face the reality that he isn't some super human. He's flesh and blood like the rest of us, and he could have been badly hurt or even killed. That's a real slap in the face, and I swallow, trying to clear the lump in my throat that just developed.

"Bullshit, you're not. I'm calling an ambulance." Jacinta's phone is already waiting in her hand, though her eyes are still trained on Dad and Emma, following his movements as he lowers Emma onto one of the steps then sits beside her.

"Okay, maybe that's not a bad idea. Should probably add in the fire department to put out the bike," he agrees, wiping his hand across his cheek, and his eyebrows jump in surprise when he sees the blood.

"It looks like someone stuck a rag in the gas tank and lit it on fire," I tell them as I study the destruction around us.

"There's a hose around the side that should reach. I don't think we should wait for the fire department. Some of the overgrown bits are still too dry from summer." Emma points to where they'd come from, and Declan quickly runs in that direction. He reappears shortly after, hose running, and starts putting out the flaming patches of grass around the bike.

"We saw someone running away, heading for the front. I think they may have come in the same way that Harlow did the first time." As Emma's shaky voice tapers off, she leans against Dad, practically melting into his side. "I shouted at them, but before we could follow, the bike exploded."

Her phone rings, and she lifts it to have a look at the screen. "The agents are here," she tells us, entering a code into some kind of app. "The front gate can be remotely unlocked, so we can wait here and stick together."

It's not long until an unmarked vehicle is driving down the overgrown driveway and parking beyond the moat gates. Out of the driver's side of the SUV hops a man who looks like Dwayne Johnson's older and bigger brother, bald head and all. He's built like a tank, and his otherwise plain shirt has DEA emblazoned across the chest. Alongside him is another man. This guy isn't as big, but he's certainly not slacking in the fitness department. He has neatly styled blond hair, and his shirt has ATF written across the front.

"How is it that we've got two different agencies coming to visit us?" Jaxon asks as the guys cross the bridge, raising his voice so they'll hear the question.

An annoyed grimace wrinkles the faux Rock's face. "Well, when the Federal Department of Counterterrorism calls and tells you that one of the richest families in the US has found a secret stash of guns and drugs that they'd like to keep quiet, the brass listens. They thought it would be more discreet if the two of us came out and assessed the situation before blowing anything up. No pun intended, given your current situation. Wayne Jackson. DEA." He introduces himself but doesn't hold his hand out to shake; he points to the other guy instead. "And my ATF counterpart Jason Adams." Both of them pull credentials out of their pockets, holding them up for us to inspect. Jason's smile is friendly and open, whereas Faux Rock is clearly pissed to be here, with his crossed arms and aggressive stance.

Declan has gotten rid of the hose, making it back to us in time to hear the introductions. He takes over, holding out his hand to greet both men. Jason accepts it, but Wayne just stares at it in disdain until Declan drops it. Wayne's little power play is not going to work on my brother. He knows them all.

"This is my father, Brad Summers, and my siblings, Jacinta, Jaxon, and Holden and our family friend Hope. And this is Emma Cullen, who was the caretaker of this property up until we discovered that Jaxon and Jacinta were the heirs." As the oldest, Declan has always been the lead in anything we do, and I'm happy to keep it that way. Tom is usually the one he yields to the easiest, and when we're in a stressful situation, those protective instincts of his kick into overdrive. It's rare that he'll relinquish control to anyone but Tom when the stakes are high. Taking charge, even in something as simple as giving our names, makes him feel a little more in control of the situation.

Jason runs his hand across his face. "Yeah, when we spoke to Jake Jennings, he filled us in on the whole story. It sounds like the plot of a movie if you don't mind me saying."

"You have no idea." Jacinta waves her hand in agitation. "Try living it."

"Does this have anything to do with it?" Wayne raises an eyebrow at the now dripping wreck of Jaxon's motorcycle.

"Actually, we're not sure if it has to do with this, or if it has to do with my girlfriend's stalker," I tell them, taking over.

"Yeah, Jake filled us in on that too. He just hung up as we pulled up to the gates. It looks like any evidence that may have been left behind has been destroyed by fire or water." Jason does a circle around the wrecked vehicle, pulling a glove out of his pocket and putting it on before he lifts a rag out of the fuel tank. "I would guess this was how they did it."

Wayne rolls his eyes at Jason. "Right now, with the record of stalking as an open case with local PD, we'll hit pause on this. Unless we can find something that connects it to our agencies' concerns, our hands are pretty tied. If we find a connection, you'll have our agencies' full support behind tracking down the perpetrator, but even a name like yours isn't enough to get us actively involved in an irrelevant case. Currently, we have a stack of drugs and guns that need our focus. If you need us to, we'll stick around and talk to any PD that are called to check out the bike scene, but I doubt we can offer you much." His voice is deadpan and he really isn't going out of his way to make friends with any of us.

"Okay thanks, we appreciate it. I'll call the detective in charge of her case and let him know about it, but I'll do that once you've finished. Whoever did it has already gotten far enough away that there's nothing we can do about it right now. Shall I show you to where the tunnel entrance is?" Dad waves his hand around toward the back of the house.

"Sure, let's get this show on the road. Then we can call our guys in if we think it's necessary." Wayne starts to head in the direction Dad pointed as Declan and I exchange a glance.

"I'm sorry. You have some doubt that this will be necessary?" I ask, unable to hide the annoyance in my tone. Hope grabs hold of my sleeve as I take a step toward the guy.

"It wouldn't be the first time someone over exaggerated the amount of drugs and guns found. I'm sure it's probably something that the local police could have handled." He doesn't bother hiding his complete lack of interest in any kind of social niceties.

That fucking condescending ass. Jason shoots him a dirty look and steps away as if to distance himself from him.

"Are you suggesting we threw our weight around? To what purpose? It's not like we're trying to make the front page of some tabloid. Not to mention, I was under the impression that Count Bucătaru was suspected of illegal activities in the past," Declan growls as another car pulls up behind the SUV. Forrest climbs out, briefcase in hand.

"Sorry it took so long for me to get here." He sounds a little frazzled, but he's already focused on hurrying over to Dad, sparing a moment to wave at me, Declan, Jax, and Jacinta. Poor guy. Our family really has run him ragged the last few weeks. The man is worth every penny, though I'm not sure he thinks that we are.

"This is our family lawyer, Forrest," Dad introduces him to the two agents. "This is Agent Jackson and Agent Adams."

The men tip their head in greeting before Jason turns to Declan, bringing the conversation back on point. "Yes, I gathered some information regarding any investigations connected to Count Bucătaru, but I haven't had a chance to read it over it yet."

Wayne shoots him a surprised look, which

doesn't say much for their partnership skills. "You didn't say anything in the car."

"You'd already made up your mind. Why should I do your job for you? You could have run the same search I did or had one of your people to do it. In my mind, it's a formality anyway. I trust that the Federal Department of Counterterrorism wouldn't have involved us, no matter who had requested it, if they hadn't thought it was needed. Not to mention you haven't been particularly helpful to me when we've worked jobs together in the past. Why should I help you out this time?"

Oh, so that's Wayne's problem. He doesn't seem to like being bossed around or having to work with anyone. Regardless of that, we need to get something settled because our family is about to depend on this asshole. "Got a problem with our family, Wayne?" I snap as he crosses his arms, stretching his DEA shirt across his large chest.

"I have a problem with rich people thinking they're more important than the little people," he throws back.

The tension between us all ramps up, and Forrest hurries to intercept it. "Shall we just show them and go from there?" Before we can go anywhere, the sounds of a siren pierce the air.

"You guys go. Dad and Emma need to be checked over by medics, so I'll wait here with them. Any questions you have for Emma can be asked over at our place when you're done here," I tell them, and although Wayne rolls his eyes, still skeptical, Jason easily agrees.

"Do you remember how to get there?" Emma asks, her eyes saying what she can't voice.

Declan steps right in to answer her, not an ounce of confusion on his face or in his voice. "Thomas and Kai are going to meet us on the other side of the island and guide us there in case we get lost," he reassures her, and she breathes a sigh of relief and relaxes into Dad's arms.

The ambulance is coming down the overgrown driveway, its siren now off but its lights still flashing, as Declan, Jacinta, Jaxon, and the two agents make their way toward the zoo.

The medics both have curious looks as we explain what happened, but they do their job professionally. They confirm that Dad has a burst eardrum from the explosion, but it will heal, which is the best we could have hoped for. They clean up their cuts and abrasions before offering a ride across to the house on the way out, recommending rest to combat the little bit of shock they're both suffering from. While Hope debriefs with Nana over the phone, I wave them off, putting on a smile that I don't entirely feel to try to put Dad a little more at ease.

Once they drive away, Hope and I head back inside, and I lock the door behind us. This house is so big I won't hear if anyone lets themselves in, so it's better to be safe than sorry. They might be still around and hiding in the bushes outside. Though I guess the appearance of the DEA and ATF might scare them off.

Jaxon wouldn't tell me where Harlow was taking Oliver, so I'm feeling a little grumpy, especially after the interaction with that DEA asshole. I can't believe neither of them heard the explosion and came to check. I should probably message them and let them know what happened. But I guess they're safer than we are if they're still upstairs. I'll let them know when they come back down.

"Hey, you look like you could use another drink." Hope brings the decanter over to the table and tops up our glasses. Our friendship is at a point where we instinctively know what the other person needs. Or maybe that's just her woman's intuition. I'm probably nowhere near as good at it as she is.

I take the glass she holds out to me. "Is this ever going to end? It seems like one thing after another, and I can't see the light at the end of the tunnel." There's no ounce of me that regrets our current situation because if things were different, I wouldn't have Harlow, and god knows I never would have gotten the courage to start things back up with Oli. But all of the stress and questions from this stalker shit are going to drive me mad.

"One day, you're going to look back on all of this and laugh. Better yet, you're going to have your own children to worry about, and this will only be a fond adventurous memory in your courtship of your lady." Something in her tone has me forgetting my own problems and looking at my best friend carefully. She's always been a fan of me finding my person, and now that I have my *people*, she's been almost sickeningly happy for me. But that… that was a weird twinge in her voice that definitely isn't normal Hope.

"Is everything okay?" I ask her when I notice the pallor of her skin and the dark circles under her eyes. I mean, I know I left her hanging and flew off to Europe in the face of the Ninja Starfish debacle, but she had it all under control. She seems to thrive on that kind of pressure, so I thought for sure she would be reveling in it. But now that I look closely, she's worn and tired. I actually don't remember ever seeing her like this before. Maybe when I first met her in college? Those first few weeks, she seemed to be dealing with something, but we were new friends back then, so I didn't want to pry.

She leans back and closes her eyes, the silence between us strained for the first time that I can ever remember.

"Yeah, everything's okay. Just a few things from my past playing over in my mind more than I would like them to. I haven't slept well the last two nights."

"Does this have anything to do with the brothers that have managed to wow my dad in such a short period of time? You've always been so closed lipped about your past. The only thing I really know is that you grew up with a foster family." I don't feel guilty about pushing her now. She knows all the good, bad, and ugly about me, so I feel like I should be able to dig at her too.

"The McCallisters," she mutters, and I put two and two together.

"Those boys are your foster brothers, but they're not related to each other, so that means your foster family adopted all of them? How come they never adopted you too?" If these guys are going to work for my father, and have our name, which no one has ever had before, I think it's time my best friend comes clean with me.

She sighs again like the weight of the world is on her shoulders. "I was placed with the family when I was sixteen. Parker and I are the same age, the twins are two years older, and Miles two years older than them. They'd been with the McCallisters for years and were adopted after the first one. I was placed with them as an emergency. They didn't want a teenage girl in the house, but there was nowhere else for me to go, so they agreed. Don't get me wrong, Judy and Stan are wonderful people, but I was watched *very* carefully. They didn't want 'some strange foster girl seducing their good boys.'"

I gape at her with disbelief, but then I shouldn't; I know all about shitty foster homes.

"It was a load of shit, of course. The twins would nail anything that would move. Miles had a long-time girlfriend, and Parker, well, he was my best friend, but he was busy trying to work out if he liked girls or boys. We went everywhere and did everything together. I guess it might have even gone further, but I was too scared to be kicked out again, so we kept it platonic no matter how much we both wanted more… until we didn't. Once the twins left school, they stopped being such big manwhores, and things between us changed. It wasn't other women that they were chasing after or flirting with. It was *me*. We fooled around a little, but I never slept with them. I knew they would break my heart." She sighs, her gaze lost in the memories. "Miles temporarily broke up with his girlfriend, got drunk, and ended up in my bed one night. I gave him my virginity, and when they made up a couple days later, I almost died inside. I told Parker about all of this. He was my rock and never judged me, probably because I never judged him when he talked about fooling around with boys. Never judged when he worked out he was bi. I accepted him for him. He's just one of those people that light up a room, ya know? What's not to love?"

She takes a large gulp of her whiskey, and I lean forward to pour some more into her glass. We're both going to be hammered by the time Oli and Harlow return, but I don't really care. It's been a trying day, and I can't do anything to solve the shit-load of problems on the Summers' list, but I can be an ear for my bestie. Maybe she'll finally feel a little lighter with something off her chest.

"Before I go any further, I need to tell you the

McCallisters never promised to adopt me or anything, but the guys always believed that if I followed their parents' rules, they would eventually take that final step. I tried so hard, but I guess I should have known it would never happen once I hit my eighteenth birthday. They'd never even brought it up!"

A tear trickles down her face, and my heart breaks for my friend. I shuffle over to sit next to her and put my arm around her shoulders, tucking her into my side.

"Anyway, I got super drunk the night of our graduation, and I had sex with the twins at a party. Later on in the night, Parker and I crossed the line together. We were so drunk we didn't think to set an alarm, and we'd totally forgotten Judy wanted to take us out for a celebration breakfast. I'd been accepted at UCLA on a full ride scholarship, and Parker was going to work with Miles in construction while doing community college courses. She was pleased as punch, but that didn't last long when she burst into his room the next morning and found us wrapped together, still naked. She hauled me out of his bed by the hair and basically tossed me out, only allowing me to get dressed and pack a bag of my belongings. By the time she dragged me down the stairs and tossed me out, all the boys were watching. The twins had this coldness in their eyes that I had never seen before, and Miles was just… indifferent. He'd been funny since we slept together, and I guess they were thinking that Judy's prediction about me had come true. What hurt the most was Parker. I wanted him to stand up to her, to fight for us or something, but he just stood there and watched. Even when I pleaded for him to help me, he didn't. I now realize he was probably in shock, but it broke my heart. I used some of my savings to hop on a bus to LA and didn't look back."

"They never tried to contact you?"

She grimaces. "They did, but I blocked them all."

"Is this the first time you've seen them since it all happened?" I ask gently, and she nods.

"I've kept track of them through social media mostly, but none of them are very active. It's more like people tagging them in things. I'm not entirely sure why their business wasn't doing well. I only knew about that because I ran into someone from my high school at a club. They mentioned it off-handedly, and I didn't push. If I didn't ask about them, I couldn't feel sad. Seeing them yesterday was somewhat of a smack in the face, and suddenly I'm that eighteen-year-old girl again being thrown out of my foster home. The reason I recommended them to Brad was I knew they were struggling. Despite all the shit that went down, Miles and the twins were good at what they did. Their company was new but it was doing well when I lived with them. Something must have happened after I left, and I knew your dad would ask the right questions.

He must have been happy with the answers because he hired them. I guess there was a part of me that still wanted their approval or for them to like me, and subconsciously, I wanted to help them."

"Aw, babe. Screw them! You don't need them anymore. You've got us and are about to get adopted into our family."

Before she can respond, Harlow and Oli enter the room, Oli waving some pieces of paper. "You should see what we found!" He's breathless with that nearly tangible energy that he gets when he's running on adrenaline. "But most importantly, we found the map."

Chapter Twenty-Two

Harlow

Holden and Hope are looking very solemn when Oli bursts into the room waving the map. Thank god it's just them because his tact leaves a little bit to be desired.

"Jesus, Oli, what about being a little more discreet? It's lucky it was just the two of them in here." His enthusiasm wilts at my scolding, but I'm more worried about the other two at the moment. Oli will bounce back quickly enough. "Is everything okay here?" I ask carefully.

Hope's smile is shaky, and her eyes are begging for me not to push right now. "Yeah, it is. I'll be okay. Oli, come show us what you found and distract me." His face lights up once more, and we chuckle at his enthusiasm as he makes room on the coffee table for the map.

"This place is like a labyrinth. There are under-ground tunnels everywhere! They even detour around the big pool in the zoo." He looks at me. "Did you get a chance to read the records to see what was in there?"

"No, I was hoping to get a chance to do it now. Where did you put it?" I ask Holden, and he points to a little table on the other side of one of the sofas. I jump up, grabbing it and bringing it back to my seat. I start to flick through it as Oli continues to explain.

"Then there are all the secret tunnels in this house. It's like they built all of them first, then built the rooms up around them." Holden and Hope lean in to have a look. "If this map is correct..." He pauses before walking over to a china cabinet on one wall, getting up close and personal with the wood before shouting, "Ah ha!" He pushes his finger into a knot in the wood, then the cabinet slides away from the door with a quiet click, revealing a dark tunnel. Motion-acti-vated lights appear along the floor to light the way after he takes a single step over the entrance to the tunnel. "This should lead to the kitchen, and there should be entrances along it to other rooms."

"Holy shit." Hope joins him. "Did you say the whole house is like this?"

He nods enthusiastically. "Yeah, upstairs has them as well. The only rooms that don't have them are the sex room and the master bedroom/safe room."

"Sex room?" Hope squeaks, and Oli laughs.

"Yeah, you should see it. It's really something."

Holden's studying the map, mumbling to himself before he starts to speak louder, directing his next comment at the rest of us. "Good idea not to let anyone else know about them. Let's keep this a family secret. From what I can see, apart from the tunnel they're showing the agents, there are six others. One leads out from a sealed room next to the vault, and that one, if I'm not mistaken, actually travels all the way under Dad's property and out the other side of it."

"That must be the one from the safe room. There's a slide that goes from the safe room to that room. I wanted to give it a go, but Harlow said we should wait until the authorities leave. Though I guess there's no point now that we know where it goes." He pouts a little, drawing the expected chuckles from the rest of us. "We still need to make sure the slide and tunnel have retained their integrity over the years, so you'll still get your chance." Oli perks up at this. "I also want to make sure there's some kind of way to securely close the tunnels at the other end. We wouldn't want some random stranger stumbling upon them."

"Holy shit!" I sit up straight as the words on the page jump out at me. I'd been skimming the details, half paying attention to their conversation and half to the words in front of me. "That crazy bastard kept an orca!"

"Are you serious?" Holden asks, gaping at me with surprise.

"Yeah. I have no idea how he managed that. He must have paid someone a lot of fucking money to catch it, not to mention what it must have cost to transport the thing here. How they did that without anyone noticing is anyone's guess. Whoever wrote this notes that it didn't do well, so they convinced him to return it to the wild. Count Bucătaru apparently had an agreement with some wildlife conservation group who specialized in aquatic creatures. The group was given access to the pool when they needed to rehab dolphins, seals, or turtles. Occasionally, a stranded whale was kept there until they were strong enough to return to the water. It says here that there was a mass stranding, and out of the fifty minke whales, they managed to save five of them by shipping them here and rehabbing them in the pool."

"Minke whales must be small, then?" Hope asks.

"Yeah, they're a smaller species. Five would have been fine in such a big pool, especially since they wouldn't have needed to stay long—just enough to build up some strength and make sure there was no underlying reason to beach before releasing them. That would have been a big operation, though. Maybe I'll get in contact with the organization, see if they have any more information."

"If we decide to refurbish the pool, we could let them know that we're ready to help them out at any time too," Oli says after closing the door on the secret tunnel and sitting back down next to me.

"Oh, what a great idea. I had just thought maybe we should fill it in, but there are always dolphins and seals that are washing up places or getting hurt by boats." I smack a kiss on his cheek just as we hear the doorbell ring. It's a loud fog-horn-sounding thing.

"Is it just me, or did that sound like something that could have been in the Addams family?" Holden asks, a small smile on his face as he shakes his head. "Count Bucătaru is really turning out to be quite a character."

The four of us head out into the foyer, with me being the one to unlock the door despite the guys' protests. I can see a shadow on the other side but can't make out who it is.

The door swings open to reveal Kai. He's a little dusty, and there's a smudge of something across his face, but he's grinning.

"Are they done already?" Holden asks, surprised, but Kai shakes his head.

"No, once they got to the entrance of the tunnel, I left them to come back here... though I might have done a little exploring a little on the way. Did you know you have a herd of deer in the zoo?" he asks me.

"Actually, I saw them on the first day, but I forgot. We're going to have to clear them out before any work starts. What's that smell?" I ask as the scent of gasoline and burned rubber wafts through the door.

"Your stalker struck again, and Jaxon's bike blew up." Oli and I step out onto the porch to take in the smoldering remains of Jaxon's bike. I instinctively press a hand to my stomach, trying to calm the rising nausea, though of course that's useless.

"Holy fuck!" Oli exclaims as I reach out and grab his hand, squeezing it.

"Should we call the police?" I ask Holden as he joins Oli and me, but he shakes his head.

"Dad's taking care of it. Come back inside," he insists, so we do as he says.

We close and lock the door behind him once he's fully inside, going back to our drinks. I think we're all feeling like safety in numbers is the smartest strategy at the moment. I'm still feeling a little shaky at the fact Jaxon's bike blew up, what if someone had been in the blast range. Surely, Holden would have told me if anyone had been hurt.

"Was everyone okay?" I ask, my gaze fixed on my whiskey. When Holden takes too long to answer, it shoots to him.

"Mostly. Dad and Emma were close by, so both

of them got a little banged up, but they're fine. Paramedics checked them over, and it's nothing a little rest won't fix." Holden sounds casual, but he can't stop his foot from tapping up and down, so I'm wondering how much he's playing it down.

"I can't believe we didn't hear it upstairs." Oli takes a big sip of his drink and paces around the room. He always gets like that when worked up.

Kai grabs himself a tumbler out of the cupboard and joins us, pouring some of the whiskey into his glass and taking a seat on the other side of me.

"You know, I was thinking about the deer." Kai changes the subject, and Holden breathes a little sigh of relief. "If there's a free paddock beyond the zoo, maybe we could fence it in for the deer and keep them in that. Then you have at least one source of food for the predators you end up keeping."

"What? Are you suggesting she let a deer loose in the tiger cage and let them hunt it?" Between the image that's now in my head and the disgust practically dripping from Hope's words, I can't help it. I burst into laughter.

"No, babe, that's a little inhumane. There are nicer ways of ending the deer's lives. That's actually a great idea, Kai. I was thinking about keeping cows, but they need a variety in their diets to keep them healthy. The deer would be a good variation for them. But that would mean having a butchering building on the premises as well." My mind is already stacking items on a list to talk about with the construction guys. Just how much would they be willing to do here? I suppose anything should be possible for the price we're willing to pay.

"I think there is one," Kai says with a frown. "I found a building that had big walk-in freezers and meat hooks for hanging carcasses. Or I hope it was for that. Who the fuck knows? Dude seems like he was a bit of a freak."

"Fuck, maybe we should show that to the police too," Holden groans, and I jump in.

"Do we have to? There's nothing to suggest that he killed people, and if the police start to poke around, they may find more things that will delay the renovations." I look down at my hands, feeling guilty and selfish, but my dreams seem to be drifting further away with every new discovery. When I look up, no one is giving me bad looks; in fact, they all have soft, sympathetic eyes.

"Let's just see what they say when they check out the vault. Wayne, the DEA agent, didn't seem like he believed any of it, but the ATF guy, Jason, seems to be on the ball. Hopefully, there's nothing in his file to suggest the count might be involved in missing persons," Kai says, trying to reassure me.

"Fingers crossed. It would be a disaster if they wanted to dig up the grounds. I only pray that when construction does start, the McCallisters don't find anything like that." That would be a disaster, and things would be delayed indefinitely.

"That Wayne was an asshole. He basically implied we were calling them in to get publicity," Holden growls, one of his hands clenching in a fist.

I pick up my book and keep skimming through the information. When I get to another section, I choke on the sip of whiskey I had just taken. "Count Bucătaru must have been crazy."

"You mean you hadn't already been thinking that?" Oli teases, and I hold out the book, turning it so they can see a photo of the front of the house. In the picture, unlike the muddy puddles in it today, the moat is full of water, the sun sparkling off it, looking refreshing and inviting.

"Oh wow, that's so cool." Hope sighs. "It's going to look amazing once you guys are through with it. Like something out of a fairytale."

"Yeah, I'm not sure fairytale is the kind of story Count Bucătaru was going for, more like a nightmare. See those things floating there?" I point something out. "And these ones here." They all lean in close, turning their heads to see if they can make it out.

"Floating logs?" Kai questions, and I shake my head.

"Nope, alligators. And these here…" I point to the two nostril-looking things sticking out of the waters. "Hippopotamus."

"Fuck off," Oli breathes out, trying to get a better look.

"Basically, they were there as security. Whenever he had parties, they were herded into the moat. Bars were dropped down to keep them in the front section so people could paddle in the lake out back risk-free."

"Dude, that's outrageous. Hey, wait! What if we —" Kai blurts out, looking dangerously intrigued, but before anyone else can say something, his phone rings. He answers it, still smiling. "Hey, man. You finished up already? That was quick."

He listens to whoever is on the other end, his smile dropping into a frown. Unfortunately, the feeling is contagious since I'm assuming he's talking to one of the three who aren't here.

"Okay, yeah, sure. Are you coming back up here? Oh, okay. Yup, got it." He hangs up and sighs.

"That was Tom. They're all on their way back up here. Wayne and Jason want to call in reinforcements. They want to transport the drugs and weapons and have the coroner pick up the body. They also want a crime scene team to go over it all before there's any more disruption to the scene even though they're not expecting to find anything. I guess that makes sense since the scene is over twenty years old. He also said they want to search Count Bucătaru's office, so Tom wants us to do a quick look in there before they get here, just to check for anything we might want to keep private for the family. They'll be taking the long way here, but we definitely don't want to get caught in the act."

We all jump to our feet, Oliver grabbing the maps while I carry my book, and we hurry to the room where we had our original sit down with Emma. All the chairs are still there, and Hope offers to find where they belong while we search for anything hidden.

Holden, Kai, Oliver, and I start to systematically search the office, each of us carefully digging through a different part of the room. It's not entirely efficient since we're attempting to leave behind no hint of our interference, but it's the best we've got right now.

"Does it say anything on the map, Oli?" Holden asks. "Let's pray that they don't stumble across a mechanism for the secret tunnels."

Oli lays it out on the desk and studies it before snorting. "How cliché. It's behind the painting of the map of the world." Kai and Holden hurry over to it. "It says there's a way to lock the tunnel mechanisms in the kitchen pantry, of all places. Apparently, there's a switch that'll lock it all up. Not sure if it works on both ends of the tunnel, but it's a temporary solution for our current problem."

"Go lock it and hide those maps," I tell him. "If you have time to put them in the car, we can take them with us when we leave. Can you put this in there, too?" I hand him the record book.

He heads out, leaving Kai and Holden to put the code into the safe. This one is just a normal safe, but it takes the same code as everything else. When they pop it open, it's surprisingly empty. Well, empty of drugs and guns and weird shit like we've found everywhere else. This one just holds a bit of paperwork, which Kai promptly pulls out.

He flips through the papers. "It's deeds to all the Bucătaru properties and what looks like a key to a safe deposit box." I pluck the key out of his hands and tuck it into my pocket before gesturing for him to put the rest back.

"I'm going to make sure Oli locked the tunnels and put the stuff in the car. Can you guys help Hope with the rest of the chairs?" I ask as she comes back, starting to feel the aftermath of so much adrenaline rushing through my system today. God, I'm about ready to collapse.

"This day can't be done soon enough. It's just one thing after another," I grumble, and Kai unceremoniously shoves the papers into Holden's hands so he can hold me instead. He wraps his arms around me and I sink into them. Kai's a master at hugging. His hugs make everything that bad in your life drain away, even if it's only for that moment. Sometimes that's enough.

"Oh, babe, it's certainly been a stressful one. When the others get back here, what do you say we jump into the car and head back to the house? We can grab some drinks and hit the hot tub. We deserve it, and we're all heading back to work tomorrow, so it's our last day off. Let's relax and blow off some steam."

"That sounds *amazing*." I slump into his hug, comforted by the soft rumble of his chuckles.

"It sure does. After the last week, work is going to seem boring and easy." Holden laughs as Hope comes back to grab another chair.

"Speak for yourself," she chimes in. "While you've all been gallivanting around the world, some of us actually turned up to work."

"See, Hope needs to relax too. Hot tub party it is. Let's just hope the agents don't take too long."

Chapter Twenty-Three

Harlow

Oliver closes the door to the car just as Declan, the twins, Thomas, and Forrest, followed by the two agents, walk around the front of the house. All of us are standing on the front porch waiting to see what instructions the agents have for us.

Forrest quickly introduces us, but Wayne doesn't stop, not even muttering basic pleasantries as he storms back to his car. At least Jason stops, a sheepish smile on his face. "Sorry about him. He doesn't like to be wrong, and you guys certainly proved him wrong. That's got to be the biggest drug haul he's had this year, and he didn't even have to do any work to get it. At this stage, none of you are considered suspects since that vault has obviously been closed up for years. We will need to speak to

Emma Cullen, but apart from identifying the body and seizing the drugs and weapons, there's not much for us to go on. We'll go through his office, but there are no leads and no witnesses, so it's looking like it's basically a dead end."

"I've got contractors coming through tomorrow to assess the zoo and what needs to be done to renovate it, or at least that was our plan. Can we still do that?" I ask him, fingers crossed behind my back.

I feel like I shouldn't be so hooked on this. I mean, it was only recently that my dream actually got the potential to become a reality. But with everything that's happened with the future of my career, all the question marks about how I'll go forward, this was sort of an anchor point for me. If I could get this going and set down some kind of cornerstone for myself, then that somehow meant I'd still work my way to the future I'd already had planned. Maybe it's silly to pin so much on brick and mortar rather than my own confidence in my skills and proving myself, but I just need something tangible to boost my spirit back up.

"I don't see that being a problem. We'll likely be out of your hair by tonight. There's no need for you guys to stay if you don't want to. We can lock up and return the key when we're done." Maybe I'm a little naive because that offer sounds pretty great to me, but Declan and Thomas exchange a side-eyed glance.

"We'll stay," Thomas says, his tone making it clear that he's firm on this decision.

Forrest steps up beside Jason, holding a few papers he'd pulled out of his briefcase. "And we would like your officers to sign NDAs before they can step onto the property, please. If you and Agent Jackson could also sign one, we'd appreciate that. I'm sure you understand our desire to keep this out of the media given the family's corporate holdings. Although Jaxon and Jacinta Summers' relation to Count Bucătaru was only recently discovered, there are some media outlets that would have a field day with wild accusations of the family being linked to such scandalous finds as a dead man and a pile of drugs. Of course, we also understand that you both have jobs to do within your respective agencies, such as reporting to your superiors and such. You are welcome to announce your findings, but we'd prefer to keep their origin, and the Summers' connection, a private matter until we can handle it in our own time."

Hope steps up, a smile on her face that says she's about to seal the deal. "We will be happy to work with your media department and release a statement. We just want to be able to control it. Tabloid speculation isn't going to benefit anyone at this stage, and Jaxon and Jacinta certainly need to be consulted about the release of any public information since it is their legacy. Once the body identification has occurred, we will know which direction we want to go in."

Jason frowns, but he takes the pile of papers. "It's certainly not normal procedure, but I think we can accommodate you."

"Like hell we will," Wayne rumbles as he returns.

Forrest's gaze becomes frosty, the man straightening his spine as he gains a determined set to his stance that makes me suddenly understand why he's responsible for protecting the Summers and their insane wealth. "Well then, I would suggest you leave and come back with a warrant. We played nice, and we've done the right thing, but we could make this difficult for you. Especially considering there's nothing yet to suggest that there would be any materials relevant to the DEA within the home itself. All we're asking is for this to be kept out of the media. We don't want to suppress anything in court or in your reports or anything like that."

Jason holds up his hands, the papers rustling in his grip. "No, it's fine. We will cooperate. Stop being an asshole, Wayne."

A satisfied smile softens Forrest's face. "Good, I suggest we wait down by the gate. Once they've signed, we'll let them through. Declan will stay with the house to make sure your officers don't get nosy and wander somewhere they shouldn't, and Thomas will do the same on the way to the tunnel. Please tell your officers that the place has been abandoned for twenty years; we do not know how stable or reliable the zoo buildings are. Wandering could be dangerous."

"Oh, and there's a herd of deer in there somewhere too. So, watch out for those," I offer up, and the agent's eyes widen.

"Just be glad there are no alligators or hippopotami left in the moat," Oliver mutters.

"That we know of," Kai follows up, playing along. Both agents stare at the moat suspiciously even though there's no water in it.

Forrest waves goodbye and heads to his car accompanied by Wayne. We leave Jason with Declan and Thomas, and the rest of us squeeze into one of the SUVs, leaving the other for Thomas and Declan to use when they finish. Jaxon's former bike is a twisted bit of miserable metal as we drive past, and I feel another pang of guilt. Yeah, I know he can afford to buy himself a new one, but we had such fun on it this morning. It's another memory the stalker has ruined for me.

"God, I'm so done with today," Jacinta groans as Kai starts the car, and we bump down the driveway. "I'm actually looking forward to going into the office tomorrow."

"I thought you were done with the office?" Holden asks her.

"I am mostly, but I still need to hire someone for the day-to-day running so that means interviews, and until that happens, I don't trust Lindy or

Rowena at all. Nana's going to be the head honcho, but I need to go in and explain to everyone what's going on."

"I'll draft up a job advertisement unless there's someone you'd like to woo away from another company." Hope leans forward in her seat to better hear Jacinta's answer.

"No, I like the idea of bringing in a newbie, maybe someone who's just graduated from college with a master of business. Give someone the chance to learn at the feet of one of the great business directors, Grace Summers. Someone with no preconceived ideas about this business, someone willing to try new things." Jacinta waxes lyrical about her ideal candidate for another few beats until the boys begin to chuckle. Can't say I blame them. The woman goes on about fashion the way I do about animals, and I know I can totally be a bit much once I get rolling.

"It's actually a pretty solid idea. You create loyalty by giving someone a chance like that," Jaxon points out, the others murmuring their agreement.

"Instead of advertising in any of the industry publications, why don't you advertise at some LA colleges? It wouldn't hurt to advertise within the company either. There might be someone who has the right skills but has never had a chance to use them," Kai suggests as we pull out of the big gates, waving at Forrest when we pass him by.

Jacinta groans. "But then Lindy and Rowena might apply."

"So? It's not like you have to hire them. Lindy doesn't even have any business education. You hired her because you felt sorry for her. She gave you a sob story about supporting an ill mother and younger siblings," Holden reminds her. Something in me twinges at that, a stirring of resignation. I knew I didn't get a good vibe from her, and hearing that she likely took advantage of Jacinta by playing on what she holds most dear—family—makes me irritated on my new sister's behalf.

"Yeah, and did you know she never talks about them? Even when I ask, she brushes it off. I think I got played," she says wryly.

"And Rowena definitely doesn't have any business management skills in her resume. I've seen it, remember," I remind her.

She nibbles on her lower lip for a minute, still looking thoughtful though decidedly more settled with our reassurance. "Okay, let's do that."

"We also need to draft a statement regarding all of this. Well, not exactly about this, but about new inheritance and all that entails." Hope gestures toward the house fading behind us. "Let's not let a loose-lipped police officer do it for us. When we get home, I'd like to sit down with the two of you and come up with something."

"Yes, okay. Let's do that," Jaxon agrees, and

although Jacinta makes another face, I can tell she'll drag her head out of the sand and face the truth.

Kai stops, leaving the SUV on the turning circle, and we all climb out. "I'm going to update Dad, then I'm going to grab a shower." He walks backward, pointing at me. "I'll meet *you* in the hot tub in about an hour. Does that sound good?"

I groan before I can stop it, and my enthusiastic nod might possibly put a bobblehead to shame. "God yes."

"I hope Nana has been cooking because I'm starving," Oliver grumbles like a cranky toddler. I think we're all a little worse for wear today. "Can Mrs. Heyton come home now? I miss her."

"If she hasn't, we'll just order something, but you'll have to talk to Dad and Thomas about the latter," Holden says, wrapping his arm around our boyfriend and giving him a kiss. "Come on, you're all dusty too. I'll help you scrub clean if you want." That's not all they're getting up to if Holden's cheesy eyebrow wiggle has anything to say about it.

Instantly, Oliver perks up, and I giggle as he drags Holden to me. They both give me kisses on the cheek before they're up the stairs and through the front door.

"Not joining them?" Jaxon asks from behind me.

"Nah, Oli hogs the water," I joke, but in truth, I like to give them their own time too. "I really want to read through this so I have all the information before I have the walk through with the McCallister brothers tomorrow." Hope stiffens at the mention of the construction crew, which reminds me that I need to get the information out of her about them. If it upsets her this much, maybe we shouldn't be using them. I'm not sure why she'd recommend them if it would be this hard for her to see them, but maybe she underestimated the impact it would have on her.

"Hope, I don't have to use them if it upsets you. I'm sure there are hundreds of other crews we could use."

The house is quiet as we enter, and my voice echoes around the entry hall. Jaxon and Jacinta are quietly waiting to see what she says, but she shakes her head.

"No, that's fine. It's not like I'll run into them all that much. Ask Holden to tell you the story. I don't really feel like repeating it today." Her eyes are shadowed, and for the first time since I've known her, she looks tired and sad.

"Ah, there you all are!" Nana bustles down the corridor from the main living area. "I was hoping I would catch you before you all disappeared. "Hope dear, Forrest informed us that he has the adoption papers drawn up if you're ready to become an official Summers."

Hope's eyes widen as her mouth drops open. "You guys were serious about that?" The shock in her voice is all too relatable. I *was* that girl, probably still am to some extent. Not being wanted by a family… That leaves a lasting mark, where even after you find a family that's worthy of you, you still feel a bit unwanted.

"Of course we were, dear. All those previous foster families were crazy. We can see what an amazing person you are and would love nothing better than to have you join our family." Nana wraps her arm around Hope's shoulders, and she bursts into tears as she pulls her into a hug and holds the sobbing girl. "We also think it would be better if you gave up that lonely apartment in town and moved out here permanently. While Harlow still has a stalker, we want to keep the family close. You can use one of our permanent rooms at the Neighpalm Hotel like we all do if you need to stay in town for business."

Hope pulls away, her face blotchy from tears. "You have no idea what it feels like to be wanted for the first time in my life." She nearly whispers the words, her voice catching by the end.

Jacinta smiles at her, and I'm almost floored. I've seen a lot of faces from her, but this is one of the first times I've seen her direct that gentle smile at anyone besides her brothers and her animals. "Actually, I think you'll find we all do. Your family is just claiming you a little later than the rest of us. Welcome to the family, sis."

"Holy shit, I have sisters!" A grin a milc wide

blasts away the tiredness that had been on her face a minute ago.

"Yeah, you certainly got a better welcome than I did, but at least Jacinta has a great wardrobe to steal from. Sister jackpot there," I joke, sticking my tongue out at her when she elbows me in the side. Where Jacinta and I are very similar in size, Hope is shorter than us both, which she compensates for with towering high heels. She's also curvier, so there's a good chance she can't steal her clothes anyway.

"I already know we take the same size shoes, so watch out." She points at Jacinta, and we all laugh.

"And don't forget six pushy brothers," Jaxon reminds, and her forehead wrinkles in a frown as she steps away from Nana, trying to compose herself.

"Not sure that's any kind of endorsement. I've lived with boys before, and that didn't turn out so great."

"These ones are well trained, and their girl-friend keeps them in line," I promise her, helping to ease some of her returning worry.

"Why don't you all wash up? Food is on a serve-yourself basis tonight. There's a big bowl of rice and a couple takeout orders on the kitchen bench. I wasn't sure when everyone would get here, so you can just heat it up when you need it."

"Are Dad and Emma okay? The agents are

coming over to see them when they finish up at the other place."

"They are. They were taking a nap, but I think they're up now. I'll get them when the agents arrive."

"Nana, what would we do without you?" Jaxon places a kiss on her cheek, taking that extra effort to make it *smooch* loudly enough for us all to hear.

"I ask myself the same thing every day. Now shoo."

Hope heads in the direction of the wing I stayed in when I first arrived. When she disappears, I turn to Nana. "If the McCallister brothers are going to be given rooms in this house, I suggest that Hope maybe take the spare room in our wing."

A sly smile crosses Nana's face, and my stomach lurches. "Nonsense, dear. Hope's a big girl. I'm sure she can cope with living close to her foster brothers."

"Nana," Jaxon growls, but the woman just fluffs her hair sashays back down the hall to the living area.

"Don't you worry, Jaxon. I helped all of you boys out. It's only right that I help my girls." She disappears, and Jaxon turns to his sister.

"You know she's got plans for you too." She blushes a pretty pink, but I'm not about to argue. It'll be kind of nice seeing it be someone else's turn.

"Somehow, I don't think Jacinta is too upset about that at all." I link my arm with hers and drag her toward our wing. "Come on, let's clean up. I'm starving, and I have a date with a sexy islander and a hot tub that I don't want to miss."

"Well, I know I'll be avoiding the hot tub then." Jacinta grimaces. "Anyway, I think I need a good night's sleep. I also want to do some research and see which colleges specialize in business and fashion classes. We might be lucky enough to find someone who majored in both."

"I have to look over the final negotiations for this cruise line."

"Now, that's exciting. I think we should actually go on a trial cruise first. Not seeing it before you buy it would just be irresponsible, Jax." The man in question rolls his eyes when Jacinta and I turn our best pouty lips on him, but he must be immune to it from too many years of Oli pulling the same trick.

"How did I know you were going to suggest that? If you *must* know, I'm booked in for departure the day after the fundraiser gala. I actually tried to get out of it this year, but Harlow came into our lives, and there is no way I want to miss seeing her all decked out for the event." He whirls me away from his sister and dips me, placing a kiss on my lips that leaves me breathless and lightheaded. "I can't wait to spend the night dancing with you."

Jacinta shoves him out of the way as he brings me upright. "Yeah, well, you and five others, lover boy, so settle down. Anyway, I expect you to demand a couple more cabins so we can all come."

"We've all just taken time off to go to Prague. I'm not sure if the others can get away."

"I'm sure the minute they hear that you and Harlow are sneaking off on a little cruise, and don't deny that you were planning on inviting her, they'll be all in." Jaxon scowls at his sister as we get to their rooms.

"Maybe I had wanted it to be a surprise," he mutters, but she only waves a regal hand at him.

"Don't be silly. Harlow has her own business to worry about now too. I bet you hadn't considered that." His scowl disappears, and he runs a hand through his hair kind of sheepishly.

"In my defense, I had planned on asking you before all of this blew up, so no, I hadn't even considered it."

I shove my hands in the pockets of my pants and watch, fascinated, as the twins bicker back and forth. There's no real malice, and the affection is real. It's strangely compelling but also warms my heart. I love seeing them this way. It's sad that the rest of the world doesn't get to know this family like they really are. Everyone sees the front they put on, and they assume they can't truly be happy because of their money, but that couldn't be further from the truth. I think Nana and Poppy and Dad have done an amazing job at keeping them grounded. I hate to say it, but it's even better than the one Chuck and Melinda did with Max. She still likes to put on airs and graces, but at home the Summers have no pretentiousness in the least.

Just as I'm about to interrupt the argument, I remember the key I had swiped from Holden earlier. "Oh, hey, we found this in a safe in the office earlier. We didn't want the police to get their hands on it, so I swiped it." I hand it over to Jaxon.

"This is for the safe deposit box that was on the list. We should probably check it out."

Jacinta swipes the dangling key. "I'll do it tomorrow when I have lunch." They start to bicker again, so I walk away and leave them to it. I really am too hungry to wait any longer, and I can't wait to spend some quality time with Kai.

Chapter Twenty-Four

Kai

When I pull back the lid on the hot tub, steam trails into the cool evening air, the coils of hot, warm air visible against the night around me. It's been a lot longer than the hour I told Harlow, but she seems to have been just as busy as I was because she's not out here yet either. I push the lid out of the way and grab us a couple of towels from the nearby box. As I climb the steps and sink into the bubbling water, I groan. I settle into the molded seat and lean my head back as the jets pound my tired body.

A jumble of thoughts and questions run through my mind, and I can't help but think back to the first time I was in a hot tub with Harlow. Back after her first accident with the saddle. I don't know what Luke was thinking; he was so very lucky she wasn't trampled. What was he trying to achieve? Did he want her to fall into his arms, or was he trying to scare her into returning to the East Coast?

I guess we'll never know his motivation now, and that only opens up a host of other questions, none of which can be answered. Who killed him? Who made it so he couldn't answer any questions? Was it related to this other stalker? Is it the same person who killed the PI and Harlow's mother, or was it about something completely unrelated? His waterlogged body wasn't able to tell the police anything, so once again, we are at another dead end —literally. I have a gut feeling it's all related, though.

Someone, probably the one we should've been worried about all along, is cleaning up all of their loose ends.

One thing I hate is feeling useless, and there's no other word to describe the frustrated churning in my mind when I can't do anything but question, question, question. If I keep turning this over and over, all I'm going to be able to offer Harlow is a bad mood. She needs more than that from me, so I push the unknowns aside and focus on what I do know something about.

My mind switches to business and the email that was waiting for me this evening. The owners of the hockey team I'm interested in definitely want to sell. I've forwarded the contracts to Forrest, and he's having his firm look over them before the meeting we have scheduled with Dad for tomorrow. The contract includes their home hockey arena, and I'd like to fly to Colorado and have a quick look at it before the gala. I was hoping Harlow would come with me, though I guess it will depend on how her meeting with these new contractors goes. I really want to be here for her, I know all of my brothers do, but we've neglected our own businesses. My box is starting to overflow with things to do, and my brothers are much the same, I'm sure. Before we know it, Harlow's life is going to be just as busy as ours. I hope we're all ready for that, but I have a feeling things will get bumpy for a while as we try to work out how our lives mesh together. On the bright side, after all we've been through so far, I have no doubt that we will make it through.

She was so excited when we were touring the house. Her face looked like a kid at Disneyland, but I know she was stressing about what we found in the vault. We should know within twenty-four hours who the body was, and that will take a load off. I hope. I mean, it can only be one of two people realistically. But it's that not knowing hanging over your head that's stressful

Thankfully, Dec said the DEA and ATF didn't care about the rest of the vault. Apparently, they didn't look too closely at all. They saw the guns, drugs, and dead body, then everything else ceased to matter.

Movement at the house has me looking up,

finding my girlfriend almost sprinting to the hot tub. She's wearing nothing but a bikini that makes her body look amazing, highlighting her gorgeous curves.

"Holy shit, it got really cold out here!" She quickly climbs the steps, sliding in and mimicking the groan that left my mouth when I did the same thing. "God, that's good." She shuffles over toward me and gives me a kiss before resting her head back against the edge and closing her eyes. "I can practically feel all the tension leaving my body. It's been a long ass week," she mutters as she reaches for my hand under the water.

The smile that I feel on my face is nothing short of ecstatic. All I can do is marvel at how small her hand feels compared to mine, how good and right it feels.

"Did you get yourself something to eat?" I ask, worried that she's not looking after herself. All the stress has been compiling, and she's looking tired.

"God yes, Nana makes a mean curry. I had two bowls. I'm surprised you couldn't see my little rice baby as I ran across the patio." My heart lurches at the thought of Harlow's belly having a baby, but that thought is marred with the reminder that a woman may already be carrying my baby. I can't help the scowl or the way my hand tightens around Harlow's. She lurches upright. "Oh fuck, Kai. I'm sorry. I was careless with my words."

She runs a wet thumb across my brow, trying to

smooth out the lines. "Have you heard anything about Veronica?" she asks quietly, and I shake my head.

"No, but the amniocentesis is tomorrow, so we should know soon."

"Have you thought about what you'll do if it is yours?" she asks, no hint of hostility, and I'm thankful for the calm curiosity. This is a lot of drama that's potentially going to spill over into her life, but she's making it easy for me to feel like this is a safe space. Do I know what I'm going to do if the kid is mine? Fuck, even if it were my brother's, I would feel a sense of responsibility for the baby. But that's all I have right now, a sense of responsibility and some kind of desire to do the right thing. I don't know anything else about raising a child, but I guess that's at least a start.

"You know that we didn't want this, that we did everything to try to avoid something like this. Sleeping with her was a one-time thing before we even knew you." She gently places a finger on my mouth, shutting down any more attempts to reassure her.

"You don't need to explain anything."

"All I know is that if it's my baby, I will do whatever it takes to have her carry it to full-term. After that, I'll make sure it grows up surrounded by love and laughter. It will never know that its mother did what she did. I know Thomas feels the same… possibly even stronger than I do. I don't want to choose between you and it. I don't usually like to admit to being selfish, but in this case, I really want to be. If this baby is mine, or his, I know I speak for both of us when I say that we don't want to lose you, but we won't let the baby not have the kind of life that we could provide. Are you willing to be a part of our lives if our lives now include this baby?" I can't quite meet her eyes when I ask this because I don't want to face seeing doubt in hers.

"Babe, of course. If that is your or Thomas' baby, I will be in its life however you want me. If you want me to be fun Aunt Harlow who can teach them how to get their pony to count on command, or if it's in more of a motherly role, I'm fine with that too. I'm all in, and not even a bat shit crazy woman is going to ruin this for us."

She climbs into my lap and rests her forehead against mine as my hands go to her waist. "Let's worry about it once we actually know the results. For now, let me try to make that haunted look in your eyes disappear."

The feel of her skin against mine is enough to have the blood rushing to my dick, starting to harden under her pert ass. She leans in and kisses me, her tongue sliding against mine, twisting and twining with one another as she grinds down on my lap. I pull away and slide my hands up her back, her panting breath soft against my cheek as I tug at the straps holding her bikini top in place. First the ones behind her back, then the ones around her neck, letting it slip off and disappear into the bubbling water. Lifting my knees, I propel her out of the water so that her breasts are now in line with my mouth. I lean in and gently bite into the rounded top of one of them, not hard enough to leave an imprint but hard enough for her to moan and arch into me, before sucking to leave a pretty red mark. Sliding both hands down, I push away my shorts, freeing my cock, then use one hand to push her bottoms to the side. Taking one of her tight nipples into my mouth, I suck hard as I lower her onto my cock. She grunts as I work myself into her, her hands tightly grasping my shoulders.

"Fuck, yes, Kai. Just like that." I have to raise and lower her a couple of times, but I finally bottom out. It's my turn to grunt when she grinds down, trying to create friction on her clit. "Suck harder. Use your teeth," she begs, and who am I to not comply?

I worry my teeth against her tight bud as she starts to undulate up and down on my dick. Her warm pussy, velvety soft, strangles me like a vice. Water starts to slosh around as her movements increase in speed, creating waves which crest over the edge of the tub and onto the ground below. I start to thrust up from below, helping her out, as she throws her head back and moans. She looks like a wanton goddess, and I feel my balls tighten. Sliding my hand down, I rub a thumb across her clit, and she tightens even more.

"Yes, god yes," she chants, and her movement starts to falter, so I take over. Gritting my teeth, I pound into her. "I'm going to come," she gasps, so I grab her head as her cunt grips down, bringing her mouth down to mine to muffle her scream. After waiting for her to ride out most of her pleasure, my orgasm finally slams into me. My toes curl as the rush of sensations flow through my limbs, my muffled groan still loud in the silence of the night around us. Thankfully, the hot tub is tucked away into a dark corner so that no one sitting in the living area can see us, but it does make it that little bit more thrilling to know that someone may walk out.

Harlow slumps against me, panting. "That was amazing." Okay, that's totally cause for a smile, and if it's a little bit smug, well, it sounds like I earned it. "And just what I needed. Will you sleep with me tonight?" she asks softly, and I hug her to me tightly, my dick still inside her.

"Of course. My brothers would have to tie me up to stop me."

We're still breathing heavily when Harlow climbs off my lap and looks into my eyes again, smiling. "Now, *that* is a much better look. Well-fucked Kai is a big improvement over sad Kai."

I chuckle as I chase after her bikini top on the other side of the tub and help her back into it. Now dressed, she snuggles in next to me, sighing contentedly.

"Tell me about your new house?" I ask, and I

know I've asked the right thing because she sits up, and the relaxed look Harlow was wearing disappears, replaced with one of pure excitement.

"Oh, Kai, you should see it! It was magnificent. I can't wait to move in with you all. Do you think Dad would be sad if we moved in right away and did the renovations around us?"

"I think he would be sad because he's only just found you, but it's not like you're going far. You can still see each other every day."

"One of the tunnels, the one that leads from the safe room, goes directly under this property and house. It actually connects to Dad's property. We could see how easy it would be to put in an entry from here, then everyone living here could have direct access. It's wide enough to be able to get a golf cart in, and we could leave one or two down there for our family to use. Jacinta wouldn't even have to get out of her PJs to come visit."

I try to hide the groan that leaves my mouth, but I don't stifle it quickly enough. "Giving her full access to a golf cart and the tunnels may become a problem. You know she's going to be over here all the time, stealing our food and drinks and encroaching on our time. She'll say it's because you need bestie time or something."

A secret smile lights up her face. "I'm fairly certain she's going to be way too busy with her own potential harem to be bothering us all the time." That makes me cringe slightly. Yep, don't need to think too hard on my sister and how many men are currently chasing after her.

"Regardless of Jazzy, I think that's a great idea, and it won't hurt for this house to access an escape tunnel too. Dad talked about putting in a safe room after Carmen and her friends invaded the place, but it never happened. Now, tell me more about your house."

"We took plenty of notes as we went around, and I'm going to order some dumpsters to be delivered. I think Jazzy talked about wanting to hire a decorating company to help us with the inside." I can see her chewing her lip in thought. "The house looks to be in tip-top condition structurally, but the decorating and furniture is dated. We're planning on stripping a lot of the rooms and starting over, but there were a few I want to leave the same. There's a huge formal dining room that has the same gothic vibe as the front foyer, as does the ball room. I think it would be fun to leave them like they are. A talking point for if we decide to throw any parties or need to have people over for business." She screws up her nose. "The master bedroom was much the same too, though I'm not too sure what to do about that."

"What do you mean? Isn't that where you want to sleep?"

"Seems like the crazy count started sleeping in the panic room instead, so the master is a little neglected. I can't say I have any issue with using the panic room. Honestly, I can't decide between the two. They were both pretty cool."

"Just use both. We keep the panic room a secret because it's a panic room, but you can transition between the two depending on how you feel. It's your place now, and if you want to spoil yourself a little and have two cozy spots of your own, I'm not going to stop you."

She gives me a thoughtful look before nodding. "That's not a bad idea. Who says I have to sleep in one place? I want the six of you to pick a room for your own too, so we need to do that, and you can tell the designer how you'd like it. All the bedrooms have ensuites, and we can redo all of them as well. For whatever reason, all the bathrooms look like they haven't been renovated since the seventies. While your bedrooms are being done, you can sleep in the spares. Or stay with me. I mean, we can make sure the bed and whatever else are big enough for you guys to join when you want."

"And you're walking around the zoo with the McCallister brothers tomorrow? Tell me what you thought of them. Honestly, I'm still surprised Dad's going to offer them our name. He's never done that before, but his gut is never wrong."

She chews on her lip, only drawing more attention to that frown of hers. "They do good work. Nyx's enclosure is amazing, so I'm not worried on that front. I'm worried for Hope."

I chuckle and shake my head. "Hope's a big girl.

She'll be fine. She's also got you and Jacinta to look out for her, and we all know that Jacinta will get rid of them if they step a foot out of line even if it interferes with Nana's matchmaking tricks." The frown softens with my reassurance, and I feel a little better knowing that I'm able to help clear her mind even a smidge.

"Hey, I wanted to ask you something. Would you fly out to Colorado and check out this hockey team with me? It will be a quick trip overnight, two at the most. I want to see their facilities, check out what we're getting for our money and how much we're going to have to put into it. I know you're busy with everything here, but if you're done with the preliminaries, then we could do it on the week-end. The following weekend is the fundraiser, and I know Jaxon wants to whisk you away to check out the cruise line after that."

Her eyes widen, and I chuckle. "Welcome to life as a Summers. It's why we make sure to enjoy ourselves when we do get time off because we don't often slow down in between."

"I'd really like to come with you. Can I let you know after I see how tomorrow goes?"

"Sure, babe, no pressure," I assure her. "If it turns out you can't, I'll be sad, but I'll also under-stand." I give her a kiss on the cheek just as a light switches on above us, and we both shade our eyes against the glare. When the black spots disappear, Declan is leaning against the wall.

"You're back." He nods, his weariness not lifting despite the smile on our girl's face.

"Yeah, they're all done over at the house, and I locked it up. The agents are in Dad's office talking to Emma now. I just wanted to help you feed the cubs before I went to bed."

Harlow stands up and moves over to get out, with Declan ready and waiting with a towel. He wraps it around her body, his touches lingering a little too long for the purpose of drying her off. "Kai, I'll meet you in bed?"

"Wouldn't miss it."

Chapter Twenty-Five

Harlow

I did my walkthrough of the zoo with the McCallister brothers, all of whom have now moved into Dad's house. The zoologist and vet that Dad poached from the MacGinty Sanctuary joined us, and with those two lovely men involved, I'm more ready than ever to begin this process. Both of them were thrilled to meet Nyx and the cubs, and the zoologist, Doug, has moved into Luke's old room in the staff quarters for now and taken over some of the cubs' feedings. It's a big help since Dec is back at work and I have meetings and things to do.

The police identified the body as Count Radic Bucătaru, and we held a small private memorial for him that only the family attended. The police gave us the all-clear to continue renovating the house since the investigation of his death amounted to no more than a cold case given the lack of evidence.

Chuck and Melinda have made the move from Connecticut to the West Coast and are busy settling into their new home. Max is still working on the movie, but she's flown out for the gala with the director and the cast, so I'll finally be able to see her tonight. A conversation is long overdue between us, and she won't be able to conveniently escape from this one.

Since Jaxon's bike blew up, there's been no stalker activity, so Thomas and Dad okayed it for Josh and all of the Summers' horses to return as well as Mrs. Hayton. Oliver wept in her arms when he saw her.

Smoothing down the fabric of my ball gown, I study myself in the mirror. The Jace-designed dress is a strapless gown, gathered around the fitted bodice and down over the hips before flaring into a voluminous train of shimmering champagne fabric. It's gorgeous, and I feel like a princess in it. The makeup artist did an amazing job of hiding the dark circles I've earned from working non-stop for the last two weeks.

A knock on the door of my hotel room has me hurrying over to open it. We all have rooms at the Neighpalm Resort where the gala is being held. I haven't been alone all day, and I finally kicked everyone out so I could get ready in peace and quiet. Thomas is in the adjoining room, but as long as I leave the door unlocked, he's fine with giving me some time alone.

When I open the door, it's to an assembly of Summers waiting on the other side. "Is everything okay?" I ask as I step aside and let them all in. Despite my room being an executive suite, the space is a little cramped after the full invasion enters the room.

"Forrest has news for us, so he requested that we all get together before we go to the gala," Dad explains, fidgeting with the bow tie of his tux. Nana smacks his hand away as my gaze scans the room. All my men are wearing tuxes, looking sexy as hell. It's enough to make a girl lightheaded, and each and every one of them is looking at me like Nyx stares at a deer leg. What makes it even better is the way they've personalized their outfits so that no two Summers are wearing the same thing.

"Harlow?" Jacinta's voice shakes me out of my thirst-induced coma, and I have to blink a couple of times before I look at her. "You've got a little something there." She points to the corner of my mouth, and my hand flies up, worried I had actually drooled. She and Hope collapse against one another in laughter.

"Assholes." I flip them both off, but there's no real malice behind it. Being teased by them is nice, homey even, and it really just feels like family, which I'd never complain about.

Another knock sounds at the door, and Holden, being the closest, reaches over to let Forrest in.

The poor man looks tired. He's been working overtime for the Summers for weeks now, and I know Dad basically had to strongarm him into taking the next week off. With the offer of a fully paid trip and use of the family's private jet, how could the man say no? His wife would likely kill him if that were the case, so I think they're heading to Cancun for a week in the sun.

"Hey, guys, sorry to do this now, but I thought we should get a few things out of the way before I leave in the morning." He places his briefcase down on a side table, clicking it open. "Okay, first things first. Harlow, that thing you asked me to do is done, congratulations." He holds out a sheet of paper, and I take it, scanning the words. It's a change of name document confirming that I am now Harlow Summers. Tears prickle in my eyes as I throw my arms around the older man and give him a kiss on the cheek.

"Thank you," I whisper, and he pats my back awkwardly.

"My pleasure, my dear."

I pull away and whirl around, waving the document in the air. "It's official!" I hand it over to my dad, and Nana and Poppy peer over his shoulder to scan it.

A sob leaves Nana's mouth as all three of them look at me. "I hope you don't mind that I did that."

I had wanted to surprise them all, or at least that's what I told myself. The truth is, I think a little fear of rejection was always sitting in the back of my mind. Old mental shit rearing its ugly head even though I knew it wasn't a real concern.

"Mind?" Dad is all choked up. He hands the paper to Declan before tugging me into his arms. "I couldn't be happier that you have my name now. Just like it was meant to be from the start." His hug is fierce and warm and welcome, drawing out a sigh of relief.

"Awesome, you don't even have to marry any of the boys to have the same last name. It's perfect," Jacinta points out. A rush of warmth fills my body with the thought of being married to these men. I know I'd legally be able to marry only one, but with all of us having the same name, there will be something permanent that connects us no matter what.

"It certainly does solve the problem of having to choose," Nana says joyously.

"Sorry to rush you, but we're needed downstairs," Poppy frets. I'm surprised he lasted this long before trying to herd the Summers horde to the party. The gala is Poppy's baby, and he's been particularly fussy about wanting things to go off without a hitch, which includes our timely presence.

"Okay, next, I would like to announce the official adoption of Miss Hope Green into the Summers family." He takes out two more pieces of paper and passes them to my friend, or I guess she's my sister now. "Or should I say Miss Hope Summers." Forrest grins widely, and it's Hope's turn to tear up as everyone surrounds her with warm congratulations.

"Oh, what an absolutely wonderful day!" Nana claps her hands together enthusiastically. "I can't wait to get downstairs and celebrate with some champagne."

"One last thing. I probably should have led with this one and saved the good news for after." He's frowning at the boys, a concerned glint in his eyes. "I'd tell you all to sit down, but I think ripping off the band-aid is really just the best course of action for everyone. I have the results for the paternity test for Veronica's baby. It's Kai's."

Kai pales and sits down heavily on the bed, shock on his face. "Fuck! I'm going to be a daddy?"

His family gathers around him to offer support as his eyes meet mine, pleading with me to say something. We talked about this scenario a little more when we went to Colorado to check out the hockey arena, so I'm not being hit as hard as he is right now. I'd been mentally preparing myself for this despite the unlikelihood because I didn't want Kai or Thomas to see anything in my reaction that might hurt them. I want them to know that we will love and accept the baby despite its horrible origins. In fact, I plan to do no less than smother it with love.

"Well, I, for one, can't wait to meet our new

family member. There was a nursery room off the master bedroom in the house. Better add that to the renovation lists, Jazzy." I watch as he releases a breath, his body relaxing so dramatically you'd think Atlas had just dropped the world from his shoulders.

"Oh, we can make it animal themed. Wouldn't that be perfect for your baby?" she says to me, and I feel my ovaries flutter. *My baby?* Hell yes, it will be my baby. My maternal instincts kick in, and a wave of fierce protectiveness hits me.

"Your first grandbaby, Brad, and our first great-grandbaby, how exciting!" Nana enthuses. How fucking amazing is this family? Ready to pivot in an instant and embrace bumps in the road like they were meant to be.

"When is she due? Were they able to determine the sex of the baby?" I ask Forrest as I push the others out of the way and sit down next to Kai, taking his hand in mine.

"Yes, they were able to determine Veronica's actually about twenty weeks along."

"Twenty weeks? But she barely had a baby bump." Oliver scowls, speaking up for the first time. "Was she not looking after it properly?"

"She was a little underweight, and she admitted to the doctors that she'd been under-eating. Told them some craziness about how she needed to look her best to make sure she could hook one or the both of you," he says, his eyes drifting between

Thomas and Kai. Forrest doesn't hide the scorn in his voice, and I'm right there with him.

"And the sex?" Kai's voice is still shaky, but I see him steel his shoulders.

"It's a girl." And that, my friends, is how you make six grown adult men melt into puddles of goo.

"Fuck me, that little girl is going to get spoiled rotten," Hope groans as the guys start talking about building her a castle playhouse and buying her a pony.

The room is filled with excitement once more, but Forrest calms some of that when he holds his hands up.

"Unfortunately, there's more. The prison is concerned about Veronica's mental state. They're worried she might do something to the baby. Their psychologist has recommended that she be allowed to think that you want her to be part of the baby's life—just for now, as a precautionary measure for the baby's health and well-being. She still thinks she's going to walk away without a prison sentence and get to live happily ever after together. She's also in denial that the baby is Kai's, and her insistence on referring to it as Thomas Jr. is implying some kind of issue with the gender as well. Really, letting her keep those fantasies will likely be very easy considering the doctors think it would be better if you all stayed away for now. We're just going to have to play things by ear, but if we want this baby to be born healthy and happy, you need to be prepared to play pretend. Thomas, if she asks for you, we may need you to go in and see her. Is that alright with you?"

He makes a face before saying, "To keep our baby safe? Of course."

Aww, *our* baby. We really are going to have to sit down and work out the parenting dynamics of this, but it can wait for now. And really, in the grand scheme of things, will it hurt the girl to have more than one protective daddy looking out for her best interests?

"Come on. Let's go downstairs and celebrate all the wonderful things that have happened today." Dad claps Forrest on the shoulder. "Thank you so much for everything you do for us." He pulls an envelope out of his inner pocket and hands it to him. "That contains ten nights all-inclusive at a five-star resort in Cancun. We really should look at expanding down there, but for now you can enjoy a stay at one of our competitors on us."

Forrrest thanks us all as he takes the envelope, and everyone starts to head downstairs until it's just Kai and me left.

"Are you sure you're okay?" I ask him.

"Yup, now that I know, I promise this little girl I'll be as good a dad to her as mine was to me. I just can't let her have anything to do with Veronica. I can already see my past repeating itself, and it frightens me."

"Don't worry, that woman is going nowhere.

She'll be someone's bitch for the rest of her life. Come on, I want to dance with the daddy-to-be. Oh, we're going to have to think of names now."

"That's going to be fun in this family," he says wryly, getting up and holding his hand out for me. I take it, and he tucks it under his arm, the two of us following after everyone. "I can't imagine what Oliver is going to come up with. He wanted Coco to be named Little Lord Fauntleroy." We're both smiling and laughing when we make it to the elevator, and I just hope the rest of the evening stays that way.

Someone jostles me from behind, causing my champagne to slosh over the side of my glass and onto my hand. Swearing, I grab a napkin off the tray of a nearby waiter and wipe it away.

The gala is a loud and jovial affair, and Nana has introduced me to what feels like a billion people, all of whom are trying their hardest to get Grace Summers' attention. There have been a few that have felt genuine but not many. Everyone wants to pitch their cause or charity in the hope that the money raised from tonight will go to them.

I've caught glimpses of Max, but every time I try to head in her direction, she disappears or I get stopped by someone else. Just now I can see her through the crowd, talking to Jacinta, and I'm determined to make it to them this time.

"Harlow dear, there you are. I have someone I'd like you to meet. This is Rose Smith, the director of the MacGinty Sanctuary." I grind my teeth in annoyance, spinning around to tell Nana no, but I quickly smooth out my expression when I see who it is.

"Oh, Nana, didn't she tell you we've met before? Haven't we, Ms. Smith? Except at the time she was basically calling me a whore and told me there was no place for me in their program."

Nana tucks her hand under my arm as the woman with her pales. "Is that right, dear? Well, I guess it's a good thing that we're not going to be able to provide the MacGinty Sanctuary with funds this year. We wouldn't want to be associated with a company that makes assumptions based on trash they see in gossip articles, would we?"

The woman scowls, her previously pleasant face turning ugly. "I wasn't wrong! What a slut. Look at you, sleeping with all six of the Summers men at the same time."

Crack. The slap Nana delivers to the woman's face sounds out through the ballroom, causing people to turn and look. "No, you self-righteous bitch, that's not slutty. That's lucky."

The woman holds her cheek and tries to storm away, but she finds herself surrounded by security.

"Please show Ms. Smith out, and, Howard,

scratch her name permanently off the invite list," Nana tells Poppy. Poor man rushed over as soon as he saw his wife starting to go in for the kill, but he wasn't quick enough.

"With pleasure," he grunts as she's thrown out, struggling and screaming ugly profanities in my direction. "I'll also make a call to the head of their board. I think we might make an offer to buy them out. Harlow can have all the animals for her sanctuary, and we can bulldoze their premises and use it for something else."

"I'm pretty sure that's called a hostile takeover, Poppy." Oliver grins and raises his glass in Poppy's direction. The man just hmphs, but there's a small smirk on his lips as he straightens his jacket and holds out his arm to a handsome older black man behind him.

"On a happier note, look who I found, dear." Nana's eyes just about bug out of her head with the man's approach. She loses her haughty sneer, and her eyes fill with tears as he takes her hands.

"Grace, you are looking as beautiful as the day I first met you." He leans in and kisses her cheek. As he pulls away, her hand moves to the spot he just kissed, and Oliver and I exchange a look of surprise.

"Benjamin, it's been so long. You're looking well." They don't drop hands, and I look to Poppy for any sign of jealousy, but he's beaming like he just won the major prize.

"Come on, dear. It's time for our yearly speech." Poppy's got a no-nonsense set to his lips despite the amused twinkle in his eyes. "We have plenty of time to catch up later. Ben is staying at the hotel for a couple of nights. I promise we won't let him escape this time." He winks in Ben's direction, and the man startles as he drops Nana's hands.

"I look forward to it very much."

"Ben, these are Harlow and Oliver, my grand-children. They'll keep you company while we do the official stuff, then we'll grab a drink and have the talk we should have had so many years ago," Poppy promises, slapping him on the shoulder. Ben nods, still looking slightly confused even as my grandparents walk toward the stage.

"Poor bastard doesn't know what's going to hit him." Oliver chuckles quietly in my ear, and I can't help but agree.

Chapter Twenty-Six

Harlow

The crowd quiets at the appearance of Nana, Poppy, and Dad on stage at the front of the grand room. The rest of the family gathers around, as do Chuck and Melinda, the latter having firmly taken Emma and Molly as her new BFFs. She's dragging them along, one in each hand, as Chuck follows. He looks nothing but amused by his wife, which means there's no hope of help in sight for the other ladies.

"Wow, Grace really gave it to that woman," she whispers furiously as we wait to hear what they have to say. I shush her with a look, and she mimes zipping her lips as Emma and Molly giggle next to her. The three women have been drinking champagne all night and are all a little tipsy. Dad and Chuck have their hands full.

"Did you talk to Max?" I ask Jacinta out of the side of my mouth, and she frowns.

"Briefly, but then she made some excuse about needing to use the restroom and disappeared. She doesn't look so great, Harlow. I think she might be sick."

My stomach lurches, goosebumps erupting over my skin at the thought of my best friend being unwell. I search through the crowd for her and still can't see her.

The squeal of the microphone draws my attention back to the stage, and Dad clears his throat. I thought it would be Poppy delivering the speech, but it looks like he and Nana are up there to support Dad.

"Welcome, everyone, to our yearly Neighpalm charity gala. Once again, it is our honor to host all of you here. It has been an exciting year for Neighpalm Industries, which I'll get into shortly, but it has also been an exciting year for our family personally. I found out I have a biological daughter, and she came out to get to know us all. It's been an eventful time, but everything is going beautifully. I also adopted another child, a daughter, so I now have three daughters and six sons." He tips his head in our direction, and the crowd applauds wildly, cheering and celebrating for him.

"My daughter Harlow is also taking on a new venture. She's a vet, and she's going to be founding and running Neighpalm Sanctuary, a not-for-profit organization dedicated to the rescue of exotic animals mixed up in the pet trade. There will be an educational branch of the operation, where we plan on offering excursions for schools to help teach why big cats and other exotic creatures don't make good pets. On the screen behind me, you'll see some of the animals that Harlow has already rescued. Each one is currently being cared for by the sanctuary staff."

My mouth drops open in shock as the crowd bursts into applause. Behind Dad, footage of Nyx and the cubs plays out, and in the corner is the new Neighpalm Sanctuary logo that marketing came up with for me. It's gorgeous, keeping the traditional horsehead and palm trees, but this one has zoo animals in the middle. There's a tiger, elephant, hippo, snake, monkey, and some dolphins. It's perfect. Beneath the applause, a few sneaky whispers creep in. Doesn't seem like everyone is universally happy for me.

"Nothing like a bit of nepotism to get funding for a pet project."

The two women startle like deer in headlights as the full force of the Summers family turns their attention on them, but before any of us can say anything, Molly steps up.

"So what charity are you from that missed out on funding this year?" she asks, and the women straighten their backs.

"The Daughters of the Confederacy," she answers quickly.

"What the fuck do they do?" Melinda whispers none too quietly to Emma, and I smother my smile.

"Did you hear that, Declan? Another one to scratch off Howard's list," Molly announces regally as she turns back around and takes a sip of champagne.

"I'm fairly certain we've never given money to that cause. I'm not even sure how they got an invite." With a frown, Declan takes out his phone and makes a note while the women shrink inward and hurry away.

"Boom!" Melinda cheers, her champagne sloshing everywhere when she tries to throw in an arm flail to go with the sound effect.

I snort in a totally undignified manner, and before long, we're laughing uncontrollably until Dad shoots us a dirty look.

"As for the Neighpalm Industries Conglomerate, I am happy to make a few announcements. Not only will Neighpalm Sanctuary be joining our line this year, but we are also unveiling three other new ventures. For the first time ever, we have partnered with someone outside of our family. We are quite thrilled to be backing them and look forward to many happy years working together to build their business. I give you Neighpalm Construction!"

The image of Nyx and the cubs disappears, and

the display lights up with a new logo. This time, tools take up the center spot to make it unique from the other branding. The crowd applauds even more wildly than before, with plenty of whoops ringing out. I think the champagne is finally helping everyone drop their reserved inhibitions from the start of the night.

"Next, I'd like to announce that we've bought a hockey team. The Colorado Grizzlies will become Neighpalm Shockwave, and we are excited to support the guys and their leadership in the next hockey season." The construction logo is struck by a bolt of lightning that becomes embedded in the team's name, with the silhouette of a hockey player brandishing his hockey stick layered behind the words.

"I can't wait to go to all of the home games. The flight is only two and half hours, and when you have a private plane, why not?! Kai said he would fly us whenever we want to go." I'm jumping up and down, my contagious excitement drawing Hope in, but Jacinta looks like we just asked her to eat dirt.

"Why would we want to go to hockey games?"

The logo melts away to show footage of the Colorado Grizzlies in training, and that skepticism gives way to appreciation.

"Okay, never mind, I see it now. Woo, go team!" she shouts, and Melinda, Emma, and Molly holler and cheer behind her.

"God help me," Chuck mutters.

"At least she'll sleep well tonight," Oliver says, but the attempted consolation only makes Chuck shudder.

"The only time Melinda snores is when she's been drinking, and she makes a grizzly bear sound delicate."

The guys wince, sharing a look of sympathy with him, and Thomas hands him a glass of whiskey.

"If you can't beat 'em, join 'em," he suggests, and Chuck grabs hold of it like a lifeline.

"Keep them coming. Thank goodness we only have to go upstairs tonight."

"Lastly, I'd like to announce a subsidiary to the Neighpalm Resorts and Clubs branch. I give you Neighpalm Cruise Lines." The final logo shines bright and clear on the screen, showcasing a cruise ship atop the waves, with a bright sun behind it.

"When will all these launch, Brad?" someone shouts from the audience.

"Neighpalm Construction is already working on projects, and the Grizzlies are transitioning to the new brand as we speak. The cruise ships may take a little longer as we need to assess them for upgrades, but I assure you there will be an inaugural cruise. Anyone on tonight's donor list will be invited to attend as a thank you for supporting all the wonderful charities we've connected with over the years."

"Sneaky," Jaxon comments, sounding impressed.

"Yup, Dad pretty much guaranteed that we make more money tonight than we've ever made," Holden cuts in.

"What do you mean?" I ask, and Declan chuckles.

"Rich people are funny. Even though each and every one of them could afford to pay for any number of cruises, they like free shit as much as the next person."

"They're technically buying their ticket by donating, but they don't see it that way," Oliver finishes up, and I watch with wide eyes as many of them move toward the donation tables set up on the side of the ballroom.

"Basically, rich people are stupid," Hope says, tucking her arm under mine. "Thank god I'm never going to have to worry about that," she muses, and Jacinta and the guys laugh.

"What's so funny?" she asks, slightly confused, and the punchline suddenly occurs to me.

"Aww, babe, It takes some getting used to, but you'll need to remember that by being adopted into this family, you just became stinking rich."

She shakes her head, denying it, and before we can argue anything else, Dad, Nana, and Poppy make their way back to us. Poppy introduces everyone to Benjamin, his best friend from college, and we all make nice, only partially thanks to

Nana's glare of steel. We make casual conversation before the three of them depart to a quiet corner of the room to catch up.

"How freaking cute was that?" Hope gushes, and Dad rolls his eyes.

"I really don't want to think about it too hard. Anyway, I forgot I had this earlier." He pulls a bank card out of his pocket and hands it to Hope. "There you go, access to the family bank accounts. I've also made sure you've been added to our accounts just like I did for Harlow. Now, this is up to you, but I would be honored if you would call me Dad. Only when you're ready, of course." He adds the last part in a rush, probably realizing he might need to hit Hope with a little less than 200% of full Summers love at once.

His cheeks become pink as she gapes at him. It seems Molly and Emma have really been a good influence on him. Sure, he's still a little socially awkward, but there's some confidence that wasn't there before.

The silence is a little heavy as we wait for her response, but I can see her scanning the rest of the siblings to check for any negative reactions. When she gets none, she throws her arms around his neck, her body shaking with emotion. Dad's arms engulf her in a hug as we turn away and allow them to have a private moment.

After a minute, Dad clears his throat and pulls back. "Now, I haven't got anyone to run the cruise lines yet, and as my newest child, I thought I would give you the first option."

"Isn't it Jaxon's?" she sputters.

Jaxon shrugs. "Meh, I don't have time to run that as well. We had always intended to hire someone to do it."

Hope looks to Holden, and I can see a multitude of things being said through their eye contact.

"Thank you, but no. I am really happy where I am and have no desire to spend most of my life on cruise ships, which is what I'm assuming that job will entail."

Dad smiles. "We assumed that's what you would say, given you and Holden are a dynamic team, but I had to offer." He claps his hands together. "So I guess we're looking for someone to run both Couture and Cruise Lines."

"Did you know that both Molly and Emma majored in business? Molly actually has a minor in fashion. They'd be a good option if you're still going the student route. They could mentor whoever you choose until they were ready to take over. That way, you can still help kickstart someone's career, but you'd also be putting a little less on Grace's plate. If things kick off with her gentleman friend, she might appreciate some of the extra free time." Melinda drops a verbal bomb as she pushes her way into our circle, and I see the two other women try to shush her. Dad looks at the two women who've suddenly sobered up, at least a little anyway, something like hurt flashing in his eyes.

"Why didn't you tell me?" he asks quietly, and they push us out of the way to get to him.

"Oh, honey bear, we didn't want you to think that's why we're with you," Emma coos, stroking his chest as Molly fusses with his tie.

"Peachy bum, I'm happy with my job at the boutique, so I'm perfectly content where I am. It's only recently that we've had to think about Emma's future. Until we found out about the count's legacy, she'd been fully committed to her caretaker duties. This is a new change in our lives."

"Nonsense." Nana steps out from behind Dad, scaring us all. Where did she come from? "It's the perfect solution. Sorry, I was heading for the bath-room, and I overheard what you were saying. I'll leave you be now that I've added my two cents. I have an old friend to re-friend." She waggles her eyes, and the boys' groans nearly drown out the women's giggles.

"Agreed," Jacinta says firmly, beyond settled and, simply put, happier than I've seen her in a long time. "So we'll still advertise at some schools and make it an internship. We could even turn this into a yearly thing. In fact, maybe we could trial this sort of program through Couture and then develop it into an internship experience in each branch of Neighpalm Industries. A pay it forward kind of thing. Not to mention good networking for us in case there are some rising stars out there who simply need a chance to shine."

"Holy shit! Who are you, and what have you done to my sister?" Jaxon's mostly teasing, but there's enough skepticism in there for her to flip him off immediately.

"My therapist has helped me see how wrong I was in the way I treated Harlow and how neither she nor Molly and Emma are to blame for what has happened to us over the years. Your happiness just makes me want to see everyone happy, and I can see how happy Molly and Emma make Dad, so it is the perfect solution."

The two women are fussing with Dad, not paying any attention to the surrounding conversation. Tucked into Chuck's side, Melinda looks awfully pleased with herself.

"I'm going to leave you to it. I have another sister to track down, one who has done her very best to avoid me all evening," I announce to my family, giving each of my men a kiss.

"We'll come with you." Jacinta grabs Hope's arm in the kind of death grip that only she can make look like sisterly affection. "I want Max to meet Hope! They haven't been introduced yet. We are *so* going to be the awesome foursome. LA isn't going to know what hit it."

It's a real pleasure to see Jacinta so happy, and that, more than anything, is proof that her therapy is making a difference. With the way her feelings are written across her face, it's impossible to ignore how brightly she's shining now that she has a unified family around her.

As we make our way through the crowded ballroom, I flinch when I hear *slut* coughs a couple of times, but I hold my head high. They can think what they want. I'm the one getting all the good dick, not them, so they can suck it.

"Now, what in the world has put such a fearsome look on your gorgeous face?" Alex intercepts us, his attention fully on Jacinta even though he greets both me and Hope with a kiss.

We exchange grins as Shane and Jace also appear. All three of them look delicious and are the perfect diversion. Jacinta's fury flows away as she melts under their attention, and we easily leave her behind.

"My sisters are dropping like flies. You and Max will be next." And, like the universe somehow heard me, there she is! She's with Cayden Storm, Jarred Reed, and Sean Walsh, the lead actors and director we'd met when Declan and I dropped off the Bostons' horses.

I wave to try to get her attention, but she seems to be in a heated discussion, so wrapped up in them that she doesn't see me. More women approach the three men, cozying up to them, and Max promptly storms off in the other direction.

"Fuck. I'm not letting her get away this time. Come on!" I tell Hope.

"Hey, will you introduce me to those delicious men?" She nods in the direction of the stars.

"Sure can, but do you really want to meet them, or are you just avoiding a certain someone?"

I've caught sight of Parker McCallister watching her all night. He and his brothers haven't really approached, I don't think they're completely comfortable with our family yet, but that will change. Nana won't allow them to be outsiders, and I've asked my guys to make an effort too. We've just all been so busy trying to catch up on everything that happened while we were away.

"I don't know what you're talking about," she mutters, not looking at me.

"Come on. Holden told me what happened, and I see the way he looks at you. Even if nothing comes of it, you should let him apologize. Don't leave it and end up regretting it."

"I'll think about it," she hedges, not willing to give in, but I *will* wear her down.

I search the crowd for my wayward sister, and my eyebrows jump in surprise when I find her in a quiet conversation with Thomas. How did she manage that? I guess our dash across the ballroom with Jacinta must have taken longer than I thought.

"Come on." I grab Hope's hand and drag her, pushing people out of the way. I'm not losing Max again.

Chapter Twenty-Seven

Harlow

"There you are," I call as we approach the two. "Gosh, I've been trying to catch up with you all night."

Thomas and Max's conversation abruptly breaks off, leaving behind awkward silence as I really look at my sister.

She's pale and thin, and her dress is hanging off her body. Her hair is limp, and eyes are missing the sparkle that they usually have. She shudders as I wrap my arms around her.

"I've missed you, my sister," I whisper as her thin arms hold on like I'm a life preserver and she's floating in the open ocean. I pull back and look her in the eye. "What's going on? What's wrong?" I'm practically begging her to tell me, but she shakes her head in refusal. Her emotions are written across her face, and I'm not liking what I see. It's surprising, to say the least. On the East Coast, amongst her friends, a show of emotions is a sign of weakness and a sure way to find yourself targeted for their amusement. You keep that shit locked down, so the fact that Max is willing to look 'weak' in this setting says a lot.

"Not here. Can we meet on Monday for lunch? I'll tell you everything then," she pleads.

"Are you not flying back to the set with the others?"

"No, I've finished all the stunts and the scene I was required for. Dad is going up to get the horses, and Josh is giving him a hand until he can hire someone to replace Luke and Peter," she tells me. Gone is the thrilled girl who had a speaking part in the movie. She's been replaced with this shell of a woman.

"Do your mom and dad know what's wrong?" I didn't think it would be possible, but her mood sinks even lower.

"No, I've been avoiding them, but I know that's coming to an end too. I'll invite them to lunch as well so I can tell you all at once."

My stomach lurches at the thought of what she could possibly have to tell me, but her eyes beg me not to press any more tonight, so I give her that. "Jaxon, Jacinta, and I are leaving after the ball for a three-day cruise out to sea and back. It's to get a feel for the new business. But you know what, I'll let them go without me. It's not like I can offer them any help. I'm just going for the free booze and to get away from all the stress."

I see the guilt in her eyes at the mention of my problems, but it's fleeting. "No, go, have fun. I'll still be here when you get back. I'll spend a few days with Mom and Dad, and we'll do lunch on Wednesday." She waves her hand around like it's no problem.

"Are you sure?" Torn between my best friend and my new family, there's a part of me that knows I shouldn't believe her. Even though it's selfish of me, the other part of me wants to just accept what she's saying so I don't have to miss out on this opportunity. It's not about the luxury of the experience; it's about the time with two people who have become increasingly dear to me.

"Absolutely," she quickly agrees, looking and sounding somewhat relieved.

"Okay." I put a bright smile on my face. I don't know what will really make a difference at the moment, but if we're ignoring the elephant in the room, I guess we have to move forward. "Have you met Hope yet? She just became a Summers too."

Max puts on a smile that absolutely doesn't fool me, then she greets Hope, welcoming her to the family. I look at Thomas, but the set of his lips as he shakes his head ever so slightly gives me my answer. She spoke to him in confidence, and even if I pushed, he's not going to break her trust. I can't say that I like it in this particular circumstance, but I have to respect his sense of honor.

Through a gap in the crowd, I see the guys from Ninja Starfish. I give them a wave, and the four of them raise their glasses to me. They look much happier than the last time I saw them. I guess getting rid of dead weight does make you feel lighter.

While Hope and Max chat, I take inventory of the crowd. Kai is talking to the Blaze brothers and his friends from Hawaii. Not far from them are Holden and Oli, the latter shifting his dress pants with a grimace. He's obviously bitching to Holden about his new tattoo, but I have no sympathy. If the silly man is going to make bets with me, he should make sure he's going to win. The chocolate milk-shake cowboy tattoo looks mighty pretty opposite his penguin one.

When I find Declan, he's in conversation with the very men that Max stormed away from. I'm not sure what it was about, but my loyalty is to her, so I think I'll just stay away from all of that for now.

I try to tune back into the conversation that Hope and Max are having, but a hand on my back and a familiar scent have me melting into Jaxon's embrace.

"May I have this dance?" he asks me as I whirl with surprise. "This is a ball, Harlow. There *is* dancing even though Nana has been determined to introduce you to every man and his dog tonight."

"I'd love to." He takes my hand and leads me onto the dance floor, twirling me under his arm before drawing me into his embrace. A breathless laugh leaves my mouth as my chest presses against his.

"Are you having a nice time?" he asks as he gracefully moves me around the dance floor. This is very different to the first time we danced together but no less seductive.

"I really am, though I'm worried about Max. I'm having lunch with her on Wednesday when we get back from the cruise. You said we should be back mid-morning?"

"Yes, it's just one of those cruises that goes out to sea and floats around for a while. It's not really meant to explore, more for some quick fun. It allows the passengers to drink, gamble, and shop duty-free before returning to port. I'd really like it if you and Jacinta tested the facilities like the beauty salons, the spa, and the shopping, and we'll try to dine in as many of the options as possible. This line isn't as big as some of them, so I'm wondering if there's a niche market we could find. If we find a group that needs an outlet, we could really personalize our venture to meet those needs."

"Well, you know what would work?" I waggle my eyebrows at him. "Why don't you make one an adults-only sex boat, much like the hotel in Hawaii. Sexify the rooms, add a bondage club, and instead of musical acts, have strippers, burlesque acts, and sex shows. You could also offer classes. Oral sex classes, shibari, pole dancing, that sort of thing." The words tumble out of my mouth, and Jaxon stops dead in the middle of all the dancers.

"Holy shit, yes, that's brilliant! We can have a couple of normal ships to aim at the families, but a few of the ships could be themed." We start to dance again as I watch his brilliant mind at work. "We could do a craft and hobby ship where we can have demonstrations and classes on things ranging from woodworking to glass blowing to lace making and shit. What about a music-themed ship? We could hire bands to perform and teach dance classes and musical instruments. Have specialized areas for jam sessions and singing classes. Harlow, you are brilliant." He twirls me out and deposits me in Thomas' arms.

"I need to go tell Dad your idea." Jaxon looks at the expensive watch on his wrist. "We need to leave in half an hour, so you might want to grab Jacinta. I'm sure you ladies will want to change out of your dresses and grab your bags." After a peck on the lips, he runs off with the energy of an excited puppy.

"He certainly looked happy about something." Thomas holds me close, the two of us swaying back and forth as I rest my head against his chest.

"Yeah, just an idea for the new cruise line," I mumble.

"Are you tired, baby?" He dances us over to the edge of the dance floor.

"Yeah, and my feet are killing me. Jaxon said that we're boarding the boat tonight so he can watch the boarding procedure in the morning. Do you want to sleep with me tonight? I think he'll be too amped up to go to bed. I'm sure he'll be doing stuff until the early hours of the morning."

It was pretty much a given that Thomas would be coming with us. After Hawaii, nobody was going to take a chance of leaving him behind. They aren't going to be complacent even though the other stalker hasn't acted again. It would be stupid to drop our guards and give the perfect opportunity for them to strike.

"I'd love to sleep with you, but I'm staying here until the end of the ball. I'll board in the morning with everyone else. You guys should be safe because no one but you and the crew will be on the ship overnight. I have a security team patrolling the ship just in case. Like you said, you'll be tucked up in bed, and I'll make sure that if Jaxon won't be with you, Jacinta will be."

"Okay, that sounds fair." He puts a little distance between us and tucks my hand under his arm so that we stay connected. "Let's find my wayward sister and get you ladies upstairs so you can get changed."

We make our rounds of the ballroom, saying goodbye to the rest of my family and the other guys. Each of them give me long, lingering kisses that raise a lot of eyebrows, but all in all, the reception hasn't been too hostile. I guess being rich has its perks; nobody wants to piss you off, so they mostly keep their opinions and their judgy looks behind closed doors.

Finally, the elevator doors open to our floor, and we leave Jacinta at her room as Thomas escorts me to mine. I'm getting better at this whole letting them look after me thing, so I wait patiently as he checks the room, not trying to enter until he gives me permission.

"Why don't you have a quick shower? That way, all you have to do is fall into bed when you get to the boat. I'll be back in half an hour to walk you down to the car."

"Are you sure you don't want to join me in the shower?" I ask, grabbing him by his jacket and tugging him close so I can take his lips with mine. Our kiss is slow and passionate, and he groans as he steps back from me.

"Harlow, you are so fucking tempting," he whispers between us. "I would like nothing more than to strip that gorgeous dress off your gorgeous body and have you on your knees, your plump lips wrapped around my thick cock." It's my turn to groan as my nipples pebble and my pussy aches from his dirty talk. "But I want to check over the car that's driving you to the port. I want to look for devices and check the brakes for leaks. Just in case."

I drop my hands and step back, knowing he needs to do this. "Okay, I'll see you soon then. But tomorrow night, I'm going to make all those words you just spoke come true." He adjusts his dick, then leaves, muttering about me driving him mad.

There's a smile on my lips as I pull all the pins from my hair, dropping them on a table before reaching behind me to unzip my dress so that it pools at my feet. Kicking off my shoes, I sigh in pure pleasure as I finally get relief from the torture heels Jacinta demanded I wear.

"Damn woman, still torturing me." Though I must admit that I prefer pain through fashion rather than public humiliation. A few semi-numb steps later, I'm enjoying the first-class shower.

"Oh, that's so good." I tilt my head back, allowing the water to flow over my hair and the rest of my body.

I don't know how long I stand there, but I just need a moment to decompress. I have so many things to think about as far as running the sanctuary goes. I think I need to hire one or two more staff members. Me, Clem, and Doug are not going to be enough to run the place. Not if we fill it to capacity. I hadn't realized how big it was until we walked it the other day. I had only touched the tip of the iceberg in my exploration. Beyond the whale pool, there were even more enclosures. At this stage we're only aiming for rescue animals, but we certainly have enough space to take on others if there are zoo closures or sanctuary closures anywhere else in the US.

I did decide that I wanted to have a public entrance to the zoo, so we're drawing up plans for another access road in and out. I'm pretty sure we're going to build a wall to separate our living space from the zoo. While the water beats down on my body, I get lost in thoughts of what else the zoo needs until I finally realize I'm running out of time.

As fast as I can, I finish up, dry off, and get dressed in a comfy pair of yoga pants and an equally soft top. I dry and braid my wet hair and pick the ball gown up off the ground, placing it on the bed. As an unexpected benefit, Nana said she would take home whatever we left behind.

Scooping the hair pins into my travel bag, I grab my trusty backpack and laptop just as there's a knock. Thomas is making a face at me through the peephole, so I open the door with a smile.

"Here, let me take that." He grabs the bag out of my hand, leaving me with only my backpack, and I pull the door closed behind me. Jacinta is collected next, acting as tired as I feel.

"Why didn't you just call one of the bell hops?" she grumps as we wait for the elevator.

"Sorry, I wanted to say goodbye to my girlfriend and sister," he grumbles back, and they stare each other down. Yeah, those Summers dramatics aren't limited to just Oli.

"Did you check the car?" I ask as we climb onto the elevator, trying to distract the two of them.

"Yup, had a good look underneath. Right now, everything appears to be fine. Go straight to your rooms when you board. No walking around tonight. It's not like you can see anything anyway. I've told Jax the same thing, so don't start arguing with me about being able to handle yourselves. It's got nothing to do with that."

When we get to the lobby, Jax is waiting, tux still on and bag in hand. "Great, let's get moving."

He leads the way out to the car, and the driver gets out. His cap is tucked low so I can't see his face, but he mutters a good evening to us as he loads the luggage in the back of the vehicle. The three of us climb into the back seat, but I linger with the door open, not wanting Tom out of my sight just yet.

"Be safe. I'll see you in the morning," Tom instructs before leaning in to kiss me.

"Get out of here. You'll be reunited soon enough!" Jacinta gives him a teasing shove to make him step back, and there's no small amount of amusement on her face as she closes the door. When Thomas taps on the roof of the car, the driver slowly pulls out from the parking lot.

The three of us are quiet and subdued on the ride, all of us lost in our thoughts and probably too damn tired to attempt conversation.

"Hey, this isn't the way to the port," Jacinta says,

her nose pressed to the window. "Where are we going?"

Jaxon knocks on the privacy screen that separates us from the driver. "Hey, excuse me, you're going the wrong way."

Suddenly, the locks on the doors snap down, and smoke starts to pour into the area where we're seated.

"What the fuck? Is the car on fire?" Jacinta's screams are the last thing I can clearly make out before I feel light headed and my eyes start to droop. Jaxon and Jacinta both stop fighting and slump down too. I'm struggling to hold my eyes open as the partition drops, giving me a glimpse of the driver in the rearview mirror. Eyes that are all too familiar look back at me.

"You!" I gasp, then all I see is blackness.

The end... almost

I know, I know. Another freaking cliffhanger. But we're almost there.

Thank you for reading!
I hope you enjoyed the book. It would be super awesome if you could leave a review wherever you bought it, because I love to hear what you thought of the story.

Want more of Harlow and the gang?
The last book of Harlow's story arc is now available for pre order and coming in April 2022
Loved Girl

Want to keep up to date with new books coming soon? Sign up to my newsletter here
Newsletter

Another way to do that is to join me Facebook group. I drop teasers and giveaways in there all the time. Here's the link
Lexie's Ladygarden

Visit my webpage and check out reading orders and what else I've written.
www.lexiewinston.com

Acknowledgments

Thank you to all the normal crew this book wouldn't be possible without you all.

Thank you…..

Michelle for your invaluable editing.

Emma for all the late night and early morning chats.

Breakout Designs for the cover.

Kerry and Jillian you keep the words flowing with your commentary and support.

My beta team for being super awesome as usual.

Leslie Arnett, for your professional veterinarian knowledge. I'd be lost without you.

To Kristine Baker, Diane Marthaler Taylor, Kylie Greenwood and Estelle Bullock for your contributions to the story in the form of dresses and animal names

Lastly to you the readers. Gosh I hope you like this one. I wanted to show life with the Summers and more relationship development between Harlow and the guys and I think I managed to achieve it. It's possibly not as fast paced as the others but I promise you the next one will more than make up for it.

I can't believe we're almost at the end of this ride. Thank you for sticking with me and I hope you enjoy Cherished Girl.

Thank you to everyone who reviews and recommends it and thank you to all of you who take the chance and preorder the next one as soon as you've finished the last. You guys are the reason I can keep writing this story.

Until next time. Happy Reading

Xoxo

Lexie

Check out something else by me. Dark Poly Romance with both MM and FF and was as many possible triggers. Make sure you read the trigger warning at the front.

Secrets Kept
Broken Promises Series

I wasn't always like this you know. I used to be one of those girls who was bubbly and people thought sunshine came out of my ass. That is until my best friend kissed me and then betrayed me with those same lips. I became ridiculed and bullied and my soul slowly died inside until I was a shadow of my former self.

But then my father introduced me and my brother to our family legacy and I became glad of the fractured, broken soul I'd become. In fact, I reveled in it. We trust no one but each other, blood is always thicker than water. Heaven help those that betray us. Because we aren't afraid to get our hands dirty.

This book is a mafia dark poly romance. There will be MM and FF and various combinations. It will contain sexual situations that may make you feel uncomfortable. There will be drugs references and violence. Please read the content at the beginning for a more concise list of possible triggers. You have been warned

Get it now

A paranormal reverse harem series with angels and demons. Now complete, you can get all three books as well as the bonus scenes in one place.
Collectors Division Omnibus

Prologue

Quiet, gentle snores drag me out of the darkness of sleep. Rolling over, I study the naked body of the man lying beside me. The long sleek lines and muscular backside of a golden Adonis who had done so many delicious things to me last night. He was a perfect distraction from the nervous energy filling my body in anticipation of the coming day, and found creative ways to use it. So much so that I was able to rest peacefully for a few hours.

But that was then, and this is now, and the incessant sexual need, awakened not long after the loss of my virginity, is building in my body again. A never-ending line of no-strings-attached fuck buddies, male or female—I'm not fussy—has been able to keep the need at bay, but not for long periods of time. And although my body's needs can be temporarily appeased, my heart and soul ache for more. Aches for love and acceptance. To be needed and wanted.

Something I thought I'd found once. A group of boys I had formed a big attachment with. Boys who had promised to wait. Boys who had broken that promise and callously stomped all over it. Boys who had caused my heart to harden.

Boys I would never have been able to choose between anyway.

A nagging, buzzing sound drags me from my thoughts. Pulling my naked body out of bed, I hunt for my communicator. Searching through our clothes, which we had dumped haphazardly in our pursuit of pleasure, I find it under my undies, now torn to shreds and useless. I throw them at a bin in the corner of the room before checking the messages on my screen. Across the screen scrolls a message from my roommate and best friend Olivia.

Mina, where the fuck are you

Mina, we've got The Gauntlet run in two hours. Get your ass home and ready.

Shit. My heart thumps hard in shock. I never expected to fall asleep and certainly not long enough that I would need to be reminded about today's challenge. Rushing quietly around the room, I throw on my clothes. Luckily, the man in the bed is also a student at the Academy and has an apartment in the same building as me, though he's a year behind and not participating today. I leave him sleeping peacefully as I make my way quickly back to my apartment. Bursting through the door, my roommates' surprised looks greet me as I rush in.

"Thanks, Livie, I just need a quick shower," I tell them both as I run past them, noticing James' sly grin.

He shouts after me, "Washing off the sex smell are you, Mina?" I throw up a one-finger salute as I duck into the bathroom and hear an oomph. Livie must've smacked him for the comment.

They both know about my problem. I've talked to them about it in the past. It's not like I could hide the amount of sex I have from my roommates, and, well, I didn't want them to think I had become careless with my body. They both suggested I speak to the Academy doctors about it, but I just wasn't comfortable sharing it. What if there was something wrong with me?

Shrugging all that off, I shower quickly and pull on my Academy uniform, focusing on the task today. The most critical challenge of the last four years. Today is the day I finally achieve my dream.

Get it here

Lila is nobody special.

She didn't have a bad childhood despite growing up in foster homes, but there was just nothing particularly good about it either. With a boring job and only one close friend, you could say Lila is a little lost in her life.

Not to mention, her romantic life is basically nonexistent. In fact, her alien erotica and her BOB are the most actions she's seen in ages. Until now...

After she receives a surprise inheritance, Lila's life becomes out of this world. With the entire galaxy and a group of sexy alien men at the tips of her fingers, she's in for the ride of her life.

Apprentice is the first Galaxy Circus novel, a fast-burn RH series that contains some

adults situations which may be triggering, such as dub-con.

Get it here Apprentice

Keep reading for the first chapter of Apprentice

"Miss Jenson, did you hear what I just said to you?" Mr. Ryding, the weaselly-looking lawyer, says to me from behind the large walnut desk. He's fidgeting with the papers in front of him, stacking them, picking them up, tapping them, and then placing them back on the desk in front of himself. While I sit there, waiting for him to say more, he straightens the pens in the holder to the right of him. Given he's done this all at least half a dozen times, it seems like he's doing everything in his power to avoid making eye contact with my very confused self.

"I'm sorry. I'm not sure I understand you. I received a letter from your office saying I have been bequeathed something. I was told that I must present myself in person to sign some papers in order to receive it. Now, you are *also* telling me it was from a grandfather I didn't even know existed, one who obviously didn't want me, as I spent the first eighteen years of my life in foster homes."

He looks up, briefly pausing his fidgeting. "Yes, that's correct. Though it's grandfathers. Plural."

Plural? I puzzle internally. *Never mind, I'll come back to that.*

"John, William, and Eric Adams are your paternal grandfathers, and it wasn't that they didn't want you." His shifty eyes soften briefly before he continues. "They weren't able to find you. Your parents were estranged from them, and they were not notified at the time of your parents' accident. When you were placed in foster care, they weren't in the States, making it even harder for word to come down the appropriate channels." He shuffles his papers again. "When they did eventually find out, John rushed back. Unfortunately, you'd been placed in the system and had your name changed, as per a request in your parents' will, by then. You'd disappeared and were well hidden. Due to the nature of their business, they decided that maybe you were better off. Their job required constant traveling, never settling in one place for very long. It was no place to raise a child, or so they thought. They believed you were safe and loved."

I scoff out loud at that one, hitting my limit of holding my tongue. Though I have to give the man credit. Despite his obvious nerves and my apparent skepticism, he soldiers on. "Otherwise, they would have claimed you immediately," he assures me.

"So, why am I finding out about this now? I'm assuming they're all dead, so why leave our estrangement until I had no chance of getting to know them?" I'm trying my best to keep my tone under control, but I'm honestly at a loss. There isn't a part of me that can reconcile these strangers leaving their granddaughter at the mercy of the system, name change or not. There had to be something terribly wrong with them, or maybe they thought there was something terribly wrong with me, if they'd chosen to stay away until we lost the chance to ever have a relationship.

The shifty look in his eyes is back, and the fidgeting obviously isn't cutting it since he gets up from his desk and starts to pace behind it. He marches back and forth in front of the big picture window which holds the view of the river his office backs onto. He stops, takes a deep breath, and turns to look at me.

"Well, actually, that's not quite true. Misters Adams have not passed on. They've decided to retire, and the family business may only pass down to a family member. You're the one that was chosen, so they contracted our firm to find you. It has taken quite a while, I can assure you."

"Excuse me?" I gasp. "Are you saying my grandfathers are alive and want to meet me?" As a little girl, I would have dreams of a relative swooping in to rescue me from the never-ending cycle of foster homes. I had finally given up around the age of thirteen. I wasn't one of those kids who were beaten or abused in care; I just never seemed to fit in. I was never really included or felt like I was one of the family. It would've been nice to know there was someone out there who wanted me.

Of course, my very skeptical nature decides this is too good to be true, turning my surprise into anger.

"Why the fuck am I dealing with a lawyer and not them directly? Can they not even be bothered, or are they too fucking chicken to face me themselves?" I can practically feel the steam escaping from my ears. It takes a lot to get me mad, but when I get there, you better watch out. Mr. Ryding swallows nervously and brings a finger up, trying to loosen his collar.

"Ah… but… They're…" he stammers. The man must be good at his job if he was able to track me down, which was apparently quite the feat, but he's horribly unprepared to deal with a woman's anger.

Taking a deep breath, I try to calm down. *Don't take it out on the lawyer, Lila. He's just the messenger.*

"Why me? I'm assuming there are other family members they could turn to?" I rub my eyes, already feeling a headache brewing. They've steadily been getting more frequent, and this meeting is not doing me any favors.

"Yes, well, no. There *are* other family members, but you are their only grandchild, and they've decided that it's time you join the family legacy. You are to be given the opportunity first. All the details are in the package." He sits back down at the desk and gestures to the stack of papers he'd been fidgeting with. "You're required to spend twelve months within the business, learning all the ins and outs. If, at the end of the twelve-month period, you're unwilling to continue, the business and the role of CEO and all it entails will pass on to the next eligible family member. You will carry on with life as if the previous twelve months had never really happened."

I stare at the package like it's a snake that's going to bite me. I just don't know what to think. Do I ignore it, sign it over now, and wash my hands of the whole debacle? Or do I take a leap of faith and at least meet the men that could be the best *or* the worst thing to happen to me?

"Can I have some time to think about this?" I ask. "It's quite a decision I need to make."

Mr. Ryding shakes his head. "I'm sorry, but this decision needs to be made as soon as possible. Our firm has been looking for you for a while, and I'm afraid we're out of time. You need to be on a plane to London in two days' time. We're going to need an answer now."

It's my turn to start pacing. Jumping out of the chair I've been sitting in, I start stalking back and forth across the room. The pounding behind my eyes has intensified, and I rub my temples in an attempt to alleviate it. What to do? It's not like I have anything keeping me here. I don't really have friends, mainly acquaintances. My best friend and roomie is head over heels in love with her partner, so she'd be ok if I left. I have a dead-end job in a bar that pays crappy but keeps me busy. Looking at the facts of my life, as totally unimpressive as they are, I guess there's nothing specifically stopping me from going. I've always dreamed of adventures, feeling sure that there must be something better in store than the life I've been living.

"All right," I tell him, making the decision, "I'm in. Show me where to sign."

He goes to the stack of papers on the table and pulls some out. "You need to sign here, here, and here. One of them is a non-disclosure form. No matter what happens, from here on, you are bound by a confidentiality clause. Even if at the end of twelve months you change your mind, everything you see and do will be confidential, and there are some very harsh consequences if you break the clause. A plane ticket is also in the pack, in your name, with the details of your flight. You'll be met at the airport by a driver who will take you to where you need to be. For your peace of mind, you can tell people where you are going and why, but there is to be no sharing of any other details. It's actually a good thing that you don't have a huge circle of friends." I'm torn between surprise that he knows that fact and being insulted by the comment despite its truth.

"We've been looking for you for so long I wouldn't hesitate to say we know everything about you," he replies to my look, a little more defensively than I expected the nervous guy to manage.

"Yeah, ok, because that's not creepy or rude," I reply sarcastically.

I busy myself with signing papers, and by the time I'm finished, my hand aches and my head throbs incessantly. Gathering my copies of everything, I shove them in my hand bag; I'll read it all when I get home. "So what business have I just signed my life away to?" I ask Mr. Ryding, thinking this is probably something I should have asked *before* signing. Fuck, I'm an idiot. Why didn't I ask that first? I mentally slap my impulsive self.

"Have you heard of the Galaxy Circus?" he asks, slightly distracted with gathering all his copies of the paperwork.

I nod enthusiastically, feeling more upbeat than I have this entire meeting."Oh yes, isn't that the circus that claims it has aliens as its performers? It pops up throughout the globe and is always sold out even though the schedule is too random for anyone to know where they'll be next. People have been trying to debunk them for years. I remember reading that PETA was trying to gain access to prove that their animals are mistreated." I laugh loudly, remembering how that particular situation worked out. Apparently, the circus claimed their animals were really shifters, a clever gimmick that allowed them some special dispensation and gave PETA no ground to stand on. Hey, if people were gullible enough to believe it, then that was their problem.

He looks at me, a strange glint in his eye. "Are they gullible or just looking to be entertained?" he questions, his words coming oddly close to the thought I hadn't spoken aloud. "Well, whether they're gullible or not is besides the point. It still attracts huge crowds when it does tour. It is one of the most popular circuses around, even outselling Cirque du Soleil despite having less shows each year."

My heart starts to beat rapidly as Mr. Ryding looks at me with an oily-looking grin, possibly the first time I've seen him smile since I walked in the door. "Miss Jenson, with the papers you signed, you just joined the circus."

Get it free on Kindle Unlimited here
Apprentice

CPSIA information can be obtained
at www.ICGtesting.com
Printed in the USA
LVHW021541080322
712902LV00002B/33